BOOKS BY RENÉ BAZIN

Published by CHARLES SCRIBNER'S SONS

Davidée Birot . . . . *net* $1.25

The Barrier . . . . *net* $1.00
  (La Barrière)

"This, My Son" . . . . . . *net* $1.25
  (Les Noellets)

The Nun . . . . *net* $1.00
  (L'Isolée)

The Coming Harvest . . . . . *net* $1.25
  (Le Blé qui Lève)

Redemption . . . . *net* $1.25
  (De toute son Âme)

DAVIDÉE BIROT

DAVIDÉE BIROT

BY

RENÉ BAZIN

AUTHOR OF "THE NUN," "THE COMING HARVEST," "THE BARRIER," ETC.

TRANSLATED BY

MARY D. FROST

NEW YORK
CHARLES SCRIBNER'S SONS
1912

Contents

CHAPTER		PAGE
I.	ARDÉSIE	3
II.	THE BIROT FAMILY	32
III.	THE HOUSE ON THE PLAINS	65
IV.	"FLOWER O' THE BROOM"	101
V.	ANNA'S FUNERAL	137
VI.	A TALK WITH PHROSINE	152
VII.	A CLANDESTINE DEPARTURE	161
VIII.	LYING IN WAIT	171
IX.	TROUBLED SOULS	192
X.	MAÏEUL'S SONG	203
XI.	THE INSPECTOR'S VISIT	232
XII.	"BLANDES OF THE GREEN SHUTTERS"	255
XIII.	THE MEETING	279
XIV.	THE RETURN TO ARDÉSIE	305
XV.	THE PERMISSION	319

DAVIDÉE BIROT

DAVIDÉE BIROT.

CHAPTER I.

ARDÉSIE.

Maïeul Jacquet, commonly known among his comrades in the quarry as Maïeul Rit-Dur or Sobersides because he laughed so seldom, had left off work earlier than usual that afternoon, and having gone behind his wind-break, where he removed his sabots, unwound the strips of cloth which served him as leggings, and hung them carefully on a cross-beam, he stood for a few moments bare-headed, gazing through a triangular opening in this wattled screen, far into the distance, doubtless with some one in his thoughts who lived over yonder toward the west.

"Are you going already?" asked one of the men who was at work within a few yards of the hut. "Is it the stones that bother you? It's the same way with me. For these three months I've had naught but waste and rubble."

"Maybe," replied Rit-Dur laconically.

"Or perhaps you are going on business of your own? You've some private reason for quitting work before four o'clock?"

3

Rit-Dur made no answer, but stooping once more under the screen picked up an empty soup-can, a pewter spoon, and half a loaf of bread. Then, having spread a checked handkerchief on the ground, he carefully tied up in it these remnants of his noon-dinner.   Meanwhile a third workman, higher up in the quarry, made answer for him.

"Why do you ask him?   He's a chap who if he has any secrets won't tell them, even when he's drunk, which he never is."

"He is a lucky one," remarked the first speaker.

"That he is for sure!"

The sound of their voices ceased and nothing could be heard save the click of broken slate from all over the quarry, rising now in sonorous musical waves as the great blocks were struck by picks of steel, then in deeper notes, from the blows of the heavy mallets and the grinding of scales of slate cloven by balanced knives which rose and fell in measured beat.   If the three hundred men at work had been smashing glass with hammers for their pastime, they would have made much the same sort of music.   Along the roads outside the quarry, which were deep with a bluish clay, tip-carts went by driven by children and laden with immense blocks of slate which clanged loudly at every jolt.   The urchins, having discharged their loads, stood up in their rimless chariots and lashed their horses into a trot, with a mighty shaking up of carts, dust, and children, while the heavy rumbling of wheels shook the ground and mingled with the cascade of lighter notes from the crashing and falling slates.

Rit-Dur's wind-break was larger and newer than the others and consisted of three fine palisades, one at the back, the two others meeting in the form of a forage-cap. It had been fashioned by its owner out of gorse and heather, closely bound between wooden laths, and held together by branches of buckthorn, that buckthorn whose shiny black bark drives the young bucks mad when they nibble it in the spring.

To the right of the entrance lay piles of finished slates, large and small, from the "poil-roux" to the "grande-anglaise" waiting to be counted and distributed as merchandise.

The morning had been lowering, as so often happens in March, and the afternoon continued damp and showery, so that the smallest splinters of the slate that strewed the ground held a raindrop on their sharp edges. The gray clouds had never ceased rolling in from the west in an unbroken mass, without a rift through which blue sky could peer. But all at once this canopy of cloud parted, revealing, on the western horizon, a belt of clear-washed green, and a pallid light, against which stood out less dimly the roofs of far-off hamlets, the billowy mounds of the slate quarries, an occasional factory chimney, and the tall outline of the well of La Fresnais looming like a windmill without sails.

Maïeul Jacquet emerged from his shelter, pushing his bicycle before him and carrying his handkerchief bundle slung across his shoulder.

"Good-night to you all," he cried.

"Good-night!"

He was no ordinary youth, this Rit-Dur. An excellent workman, he had been doing a man's job since his eighteenth year, and was what is called a four-load slate-cutter—that is, one whose supply of blocks to be cut is renewed at each distribution. But it was more especially in his independence of character and his love of solitude that he differed from his comrades. He had come originally from one of the small islands lying between two branches of the Loire at Savennières, and even when he arrived at the quarry he was already taller and dreamier than the other lads, with something in his face and manner which attracted every one. If he was no talker, he was a bit of a musician and poet though he never wrote songs for the village revels. But the stone-cutters behind their wind-breaks could often be heard singing ditties which were said to be his, and sometimes at night there came across the heather from the slopes of La Gravelle the sound of airs played upon a rustic flute which brought tears to the eyes. No one ever saw the player, but the neighbours said to each other, "That is Maïeul having one of his nights!"

He walked for a few yards over the crackling slates, then mounted his machine, and, without haste, took the road that led to Ardésie, the little neighbouring commune where he lived. Every morning and evening he followed this road almost as far as the village, but not quite, for, to reach his house, he was obliged to make a slight détour. La Gravelle was situated—and very wisely too—at some distance from the high-road. If Maïeul was in many ways unlike those about him, the same may be said of his house, which stood, old, high-perched, and isolated, amidst the mounds and hollows of ancient slate-quarries, abandoned a hundred years ago.

What a droll idea it was of his, every one said, to go and settle himself so far from the inn and the neighbours who always have at least some news to tell, a newspaper to lend, or a joke to repeat!

He was in no hurry now, and being a muscular youth he could mount an occasional steep rise without apparent effort. In a few minutes he had reached the little square of Ardésie, in which there was not a single house of the good old kind, with fine steep roofs, a turret or a mullioned window; nothing but a new grocery, a tobacconist's shop, two tumble-down cottages newly painted and whitewashed, and an immense shed, the disused storehouse of a slate-quarry, whose shattered roofs let in the sun and rain and stars.

No one was crossing the square as he entered, but as he turned into the street leading from it, a troop of romping girls rushed out of the village school, laughing and shouting and flourishing their arms about. Two of them, in their rush, collided with the bicycle and would have thrown the rider off if he had not whirled his machine round and lighted on one foot. Thereupon the whole crew of twenty little girls set up a shout of joy and triumph at having nearly upset the tall young quarryman, and without damage to life or limb.

"Oh, Monsieur Maïeul has fallen!" they cried; "he has fallen off his wheel! It is a hurdle race!"

A clear firm voice arrested the tumult.

"Ernestine," it said, "you will be kept after school to-morrow evening."

The noise ceased at once as the children formed into two groups and disappeared rapidly in opposite directions.

"Monsieur Maïeul, I am very much annoyed."

"I am not at all. There's no harm done."

He said no more, but shrugged his shoulders slightly in the direction of the retreating children. The school-mistress had been watching the departure of her pupils from the threshold of a doorway whose tufa side-posts were roughcast with brown and purple-shot clay up to the height of a man's head—that is to say, a little higher than the head of Mlle. Davidée Birot. She was young, and very erect, and her eyes, weary with writing and reading, were gazing with pleasure along the road, at the rift of light on the horizon, at the melancholy landscape, and at the figure of the young quarryman dismounted there in the middle of the highway.

Between her black skirts and the sides of the door-way one caught glimpses of the court-yard of the school, its sandy floor flecked with puddles, its leafless pear-trees, and the arched trellis of an arbour.

When Maïeul had followed the children with his eyes a moment, he seized the handles of his wheel, replaced his bundle with a toss over his shoulder, and was about to move on when the thought seemed to strike him that it would be uncivil to go without a word to the young school-mistress. As he turned toward her, an expres-

sion of astonishment crossed his face as he exclaimed:

"What is that I see, Mademoiselle, alongside
of you?   A spade?"

"Certainly, Monsieur Maïeul."

"But it is as big as mine!"

"Is it?   I found it here at the school; we have
no other."

"You are not going to use it, surely?"

"Pardon me, I *am* going to use it, and at once."
She laughed as she spoke, not with the wide-
mouthed ringing peal of the countrywoman, but
discreetly and with reserve, as if her mind were
just hovering on her lips.   There was no mockery
in her laugh.   She knew Maïeul by sight, and said
to herself: "This good fellow evidently regards
me as a sort of princess!"

"You imagine then that we have a gardener,
Monsieur Maïeul?   No, the commune has not
offered us one.   The Mayor of Ardésie would be
highly astonished if I asked him for such a thing.
We hoe our own beds and sow our own carrots,
onions, parsley, and little radishes.   It certainly
is not expert labour, but here is spring coming upon
us, and if we wish to vary our fare a little, we must
set to work.   And, as you see, I am about to do
so!"

Her jesting tone, which implied more than she
uttered, at once intimidated and attracted the
young slate-cutter.   Mlle. Davidée had already
turned away, crossed the court, and opened the
wicket gate which led through a low wall into the
kitchen-garden.   She entered, stepped across a

border sown with corn salad, and took up her position firmly at the end of the adjoining bed. Was
she actually going to use those hands—which
seemed fit only for handling a pen, so white and
slender were they and no bigger than a fennel
apple—to dig great shovelfuls of earth and turn
them over and over, and keep on at this work until
dusk? She had already raised her left arm and
planted her foot on the spade, when Maïeul
grasped the handle and with a vigorous movement
drew it away from her.

"There! there! let me have that spade," he
cried; "it is much more used to me than to you.
I will dig your garden for you!"

"You! Not really?"

"And take much less time about it too—and
maybe give pleasure also to—but enough said!
I must get to work at once."

Mlle. Davidée was standing in the middle of
the salad bed, half inclined to laugh and half
touched by this attention, and not at all sure which
was the more appropriate feeling. As for Maïeul,
he had already pulled off his vest, thrown it over
a small pear-tree, and set to work digging the rich
earth which, at touch of the hoe, crumbled away
in soft heaps, intermixed with straw and ground-
sel.

"Very well, then, since you really mean it,
Monsieur Maïeul; I thank you heartily. I have
in fact some papers to correct and you are doing
me a great kindness."

But to this he made no reply, not being given
to expending his energy in words. Already, with

half-a-dozen strokes of the spade, he had dug up a strip of earth a foot wide and was beginning on a second one.

The young girl walked away along the garden path which was imprinted with the marks of tiny heels, her own and those of Mlle. Renée Desforges the head-mistress. She mounted the three steps of the porch at the end of the playground and in full sight of the garden, unconsciously holding herself very erect without any swaying of her light figure. As she opened the door she turned back to gaze up at the sky, which was again covered with dark clouds, the rift in the west having closed in.

"What a dismal light, Mademoiselle!" she exclaimed to some one within. "It gives me a very despondent feeling."

"Don't be over-sensitive, my child, and beware of humbug! I heard you joking a moment ago."

"Yes, with Maïeul Jacquet who insisted on hoeing our garden for us. It was droll of him, was it not?"

"Perhaps so."

"Why do you say that?"

"He has reasons of his own, no doubt."

"All the same it strikes me as rather odd, though I have no wish to look deeply into his motives. But, Mademoiselle, it is quite true that owing to all these dark clouds, this fog and rain, I am feeling a little——"

"A little what?"

"Depressed?—No, hardly that. Sad?—No, not actually sad, but a little inclined to sadness."

"You must tell the Inspector so the next time he comes to Ardésie. He will advise you to get married, or perhaps he will have you appointed to some place on the Riviera—the sky there is always blue, you know!"

Mlle. Renée Desforges' wide lips curled with a slightly disdainful smile. Then of a sudden she ceased smiling, the bodice on which she was working fell from her lap, and she spoke volubly and passionately.

"You are still a novice in spite of your three years and a half of teaching, and as naïve as a newcomer after your six months in Ardésie. Positively you rouse my pity! You do not talk about marriage, but you encourage, you cultivate, and cherish your emotions, whether over a sick child or a dying woman, a strike, a mewing cat, or a small bird that breaks its wing against a telephone wire. You are always in a state of agitation and suffering, trying to solve the problem of evil, while you are nothing after all but a poor little assistant school-mistress exiled to this remote hamlet of Ardésie, regarded with jealousy by the curé, scarcely listened to by the inhabitants, closely watched by the school board, and on the whole pretty badly off. You are on a false tack, my dear, believe me! Live for yourself, do all that is required to get on, have a good class-room in excellent order, and neat papers; the rest is superfluous, and nobody will thank you for it. Give up your zeal for helping the human race. Cultivate a universal scepticism such as is in favour with the authorities. Above all, indulge in no dreams of conjugal affection! Any other kind you may dream of, if it is not against your principles. But the husband of a village school-mistress, what is he? Three times out of four he is a man who lives upon *us*, upon our labour, and if we take one from among the instructors we renounce all hope of promotion, for it would be the height of luck to find two posts vacant at the same time, side by side. And moreover, my child, I do not see many of our masculine colleagues whom *I* would consent to marry. No, no, my dear, we must love our profession for its own sake, we must lay our hearts between two sheets of blotting-paper so that they may dry thoroughly, always say yes to the school-committee, and attain to a tidy little pension at last without over-exerting ourselves."

"What a profession of faith! And what ardour you put into it, Mademoiselle! I assure you that I have given you no pretext for lecturing me on the subject of a possible or impossible marriage. There is not a suitor on the horizon, I swear to you! The horizon is quite misty; I have just looked out. There is not a gleam in sight." She laughed gently as she spoke, bending her slender neck a little. Mlle. Renée resumed:

"However, you have perhaps a right not to be like the rest of us school-ma'ams; you have a dowry and a rich father, you are a sort of aristocrat."

She rose as she said this, carefully folded her work, stuck her needle in it, and laid it on the kitchen table.

"As it is my week to keep house, I must go and make the soup. Come and correct your papers beside me, will you? And perhaps you will correct some of mine at the same time."

"Oh, yes, most willingly."

Mlle. Davidée crossed the little corridor at one end of which was the stairway leading to their bedchambers, and entered the scantily furnished, tilefloored room which the young teachers called their parlour. Taking up a pile of exercise-books she carried them back to the little kitchen, where she seated herself at the table and, turning her eager young face toward the window, began to read. "Middle class,"—this was Mlle. Desforges' class —"Madeleine Bunat's copybook, Friday, March 26. Writing: Imitate good examples." With one stroke of her pencil Mlle. Davidée marked the page "fairly good." "French composition: Describe how you intend to spend your Easter vacation in useful ways while resting from your studies."

"Upon my word, this of Madeleine's is not bad. Are you listening, Mademoiselle Renée?"

"Yes, yes, I am listening."

The head-mistress was bending over the fireplace, hanging the kettle on the crane. She raked up the dead ashes, threw on a few handfuls of dry thorns, took a newspaper which she folded in a narrow strip so that it should not burn too fast, lighted it, and set fire to the thorns which crackled and threw out a white blaze. This done she put her foot on the paper to extinguish the flame and carefully laid the rest of it aside for next day, a housekeeper's movement and a frank avowal of poverty. All the women in Ardésie did this. Davidée looked on curiously.

"Well, read this masterpiece, then!" said Mlle. Renée.

"Oh, yes. Here it is: 'I intend to spend my holidays usefully, for I am too old now to play all the time. The first thing in the morning, I will help about the housework, I will run errands, and peel the vegetables. Then I will spend my afternoon in manual work, embroidery, sewing, and the like. But I shall also have my hours of leisure. When I am alone, I will employ them in reading and drawing, and quite often I will ask my little friends to play with me. I shall thus have spent my vacation usefully and at the same time pleasantly.'"

"You are right. That is very good!" said Mlle. Renée as she rose from her knees with her face scarlet and her eyes glowing from the flames. "I have always had great confidence in Madeleine Bunat."

Mlle. Davidée, as often happened, shook her head, and proceeded to deny what she had just asserted. Speech was prompt with her, judgment followed later, and often contradicted her first words.

"All the same, do you not think Madeleine Bunat's ideal of a vacation rather a tame one?"

"What would you ask better?"

"I hardly know, but as I reread the composition I thought to myself: A formula, just a formula she has learnt by heart, and which will not protect the child. Let us suppose that——"

"Well, prater, I will suppose that you are not looking after your gardener. Is he still there?"

Davidée Birot, light, swift, agile, rose from the table, glided past Mlle. Renée, and pressed her face against the window-pane.

"Yes, he is still there. He looks terribly heated. The bed is almost dug. If you could only see him! If we were hiring him at exorbitant wages he could not work with greater ardour. There now! What a shovelful, my poor Maïeul Rit-Dur! I really believe the darkness has made him taller. He looks like a giant toiling away among our pear-trees."

The young girl turned from the window and came back to her papers, saying as she bent her head over them, "It is very kind of this young man to be doing what he is!"

"Perhaps I should think so too if he were doing it for me."

"Oh, nonsense!—Poor fellow!"

She said no more. The two school-mistresses of Ardésie exchanged a glance. Their eyes questioned each other mutely. "What are you really thinking?" They were both young—though with some years between them—and their youth gave a strange depth to the emotion which the half-implied word of love had awakened in them. Their long years of hard study were there, ready to speak and say: "Shall we have our reward? Will there ever be any truce to this labour?"

Such striving and effort! Such solitude! Such weariness over the daily monotony! No reward but the passing affection of a few children and the ingratitude of all the rest! The present moment stirred them both and awoke their self-pity. The same thought murmured vaguely in the soul of each: "Look at this kitchen, this dull court-yard, this pile of papers, this pot boiling on the hearth, this whole humble life! We have barely courage to go on living because it is for ourselves alone; but if it were for him! for him the unknown, the impossible, perhaps!" The dream was the same in the eyes of Mlle. Davidée and of Mlle. Renée. But the latter no longer believed in the words that came in the silence with their subtle music and tempting visions. She had known disappointment; she was growing old. Her beautiful fair hair was beginning to lose its golden lights and reflections. The rosy tints in her cheeks were turning too fixed a red.

They still looked into each other's eyes; the smile tinged with irony on Mlle. Renée's lips never changed. The younger girl, the little one who had been teaching for four years, had in one moment lived through a happy future and seen her spring-time fade; she grew sad the first, with a passing impulse of gratitude for the sympathy which she thought Mlle. Renée expressed for her. Then she went back to her task of correcting papers. The two young teachers had not exchanged a word. Mlle. Renée now took from the sideboard a tin dish containing cold meat sliced in gravy, and set it on the fire, while Mlle. Davidée went on reading:

"Elementary course. Writing: 'Temperance preserves the health.' She is incredibly lazy, that little Philomène Letourneur! If you could see her page of writing! I shall give her a bad mark."

"Then her father will beat her!"

"No, he drinks; nothing matters to him. The mother is a nice woman, however."

Mlle. Davidée took up her pen again, erased the bad mark and substituted: "Carelessly done."

"Elementary course. 'Temperance preserves the health!' This time we have little Anna Le Floch."

"The Bretonne? We have too many children from Brittany in school now. They come in troops from Poullaouen and Huelgoat and Redon."

"This is very badly written, all ups and downs. Temperance—preserves—health. Besides, the poor little thing has no health, although she observes temperance strictly enough! I am always afraid of her dying on our hands. She would be the first of my pupils who has ever died. I am going to put 'Fairly well' for her mark; it will save a few tears."

She continued to skim the copybooks, her head bent lower over the pages as the light faded. Her serious mouth with the red lips, which enunciated so clearly, murmured each name in turn: Julie Sauvage, Corentine Le Derf, Jeannie Fête-Dieu. From time to time she addressed a remark to Mlle. Renée who replied as she moved about the kitchen.

When she had finished correcting her papers and laid them in a neat pile, Mlle. Davidée rose and went to the door which led into the court-yard, opened it cautiously, took a step or two on the sand outside, bending her head to listen, then re-entered the room.

"He is gone," she said.

"What! without taking leave of us?" returned Mlle. Renée. "What manners these people have! They are perfect boors."

"But he has dug our garden-bed," said Davidée, "and after all—" She did not pursue her thought, but added only:

"We must light our lamp; the night is coming on," and, so saying, she took down from the buffet shelf a glass lamp whose opaque shade was tastelessly decorated with a design of playing-cards on a greenish ground. She lighted it with the care she gave to whatever she did and began to set the table.

The two young teachers always spread a cloth for their morning and evening meal; it was of coarse linen, but white and fresh, and served to distinguish their simple meal from those of the peasants around them. Mlle. Davidée spread it, smoothing the folds with her hands, while Mlle. Renée took the soup kettle from the hob and poured its contents into a tureen, which stood on the hearth half-filled with morsels of bread. Then without turning her head she remarked:

"It is a pity Maïeul Jacquet leads such a sad life, for he is not a bad man after all."

"What do you mean by a sad life?"

"How simple-minded you are!"

"But what is it you reproach him with?"

Mlle. Davidée bending forward across the table, her hands still smoothing the cloth, was vexed to feel her blood mounting suddenly in such an absurd way to her lips and cheeks and brow.

"Do you never hear any gossip then?" the other

rejoined. "I knew it six weeks after my arrival in Ardésie. Maïeul Jacquet, whom they call Rit-Dur, is Phrosine's lover."

"What! the woman who sweeps our class-rooms?"

"Certainly."

"And whom I shall see to-morrow?"

"Yes, to-morrow, and all the following days; Anna Le Floch's mother."

"Oh, how you have lowered her in my eyes! I shall never be able to look at her again without thinking of this."

"Oh, you will grow indulgent in time."

"I am so now. I make no open reproaches. I pass as unconsciously as I can in the midst of their vices. But I would like to rest my eyes some-where. And as to this woman, I guessed her to be unhappy, I saw that at times she looked shy and rebellious and that her face was hard and stern, but I was always struck by a sort of dignity about her."

"Trust to that if you choose, my dear! She certainly cannot live on what she earns from us."

"I never could have believed it. She was one of the last among the younger women to wear the pretty cap of Ponts-de-Cé with the fluted wings."

"Do you think those caps protect a girl?"

"But I thought she had such a steady air, the look of a mother who misses her child. I have never talked with her except to say: 'Do this or do that, do not forget to put the broom in the closet, good-by.'"

"You are not regretting the fact, are you?"

"But how many fellow-beings there are whose minds never touch ours except in trivial words like these, and their equally trivial answers: 'Yes, Mademoiselle! No, Mademoiselle. Good-by till to-morrow!'"

Mlle. Renée's sonorous laugh broke out in the peaceful room, disturbing the silence which enwrapped the house and swathed the court-yard outside, the garden and the highway in a shroud of mist.

"Eat your supper, my dear; you evidently need fortifying. You can philosophize to-morrow. Are there many philosophers of your stamp in Charente? Ah, I confess frankly that I am incapable of following you, and that I cannot worry as you do over everybody's troubles. As long as I conduct my classes properly, I am content to let humanity alone. Will you have another spoonful of soup?"

"No, thanks; I am not hungry."

"That is the way things go! If you had hoed the garden-bed yourself you would be eating your supper with the appetite of a young wolf cub."

Sitting opposite each other the two young teachers now resumed their usual evening talk on the uninteresting but necessary subjects of the next day's work, the order of studies, the themes to be given out. Mlle. Birot, while doing her best not to appear absent-minded, was evidently thinking of other things: a deep undercurrent of thoughts and emotions was flowing beneath the surface attention she gave and the partly veiled glance of her dark eyes. At this moment she, too,

was of those who give nothing of their real mind
and heart to their neighbour; she merely answered
"Yes, no, precisely," with a face void of thought,
like so many faces which reveal nothing but
the material life that animates them, the blood
flowing through their veins. And yet hers was
a face which, although without regular beauty,
could not fail to interest, such was the charm of
its soft pallor lighted up by her large dark eyes
and the deep red of her lips.

The plump, blonde Mlle. Renée would have preferred to have her companion in a more commu-
nicative mood. Had *she* ever known the eager
concern in everything about her which agitated
Davidée? If so, she had speedily conquered it.
This woman of thirty-two lived her life wholly free
from that cold shivering breath which blows in
upon us from the open sea. She had no taste for
melancholy and fought its attacks, which grew
constantly rarer, by striving to drown reflection,
to avoid looking forward or facing any problems
which she had decided to be insoluble. There
was about her a prompt and easy gayety which
was not due to courage, though it produced that
illusion, but was rather the means of escape from
thoughts of sorrow, moral perplexity, and death.

"She is always in a good humour," said the
parents after a visit to the head-mistress, but they
left her without a spark of feeling or a glow of
comfort, with the memory merely of precise colour-
less words, relieved by little familiarities of manner and studied pleasantries. No one could cite
more than three or four instances in which Mlle.

Renée had shown herself violently aggressive or harshly vindictive. The curé of Ardésic was one of its inhabitants whom she cordially hated, though she scarcely knew him. Her other enemies were both women, and young, of whom one had complained of the head-teacher for tearing up a pupil's catechism in the class-room, while the other had ventured to say of her, "That blonde is growing stout and red."

To distract her assistant's mind, she began describing the last teacher's reunion she had attended in the neighbouring town. She dwelt upon the toilettes—"Oh, very pretentious in a small way!"—related some local gossip, and commented on the latest school appointments, of which she approved only those which did not arouse her envy, and finally she wound up by exclaiming:

"Come, child, let us go for a walk. The weather is bad, to be sure, but it will make our blood tingle and change the current of our thoughts. You evidently need distraction. Oh, how young you are!"

The girls rapidly washed the plates and soup tureen, performing this task with nervous haste, the principal especially, who had long aspired to a better-paid post, where she could hire a little maid for these homely offices.

They were soon out-of-doors. "How soft the air is!" exclaimed Mlle. Renée.

They had put on sabots over their shoes, which clicked at every step and raised them above the sticky mud of the road. After leaving the school behind they passed a larger whitewashed build-

ing, then the roofs grew lower and the one-storied
houses whose age was past reckoning, stretched
out to the cross-roads and beyond, the dim evening light showing their long lines of roof thatched
with dusty moss and looking as if patched with
bits of gray cloth from the cast-off garments of their
peasant dwellers. They all lay wrapped in such
deep slumber that the village seemed dead. The
two "demoiselles" descended toward the square,
which is built up only on the south and east. The
café was still lighted and the dull glare from its
windows streamed out across the miry road. On
the east was a tumble-down wall and a house
before which stood a tree, the solitary tree which
vouchsafed the shade of its quivering leaves to
this poor toiling hamlet. On the north there was
one deserted house, whose outside stairway served
as a sleeping place for tramps and homeless dogs
on summer nights. Work at the cross-roads had
ceased, the earth no longer groaned beneath the
heavy slate-laden carts, and only these two girls
seemed to be abroad to listen to the wailing of the
night wind. All the life of the village was con-
centrated in the two streets diverging from this
open space. Streets crowded by poor hovels,
workmen's tenements, and drinking places whose
patrons were no longer entering them, but where a
few obstinate topers still lingered over their cups.

It was in this quarter that most of the school-
children lived. Mlle. Renée and Mlle. Davidée
stared up at the house fronts, with their dimly
lighted windows, which they could distinguish by
certain vague signs.

"I must go, one of these days, to call on Jeannie Fête-Dieu's grandmother," said Mlle. Davidée. "The child tells me she is growing worse."

"Ah, my dear, you will be doing a kind act. I envy you. For my part I cannot see people suffer. It is too much for me."

The younger woman felt tempted to reply, "Then do not look at me," but she kept silence, for in truth she hardly knew why such bitter sadness had taken hold on her and could not be shaken off, or if she knew she could as yet find no words to express it. She only said, after a moment's pause:

"We are real personages here, you and I, are we not? At all events, I feel the need of saying so to myself."

"Fine personages indeed! I with my hood on my head, sabots on my feet, and solitude around me! My poor Mademoiselle Davidée, when you have lived six months longer here you will find out that we are merely victims, sacrificed if not condemned!"

A discreet and musical peal of laughter rang out on the astonished night, like the note of a waking bird. The cross-roads, the two diverging streets stretching out and losing themselves in the darkness, all were a desert. But humanity was nevertheless there, innumerable, borne upon the night wind—that wind which drove the noises of the town before it and scattered them over the lonely fields. There was a confused murmur in the distance whence issued from time to time, as bubbles break on the surface of a wave, now a voice, now the whistle of a passing locomotive, then two distinct measures of a waltz played by a military band on some square in the distant town. A bell rang in muffled tones, then came the blast of a siren releasing a gang of men from their work, or again the whistle of an exhaust pump in the quarries beyond the well of Champ-Robert. Then all these sounds mingled and lost themselves in one vast harmony, and this song of life was made up of a vast interblending of toils and pleasures, sorrows and joys, indistinguishable one from the other. Great searchlights kept watch through the darkness over distant quarries and formed islands of light here and there, a soft warmth exuded from the enveloping folds of mist and dripped from stones and walls and bushes—one could feel the breath of spring which had not yet fully come and which exhaled itself as yet only in stray perfumes and fugitive sighs borne on the soft mild air.

"You were right," said Mlle. Davidée; "the night is sweet."

"What the poets would call a voluptuous night," replied Mlle. Renée, and as she spoke she wound her arm around her companion's waist and together they retraced their steps toward the deserted house at the head of the square, where another lonely road led away through pasture-lands and rough fields strewn with bluish pebbles where only sparse tufts of grass and moss could grow. The girls followed it slowly and a little timidly, scarcely uttering a word; they were bound for a neighbouring hamlet where stood the parish church and thence homeward by another road. Half-way along this lonely stretch, they both started at the sound of some nocturnal bird, an owl or bat, rustling through the shrubbery as it flew by them. They stopped short for a moment and then moved on. But instead of smiling at their passing fears, Mlle. Renée wound her arm more closely around the other girl's waist and stooped to embrace her.

"Let me kiss you, dear," she murmured. "I am very fond of you; are you fond of me?"

Davidée, a little surprised but grateful for this unlooked for kindness, answered softly:

"Yes, Mademoiselle."

They resumed their slow pace, avoiding bogs and pitfalls and passing a lonely house here and there, until they caught a glimpse of the church tower, a dim shadow rising a little darker against the night sky. Then they turned back to the house where they were living in order to teach the village children how to live. They were influences there—if not personages, as the younger one had said—strong, youthful influences—one in the fulness of her ardour, eager to spend herself for her scholars, the other already disillusionized, having exhausted an enthusiasm which had never been very keen, and fallen back on lower ambitions though continuing faithful to the letter of her duties.

Both had studied hard and knew more than all the other dwellers of Ardésie put together, with the exception of the curé and one or two engineers established in the village. Ardésie, owing to its slight importance, had no school besides theirs, the boys being sent to school in a neighbouring commune.

These girls had left their homes and families as all their colleagues had, in order to teach and live among the poor, absorbed in their professional duties, far from the pleasures of town and congenial society, and surrounded by a stern and desolate landscape. They could lay aside but little from their slender salaries, and marriage was a difficult question for them, since they belonged to an exceptional world, unclassed as they were by their very education, with minds sufficiently cultivated to make an unequal marriage unendurable and yet bound by close ties to the class in which they taught and from which they had sprung—bound to it by their early education, by many of their tastes and some of their jealousies and ambitions.

Nine o'clock was striking as the young teachers opened the school-house door. They lighted a pair of candles set in twin candlesticks of blue and white china, and mounted the stairs to their rooms, but as they parted on the landing, the two faces, dimly lighted by the gleam of the candles, smiled upon one another.

"Good-night, Mademoiselle!"

"Good-night, Davidée!"

"Is it the dawning of a new friendship?" the younger girl asked herself. "Is the Principal really about to be something beyond what a head-mistress is apt to be; that is to say, a near neighbour, a watchful authority, but a moral life totally apart from ours, a judge useful to consult and difficult to love?" But her thoughts did not dwell long upon Mlle. Desforges. She drew aside the white curtain of her one little window and gazed out toward the north, trying to discern the light from an upper chamber which often burned far into the night. For there Maïeul dwelt, in a large, almost noble house, standing as it did on one of the mounds left by a forgotten generation and overlooking the whole slate-country. But she could see nothing save a few twinkling lights in the foreground which seemed to indicate the hamlet of Morellerie.

"That Maïeul! I detest him now!" she said to herself as with her finger tips she rubbed away the mist her breath had left on the window-pane. "Ah, those men who live with a woman for years and then abandon her! The species is common enough and odious enough! Phrosine may have tried in vain to persuade him to marry her, for she is older than he, much older, ten years at least. And those are the surroundings in which little Anna Le Floch lives! I no longer wonder that she is shy and sad, and yet I have sometimes scolded the child! She is not one of my pupils, to be sure, but how I wish that she were, so that I might clasp her tenderly to my heart, since her mother is unworthy! How hard it will be to show a friendly face to Phrosine to-morrow! But it would be useless for me to speak out what I think. One may pity but never blame! Blame! Oh, why did this Maïeul offer to work in our garden? Why was he so eager to do something for

me, or rather for us?   One never can tell, and he
is so silent.   How glad I should be to see him the
head of a decent family such as are not lacking,
even in Ardésie!   To see him a good husband, a
steady workman, living in his own little cottage,
well-kept and tidy, with a swarm of children on
his knees!   Three or four or even five, if it is
possible to hold so many at once!"   She smiled
as she conjured up this picture, for the maternal
instinct was strong within her and her thoughts
now reverted to her own little pupils and the
morrow's work.   She undressed rapidly and lay
down on the narrow cot-bed protected from the
wind by one thin curtain only.   The wind whistled in chilly blasts and set her candle flickering,
so Davidée hastened to blow it out and was soon
asleep.

Night had come with its needful rest, but not
to all.   Suffering and pleasure, poverty and duty
still kept their vigils!   At that very hour, in a
pothouse on the lower road which the two girls
had passed in their walk, a young slate-cutter
was being enticed to drink away his week's earn-
ings.   At that hour, in a poor house in the village street, little Jeannie Fête-Dieu had risen and
crept with bare feet to her grandmother's bedside and stood beside it holding her flickering
candle—the only being awake in the house—
watching the worn pallid face of the sleeper who
had called to her in her dreams.   Beneath the
great searchlights carters were still busy in the
quarries carrying off the refuse of the day's work.
Here and there a rabbit-snarer, a tramp or a

poacher was prowling along the tracks of one of the deserted quarries, while above them all, the moon was making her tranquil way through heavy banks of cloud.

CHAPTER II.

THE BIROT FAMILY.

WHERE was Davidée Birot's home? It was a small village by the sea in the Charente region where the coast-line rises softly like the bevelled edge of a mirror, and the long beach slopes gradually beneath a shallow tide.

She came of a land-holding family which, however, had long been settled on the water's edge within sight of the open sea. The father had not always lived as now upon his income. A journeyman stone-cutter, skilled in his trade, tenacious in his business dealings, surly but intelligent, Constant Birot had made his tour of France, and had chiselled, hammered, and carved every species of stone, hard and soft, marble and granite, from the ancient lava of the Central Range to the cream or rust-coloured agglomerates in which he delighted to find the shell-deposits.

On his return to his native province after amassing some hundreds of francs, he had entered into partnership with the son of a good family there, named Hubert. Together they had purchased a granite quarry outside the village, on the wide treeless plain encircling "Blandes of the Green Shutters." Hubert had furnished the funds, Birot undertaking to act as overseer, and the business developed slowly. Birot, who was defi-

cient in general education, had found this a great
disadvantage in his trade, and as his ambition to
rise in the world increased, he became more and
more irritated by this drawback which he regarded
as an injustice of fate, and through a delusion
caused by vanity, he had grown to exaggerate the
value of that learning which he had not acquired
and to attribute to this cause alone all his limita-
tions and failures.

Accordingly, when, after his marriage with a
woman of modest means, two children were born
to them, he announced that his son was to be an
engineer, and that his daughter also should have
a fine position in the world. The son's career did
not turn out a success, and after proving an indifferent scholar at the Lycée, where he was more
than once threatened with expulsion, he finally
obtained a clerical position in a prefecture in the
south, and was thenceforth rarely seen in Blandes.
Madame Birot's friends asserted that he only
retained this second-rate post through the influence and political relations of Birot the father.
This latter, in fact, who was already rich and still
engaged in active business, having bought out his
partner and become the sole proprietor of the
quarry, had grown to be an important figure, not
only in Blandes, but throughout the region, even as
far as La Rochelle. At Blandes itself he ruled supreme, he had been elected mayor and constantly
re-elected, and was always sure of being so, having become what may be styled an absolute
mayor. He even aspired to the prefecture.

He had all the requisite gifts for the forcible

conquest of municipal supremacy in a period of
local jealousies and violent transitions. He had
a methodical mind and a memory as implacable
as were his hatreds, but he could show himself
obliging and serviceable enough toward those
whom he did not hate. Always jovial and a
good fellow at first sight, and continuing so toward
those who yielded to his will, talkative and apparently open, with a hand ever extended in cordial greeting, he was, nevertheless, beneath this
expansive exterior, a keen, suspicious observer.
The first offence, the smallest failure on the part
of a subordinate which touched him officially or
in his private interests, called forth an immediate
response, and often one of startling brutality.
Every word, every gesture, every threat, all the
damaging stories accumulated for thirty years in
that tenacious memory, every insinuation that
might be brought, sustained as it was sure to be
by ready proofs, overwhelmed his victim. Birot
never denounced secretly; he proclaimed his
wrath loudly and demanded vengeance on his opponents, sustaining his demand with promises of
reward which were invariably fulfilled. Accordingly the public school teacher was discharged,
the postmistress dismissed in disgrace, the municipal counsellor saw his demand for the reprieve
of his son as reservist refused, and the son of
an old peasant woman, a soldier, was unable to
obtain leave of absence for the harvest. Neither
sex nor youth nor penitence on the part of the
culprit availed against the sentence of old Birot
whether already pronounced or about to be so.

Never had he been known to grant a pardon. Never had a debtor obtained a respite from this burly red-faced creditor who laughed as he cried, "Pay! pay first! we'll see about it afterwards," but his laugh was merely a tribute to his own power, to his sense of his rights, and the force of legality. No one had ever accused him of cowardice. It was his habit to go straight to any citizen who had been accused of speaking ill of him and ask him outright:

"Is it true that you have been running me down? Or is it a lie? Are you my friend or my enemy? This is your time to speak openly." He was accused of being pitiless and it was true. It was also commonly said of him: "This man has no heart;" and this was false. He loved his trade and his quarry at Blandes, he loved his blocks of granite and fine ashlar, his solid foundation-stones, well-hewn and laid in perfect equilibrium. Although he was beginning to walk with difficulty on the bow-legs which ill-sustained his mighty paunch, he would gladly travel six kilometres across country for the sake of seeing a new façade, the fine span of a bridge, a milestone or a pedestal which did honour to the workman or the mine from which it came. But above all, he loved his daughter. Davidée had been born during what he called his hard-times, that is, the period when he had laboured with his own hands with exemplary ardour, conscientiousness, and diligence. When he returned home at night she was there, a dainty creature with little hands outstretched to greet him, delicate hands which filled him with wonder; the nose a little tip-tilted, the eyes fixed eagerly on him, full of infantile admiration, and the memory of yesterday's gambols, eyes moist and brilliant with a tenderness whose power she already knew.

In her he recognized himself, not perhaps as he was, but as he might have been. He would often say to her:

"My little Davidée, you are intelligent. I am no fool, but I lack education. You shall have the best of educations. I will buy books for you, the biggest and the most expensive, all you want. I will hire teachers for you, teachers of writing, reading, and arithmetic, of all that can be taught. I will spend my last copper on you so that you may do me credit, for you see I no longer count on your brother! Come here and kiss me, child!"

And he would lift her proudly in his arms, those arms whose muscles, long used to lifting heavy weights, carried the child as lightly as if she had been made of thistledown. He would then seat her in a wicker chair, perched on four high legs, bought for her at the same time as her nursing bottle, and which still served—in spite of her mother's shrugs—for the little maid Davidée, now grown as tall as a sheaf of wheat. Her father wished it to be so because his heavy heart knew but one joy on earth and feared to lose it, and seeing the child still seated in her baby chair, he could persuade himself more easily that nothing was changed. Birot drew the chair to the fire, which the mother had built sparingly, and threw upon the heap of smouldering coals and embers

an armful of vine fagots from a tall pile he had
made under the winding kitchen stairs.

"There, warm your little hands, laugh, and
show your tiny teeth. This is the fire I have
earned for you with these arms! This is the wood
from my vineyard whose wine I have sold to the
cognac makers. Draw nearer, child! This has
been a sorry day, mother! A big block of free-
stone, split by the frost, wounded one of those
confounded workmen in the knee and he expected
me to pay him damages! You know him, Blazoin,
that swarthy fellow, with his hair in his eyes?
Haven't I been a workingman too? Have I never
had my carcase injured? Do you suppose I
minced matters with him? No, I just put my
two hands on his shoulders and shook him till his
bones rattled. That scared him and I heard no
more talk of damages. Come, little one, stretch
out your feet to the fire! these vine branches burn
like one's heart."

The child did not laugh as much as he would
have liked. She condescendingly allowed herself to be spoiled. Children divine so early the
power they have and how they can increase it.
Davidée stood more in awe of her silent mother
than of her violent father. When she wanted
anything hard to obtain, such as a journey to La
Rochelle, a day of mussel fishing in the bay, a
party of her little friends, or a fine new doll from
Paris, she asked Papa Birot, but cast anxious
glances meanwhile at her mother, moving about
silently in the background in her felt shoes, dark
and slender, noiseless, tireless, dusting, sweeping,

polishing, always busy but never satisfied. A soul enamoured of material order and finding all perfection there. When her mother had said yes by a nod, or no by a slight turn of the chin, Davidée cared no more for Papa Birot's opinion. Her case was already lost or won.

Soon the chair was too high for the child. Davidée like all big girls preferred to touch the floor with her feet. Birot who read slowly, stopping to spell the complicated words, now begged her to read the newspaper aloud to him. Through a scruple which would have astonished his friends, this foul-mouthed man ran over the head-lines of his radical sheet beforehand, saying:

"Davidée, you may make a little skip just there, and another here, just a lamb's skip." He bent forward intently while his daughter read, striving to follow everything, however fast the words came, on the trot or the gallop, according as the article amused or bored the youthful reader. She had a naturally delicate enunciation, and an alert mind which played between the lines like a dolphin in the waves. Ah, the sharp little thing! She much preferred to read to herself, her lesson books or other volumes which Madame Birot took out of the school library for her; or those she could borrow from her friends who sometimes possessed as many as two or three dozen in a row on their shelves. She brought home very high marks from school. When she had gone to bed in her own chamber just over the dining-room, which served as a parlour for Madame Birot and a smoking-room for the old man, the couple pored to-

gether over the marks on Davidée's papers,
and pride filled their souls as they counted up
the high marks which invariably signified "well-
done."

But Madame Birot, whose imagination was less
unbridled than her husband's, and whose judgment was sounder, did not always conclude with
him: "She will go far!" but took care to add:
"Yes, doubtless, well-established near home, she
will do us honour. But you must beware, Birot,
of your ambition. It has already driven away
our son, it must not drive away our daughter."

This advice irritated the man, who, in return,
taunted his wife with being a *bourgeoise*. He
held forth on the subject of learning, repeating
the phrases he had caught up in the workshops,
or at public meetings, and which returned to his
memory, welded together like the links of a chain.
He knew the world, he affirmed; he saw men and
understood progress; he would be willing to sacrifice his interests, even his pleasures, for his child's
future. He did not specify, however, what he
was prepared to do. But it became known in
time. The head-mistress of the girls' school at
Blandes had long ago laid her plan before Constant Birot. She had offered her services gra-
tuitously in preparing Davidée for the normal
school, and securing her admission there.

"Such an intelligent child, Monsieur Birot,"
she said to him; "such a favourite with her companions, so clever and with so much distinction.
Yes, I can truly say it, such distinction! She
is formed to succeed as an instructress. She has

perhaps too much sensibility, but life will soon cure her of that defect."

"Yes, you may well say that," replied Birot. The directress continued:

"At fourteen, after she has rested for awhile, I will take charge of her. You will have no further responsibility. You will merely have to supply remittances."

It was on a spring afternoon, to the sound of bells which were ringing for vespers from the tower of the fortified and crenelated church of "Blandes of the Green Shutters," that Birot announced to his wife that he had selected a profession for their child. The couple were alone in a first-floor chamber, scantily furnished with a black walnut bed, with red cretonne coverlet, four chairs and a round table, part of the stone-cutter's dower, duly appraised and detailed in the marriage contract exacted by the father of the future Madame Birot. A door which stood open connected this plain, bare, tile-floored room with a larger one, whose parqueted floor and muslin curtains, its brass bed and mirror, with its gilt frame always shrouded in gauze, and its fine china ornaments over the fireplace, seemed prepared for a coming guest. The parents' room had no fireplace though the atmosphere within the house was colder than without.

Davidée had gone with one of her friends on a visit to the neighbouring village of Villefeue and accordingly the larger, handsomer, warmer chamber stood empty. Madame Birot, standing upon a wooden foot-warmer, which made her look un-

naturally tall, with her head turned toward the
window, was preparing to iron three spring waists
for her daughter—a lilac and two white ones—
which now hung damp and rumpled, on a tempo-
rary clothes-line stretched between two chairs.
An ironing-board was before her. Birot on her
right hand, with his back to the light, was superintending the heating of a posset of red wine and
sugar, which stood on the little stove beside the
flat-irons.

This universal remedy was intended to cure an
obstinate cough which the master stone-cutter had
brought back with him from the works. The oppressive odour of burning charcoal filled the room.

Birot, who had not spoken for the last hour, but
sat gnawing his short moustache, suddenly raised
his resolute face.

"Well, I have seen Mademoiselle Hélène," he
said. "She is quite ready to undertake Davidée's
instruction, and to teach her everything—everything. She answers for it that three years hence, at
the latest, the child will be capable of entering the
normal school on the rue Dauphine in La Rochelle."

The slender housewife, with the brown braided
locks, started slightly but did not speak at once.
She seized the lilac waist and spread it out on the
board, smoothing its folds nervously with fingers
that trembled slightly, as eyelids do that are heavy
with tears. Her husband had time to add:

"Nothing to pay. Only for her books, a mere
trifle."

"We ought to find out first whether she wants
to be a teacher. It is a poor trade."

"The finest of all."

"What do you know of it? Attending to other people's children when one might have some of one's own!"

"Well, what will hinder her from getting married?"

"To another teacher, I suppose? To a man who can be sent hither and yon, away from us, as a soldier is, and you who do not love soldiers! It is just the same thing. Not to mention that he will look down upon me, and on you also, for that matter. But your pride prevents your judging intelligently."

"Why don't you say at once that I have never been successful?"

"In business, yes; in elections, yes; but it goes no further, Birot. You and the world are two."

"The world and you and I are three, then. For you are of no different species from your husband, my lady. You are nothing but the wife of a workingman, who puts on gloves on fête-days, but is nobody after all. Look here! Of us two, it is I who have travelled most and heard how people of the world talk. I hold my tongue, to be sure, when your friends come to call on you, if I happen to be around, and I appear like a man who thinks about nothing. But I make it up among men, I can tell you. I am listened to; they tremble when I get angry; they seek to know my opinion, to guess at it in order to agree with me before I open my mouth. The gate-keepers, the gendarmes, all the functionaries of La Rochelle, even the big fellows, bow low to me as if

begging my leave to keep their places. The curé
never looks at me when we meet on the road,
probably for fear of seeing how I despise him.
The prefect would ask me to dinner if I cared to
go—me the stone-cutter! and he would even ask
you with me if I cared to have him. I could go
to his house in my blouse and sabots, with my pipe
and my oaths, and he would laugh, the poor coward! I have the sort of power men don't gain
without being intelligent. You can't understand
the pleasure of that! To give orders without a
sergeant's stripe, to be a gendarme in a blouse!
Only it brings obligations with it, you see. I must
have children who will carry out my ideas and
serve the cause, do you understand? To have
Davidée married doesn't raise me in the world,
but to have Davidée a state-instructress does raise
me! And besides, I can look after her promotion."

Little Madame Birot, who was still ironing away
at the lilac waist, pointed the smoking flat-iron
toward her husband.

"So you are choosing for her! That is a pretty
business," she said.

"No, I want her to choose for me."

"Egotist that you are!"

"Isn't she my daughter, then?"

"She is mine still more, as I am her mother.
Do you never think that you are taking her away
from me?"

"Three years from now!"

"Three years from now seem like to-morrow!
The fear of losing her will stand between us all
those days! Birot, do not do this! Neither for

yourself, nor for me, nor for her! We shall all suffer if you do, each in our own way."

Birot rose with purple face and hard eyes, and stretched out his hand toward the hot iron which his wife drew back quickly, and which she began to move to and fro with frantic haste over the light muslin, murmuring as she did so:

"Hard heart! Hard heart!"

The man was standing before her between the ironing-board and the window, and she paused in her work so that she could look him straight in the face; she, facing the light which streamed into the depths of her brown eyes, showed him plainly that she did not fear him.

"*Bourgeoise!*" he exclaimed after a moment's silence, during which he recognized that his anger would not prevail this time over the wounded mother who resisted him.

"Bourgeoise! you are better educated than I in some ways, but you have no longing for education. As for me, I would give half my savings to acquire learning, to be able to speak well, to write well, to read books without my head's splitting, as I see others do. You think I only want to please my friends by making my daughter a teacher? Well, no, it's not merely that. I want her to have what I have never had. I want her not to be below anybody, not to be ashamed when she meets learned people. Knowledge is the thing I am jealous of. I never own it to the comrades; they think me strong because I talk big; but it is only because they are such cowards that they always give in to me. I am in the wrong sometimes; I can't invent everything. It enrages me, when I have to answer back to a bourgeois or to silence an enemy or a comrade who refuses to obey me, that I can only swear at them. I want to have ideas, knowledge, all that makes one able to laugh at others instead of getting mad with them. My daughter shall turn the tables. She shall talk for me, she shall think for me. People will say: 'How well she talks, the young lady! What a lot of things she knows! What an education she has!' While of me they only say: 'That old Birot! It is not safe to be one of his enemies! He hits hard and fears nobody.' That's true enough, but it doesn't content one."

"And who is content, Birot? Are you? Or am I? Or the comrades in the stone-yard?"

He replied by stretching out his big broad hand and seizing between two square-tipped fingers the half-ironed waist, puffed out by the pressing, and transparent in the light. Under his harsh moustache, reddened by the pipe, his lips spread wide apart:

"It's this pretty rascal, Davidée Birot!"

"Will you stop saying words like that!"

"When she's through school at twenty, how the suitors will swarm around her like flies around a block of stone at noonday!"

"Don't touch that muslin, Birot. It is too fresh and fine for your fingers. Give it back to me."

He merely kept up his big laugh, trying to soften his wife.

"Give it back to me, I tell you!   I tell you not to touch it."

This time he threw the waist down and his wife seized it, holding it up to see if he had left any trace of his fingers on the muslin and cried angrily:

"You will live to repent, Birot.   You who sell your daughter to serve anybody's children!   You will have grief enough when you are only a poor old man and your daughter is no longer here beside us and you can see her no more!   You never yield, to be sure, but old age will make you bend.   You won't know how to bear it, and then you will shed bitter tears at having driven away our little one, the pretty, the sweet, the well-beloved!"

He felt the force of these images which gripped hold of his heart.   He turned aside and coughed to show that he was ill, leaning his head against the window.   "There she is!" he suddenly cried.

Madame Birot stepped down off the foot-warmer.

"Let me see!" she said, pushing him aside. He did not protest, for he obeyed his wife in everything which did not concern his "ideas." Each exercised their own tyranny, hers within the home, his without.

"You say that you love her, the poor darling! I know you only too well; you have a fashion of loving others which takes no account of their tastes or their wishes.   Look at her there!   How she walks between the tinman's two daughters! How rosy she is and how soft-hearted and pleased

with life! She has already turned her eyes this
way; there again! She sees me. She is saying
to her companions: 'That is mamma!' Poor
innocent! The idea of making a teacher out of
her with that smile, and lips like apple blossoms!
The idea of making *her* teach b–a *ba,* and dip
steel pens in ink! Now she is crossing the street
alone, and looking out for the carriage that is
coming. I have so often told her she must look
out for carriages! Do you hear her on the
stairs?"

They had both turned at once. They were
listening for Davidée's light, even step on the
wooden stairs. With the same emotion they
watched the door open and saw in the rift of light
from outside the head of a slip of a girl, the quick
hand turning the handle and throwing the door
wide open, and then Davidée standing there in
the full light.

"Good-morning, papa! Morning, mamma!"

Her cheeks were sunburnt, and her features
still unformed; her long brown braids were loosened by running; her cotton dress with white
polka-dots was stained and too short for her; her
boots were muddy, and her legs in their black
stockings too stout for grace, and yet she had
about her a radiancy of youth, a dazzling air of
health and vigour, an awkward grace, a mysterious but evident promise of intelligence, of capacity for happiness or suffering—perhaps for
making others suffer, perhaps for consoling them
—a something, in short, which already out-
stripped the poor calculations of the parents who

now embraced her, the father brusquely, the
mother with a slow, tender clasp.

"Good-morning, my darling, darling Davidée."

"Good-day, little one."

She seated herself on her mother's knee and
nestled in her arms, and Madame Birot's face
grew young again. It relaxed, softened, and
became beautified, in its perfect happiness. A
little more and she would have rocked her child
in her arms. Even Birot, little given as he was
to idle sentiment, gazed with complacency on this
group formed by the two beings who belonged
to him wholly, his wife and his daughter. His
mind, uncultivated as it was, controlled his feelings; his emotion at this moment was purely mental. He admired Davidée's look, her happiness
at being petted, but a happiness which did not
exclude thought; he divined that those brown
eyes, half-hidden on her mother's breast and yet
peeping forth at her father, around the room and
out of the window, held a strange fulness of life,
and he was proud of her; he was confirmed in his
views as to her future, while the mother merely
rejoiced in clasping her child in her arms and
defending her body and soul.

They were alike, Davidée and her mother, but
the child had a mobility of expression which the
mother lacked. Her delicate ears, small and
well-modelled, came neither from her father nor
mother; her red, half-parted lips exhaled a fresh,
even breath which her mother drew in like the
breath of spring. All three remained silent,
father, mother and child, because their minds were

each absorbed in a different thought, and an obscure sense of separation lay between them.

The father spoke first.

"Did you enjoy yourself?"

"Yes, well enough." She often answered in that way.

"Did you run?"

"Yes, as fast as a doe."

"Did you drink milk?"

"I dipped my nose in it."

"A big cupful?"

"Yes, with cream as high as that."

"Who did you meet on the road, gentle-folk, or men from the works?"

"Your men, papa."

"Did they bow to you?"

"They didn't seem to recognize me."

The man gave a scowl and muttered:

"If you were the daughter of a rich patron, who did no work, of a noble or a half-noble, they would have recognized you fast enough. But the daughter of one of themselves, who has worked harder and earned more than they, her they pass by as if she were nobody. The jealous dogs! How disgusting it is to get on in the world and yet not be looked up to!"

He snorted furiously through his bristling moustache as he spoke. Davidée's mother was bending over her, unbuttoning her damp, muddy shoes and struggling over each button. When she had pulled the shoes off she carefully felt of the child's feet.

"They are wet, you naughty girl; you will catch

cold. Oh! how I hate letting you go away from home like that. Wait while I get you some dry stockings from the closet." So speaking, she drew off the clinging stockings as if she were skinning a little rabbit, while the child's long legs steamed in the warm room. Davidée was laughing, her head leaning against the chair-back. Her mother had lifted her in her arms as she rose and set her down again a little sideways, telling her not to touch her feet to the ground, while she ran hastily to the clothes-press and turned the creaking lock, which invariably resisted.

Papa Birot seized the opportunity to approach without rising from his chair, by dragging it along with him, and seized one of the girl's hands as it hung at her side.

"Look here, child! tell her it is all settled."

"What is settled, papa?"

She knew perfectly what he meant, but she hesitated, because she had a tender heart which suffered at the thought of giving pain to others. She divined that at the farther end of the room an ear was bent to listen to them, as the lower drawer slid softly open and was softly closed again.

"Tell her that you want to be a teacher. You must speak out frankly now that you're a big girl. Who did you meet over yonder? Did you not meet a lady whom father had asked to meet you?"

Davidée was a resolute girl as well as a sensitive one. She rose now and stood barefooted on the floor, saying solemnly and in measured tones as if pronouncing an oath:

"I will be a teacher. I have met the directress. I will begin to-morrow."

But no sooner had she spoken than her heart resumed its sway; she was about to throw herself into her father's arms when she found herself seized by the waist, lifted and forcibly replaced in the chair, while her mother kneeling in front of her pressed the two small feet against her breast so vehemently as almost to crush them, as unrolling a pair of black stockings she exclaimed:

"Just wait till I give you a scolding. Can't you stay where I put you?"

But whether the child's limbs were still damp or the mother's hands trembled, the woollen stockings refused to slip on, and Madame Birot, bending over them, was nothing now but a poor unnerved mother, helpless between her husband and child.

"God have mercy!" she murmured.

"There is no God!" replied Birot.

No one resented this blasphemous utterance, neither mother nor daughter, for they were used to such words. Birot pushed his chair back with his foot, and began walking up and down the chamber without removing his gaze from his wife, who still bent over her task with blinded eyes. Davidée had turned pale, youth for a moment seemed to have vanished from her face; there where it was wont to bloom and play over the curves of her cheek, her low forehead and the darkly arched eyebrows that nearly met, there was now only the shade of pity for her weeping mother, and the gravity of a child who for the first time is conscious of another's grief.

"You look like the directress, yes, already!" exclaimed her father.

Davidée tried to smile but did not succeed. Her mother, wiping away her tears with the hem of her apron, rose and said:

"Go and draw some water, Birot, for me to wash my hands!"

She was making him pay for having won the day. She had yielded to the man who would not tolerate the least opposition to his "ideas," but she now recalled to him that at home, in household affairs, it was she who ruled. Her husband made no resistance, but descended the stairs heavily, and they heard him push open the door which led into their little garden.

When he re-entered, puffing and panting, with the water-pail on his outstretched right arm while the left was bent to serve as a balance, he found Davidée in her mother's arms; the little one was caressing the thin temples where the hair was wearing away.

"I shall come home," she said; "you will see how nice it will be during the vacations. You will be proud of your little girl. Mamma, do not cry; do not put such grief into my heart that it will never go away. I have a friend who is going to be a teacher too. She is the best scholar in the class, so you see!"

Her father set down the pail, which, being full to the brim, spilt over on the floor.

"Can't you be a little more careful, Birot?"

He pulled at the ends of his moustache and said, with no ill-temper left in his voice:

"I am going out to see my friends who are waiting for me at the café. Don't you worry, Davidée; before you leave home I shall have built a fine new house with a parlour, and running water in the bedrooms, and the year inscribed by me in the key-stone over the front door, and a porch, and a garden with a fountain in it. Yes, if business goes on prospering as it is doing now, I shall certainly build that house. And all the ladies in Blandes will envy Madame Birot. She will be quite happy, your mother, in her new house, where she will spend all her time embroidering underclothes for you, child, and doing worsted work."

Madame Birot turned her head at this.

"And alone of course! You think I shall be happy in a house where I am all alone?"

"And what of me, and our son? Don't we count for anything?" And shrugging his shoulders, Birot left the room.

Spring came at last and Davidée began her studies. She had good marks and was in excellent health. Little by little her mother, who from the first moment had recognized the inevitable, grew resigned to living with her grief as if wedded to it, and made no further complaint. Birot declared:

"She has grown used to the idea. She will be as proud as I." But it was not so. This woman who had great powers of self-control and who at another period and under other conditions, might have developed a deep inner life and habits of meditation, continued inwardly rebellious as at first, but kept silence for the sake of peace. What would it have availed to struggle? Their son already promised little comfort to his parents; he would never attach his father to the house, and, far from being a bond of union, he was a subject of mutual reproaches: "He is like you!" "That may be, but it was you who spoiled him." If Davidée were made the subject of fresh quarrels, Birot was capable of any violent action. The mother, therefore, having once uttered her grief, kept it hidden like a treasure, like a secret all her own, in the depths of her soul where she visited it when she was alone and wept.

But before Birot, before her friends, before the "world," she wore a placid smile, which no one distinguished at first from an expression of tranquil contentment, of vanity flattered by her child's successes.

"She is as ambitious as Monsieur Birot," said the neighbours; "and moreover, who is it that rules the house? Isn't it she?" They could not draw the distinction, nor recognize the curious phenomenon by which this stone-cutter, docile in all domestic matters, became a tyrant where his "ideas" were concerned. Even before her daughter, Madame Birot never showed the trouble which seldom left her. She had but one little hobby, which was to dwell constantly on the past, as if the best of life for her was already there in the years that had flown.

"I remember one day, Davidée, when you were only four years old. Oh, how pretty you were with your long curls, and the arms you threw

round one's neck so coaxingly! I remember something you once said . . . a walk we took . . . and
one night when you woke feverish and with a
hard cough, so hard that I jumped out of bed and
ran to your crib in my night-dress, crying, 'It is
croup, Birot; our darling has the croup!'"

In her heart she was constantly counting the
days between the vacations, and the examinations
which succeeded each other so rapidly. She had
a horror, barely dissimulated, of all books and
copybooks, and of the black-board which they
had been obliged to purchase and set up in the
white chamber.

Davidée worked diligently; she brought to her
daily tasks a clear mind, marked taste for study
and pride in learning. Her father was right in
saying of her: "You are the picture of me—
flattered of course—when you are bending over
a book. Oh, how I should have loved that!"
But her kinship to her mother showed more
plainly still. Child of an anxious, self-tormenting
mother, Davidée was already a dreamer at the age
when most girls are thinking only of the sports
of to-day, or the lover of to-morrow. Possessed
outwardly of a calm nature like her mother, but
not limited, in her capacity for dreaming and
suffering, to her home or her village. She pored
over books; she read, she sought, she divined, and
soon became conscious that her intellectual long-
ings would never be appeased by the teacher who
had first contributed to awaken this thirst for
knowing and understanding. She was but slightly
concerned about religious questions. Madame

Birot, in the early days of her married life, had
renounced all genuine religious observances. At
the great festivals, like All Souls and Easter, she
was to be seen in the Blandes church directly
under the spot where a small model of a three-
masted vessel was suspended as a votive offering,
and this sufficed to prevent her being ranked as
anti-religious. Her husband, on the contrary, was
openly and violently hostile to religion, to priests
and to all religious schools, and regarded the
Catholic Church merely as a political institution
opposed to the State of which he considered himself an influential adherent. Under his roof no
word was ever uttered in favour of religion. Sacred
pictures or books expounding the faith were never
seen. Outside her home, on rare occasions, Davidée had heard some acquaintance complain of
the tyranny of the existing laws and their functionaries, and express regret at the closing of the
convents, especially of the school conducted by
nuns, in which many mothers of families in Blandes
had received their education. But having no
comprehension of the religious life, she felt no
sympathy for those sufferings which reach above
the merely human order of emotions; she pitied
only those aged nuns of whom she was told that
they were "dying of hunger." For her, Catholi-
cism was a religion which had had its day; she
confounded the complaints of the faithful with
opposition to the party in power. She heard
perpetual talk of "the clericals, those eternal
enemies of the Republic," and she regarded them
as troublesome malcontents whom Monsieur

Birot's journals accused of opposing all progress.

One religious memory alone flitted across the
solitude of her heaven, above her little plot of
earth, fertile, cultivated and overflowing with
abundance. The shadow of its wing was light,
and yet the earth had felt it. Davidée remembered her first communion, never renewed, and
ill-prepared for, but fervent. Certainly she had
missed many lessons in the catechism, which her
mother had barely consented to hear her recite
in her father's absence. And yet there had been
for one day a response of this pure young soul to
the touch of a divine joy which left her still won-
dering. A solitary impulse of the heart, a desire
to be good forever, and a luminous peace had settled over her. For a moment, more or less, she
had felt the reasonable and sweet persuasion of
being a soul, a power capable of the loftiest flights,
a frail being lost and glorified in a Greater Being.

No one ever spoke to her again of that moment
which so many other moments had covered up
and buried. Her white dress had been given
away; her crown of roses, preserved for awhile
among her girlish treasures, had lost its petals,
and finally, when the family moved from one
house to another, had been thrown away, with
her mother-of-pearl rosary and gold medal, without either her father or mother's admitting the
least remembrance of having seen or touched
them. Of these sacred relics of her first and only
communion the sole remaining one was a little
prayer-book bound in fawn-coloured morocco.

Davidée was admitted to the examination for
the normal school in July, 1902. During the
vacation she paid a little visit in the south to be
near her brother, who was a clerk in the prefecture. At the same time the master quarryman was superintending the construction of the
fine new house which he had long aspired to possess; he studied plans; he himself drew designs
for the flight of six broad steps leading up to the
porch, and for the cornices and window sills. He
rarely left the workshop, but received there the
envious homage of his cronies who now invariably styled him *Monsieur* Birot; who mentally
calculated the cost of the building while they
openly praised the quality of the materials em-
ployed, the size of the dining and reception rooms,
and the plan of the two connecting gardens, the
lower and smaller enclosed by an iron railing, the
larger which sloped upward toward the church,
surrounded by high walls. Along these walls, as
Birot explained, with a sweeping gesture of his
arm, was to extend a plantation of peach and
cherry trees, garden grapes and even a mimosa,
the latter ostensibly because "Madame Birot was
wild to have one," but actually for the reason
that no one in Blandes had ever possessed a
mimosa.

The three years at the normal school were
years of success for Davidée and of pride for
Monsieur Birot. Davidée was now a young girl;
her large black eyes, her scarlet lips and the raven
hair piled above her forehead like a casque or
crown made her look like a daughter of the south.

She walked well, with a supple grace, though she
was not tall, being only an inch taller than her
little mother and two inches shorter than her
father; when she laughed she showed two rows
of dazzling teeth. But there was nothing of the
south about her mind. She had acute sensibili-
ties which her reason was powerless to control,
though outwardly she appeared to dominate them.
She was never seen to shed tears, her face remained calm, her speech clear and deliberate under
any stress of emotion, something of her father's
sturdy will revealing itself in her bearing. Her
friends, little expert in reading souls, would say
to her: "How lucky you are to be so entirely
mistress over external impressions! Have you
any emotions which are not swayed by your reason?" They were unaware that the immovable
green earth, a shallow crust, hides deep internal
springs, and that every oscillation of the surface,
every slightest vibration, stirs these quivering
unknown deeps. A reproach, an injustice, a
sorrow, agitated Davidée for weeks, and ideas
and thoughts, with her, prolonged themselves
in emotion. She asked herself perpetually:
"Whence comes this feeble light which is granted
me? How does it serve to illuminate my path,
or that of others, or the world? Have I understood such and such a daily problem? To what
conclusion will these principles lead me? How
will they affect to-morrow's actions, and in the
past how should I have acted if I had known this
earlier?" Her mind wearied itself in following
these paths without a landmark, with no leading

by her parents, nor by any later guide. She turned
on her tracks amid these mazes like a pursued and
panting hare which ends by falling exhausted.
She felt an actual sense of pain on hearing Mlle.
Hacquin, the professor of psychology, assert, in
one of her first lessons, that morality should be
entirely independent of all religious basis. She
revolted at this conclusion and during the recrea-
tion hour that followed the class, she went bravely,
for hers was the nervous courage that cannot
brook delay, to expose her doubts to the professor. "I was expecting you," said Mlle. Hacquin. "I saw by the knitting of your brows that
I had surprised and possibly pained you."

This preceptress, a lean, spare person, who
veiled her irony under a caressing manner, possessed the art of calming rather than confuting
her opponent, leaving the arguments she did not
wish to attack openly in a mid-region of vague-
ness and uncertainty. She thus destroyed in-
sidiously, counting on the gradual crumbling
away of those ancient edifices of thought which
were no longer kept in repair. And so it happened almost invariably. Her pupils lost hold
on the faith, often uncertain and barely conscious, with which they entered school. In
exchange they adopted the views of Mlle. Hacquin, shallow views on the whole, though dressed
out in a specious affirmative guise, forming a
system which seemed at first sight to be supported by reason. But on being subjected to the
slightest practical test—as those of her pupils
discovered who still recalled their teacher's les-

sons—this system of ethics proved of no real
help in the exigencies of life, this wisdom lacked
the power to direct or to console.

Davidée Birot resigned herself like the others,
though with more reluctance, to calling God the
Unknowable. She suffered at feeling herself
bereft of support and love, gazing up into an
empty sky, with no invisible protection above her,
no Judge to whom she could appeal for laws of
perfection and beauty in the inward life, no
Redeemer, no resource in the hour of death. Like
the others, she noted down with care and reduced
to formulas the contradictory philosophies of all
the modern and most of the ancient sceptics, and
she strove to find in their theories repose for her
soul. This vain attempt wearied her, but at
least she never relinquished it. Many of her
companions, who experienced none of her mental
disquiet, speedily learned to disdain all religious
ideas. Davidée could not become a mocker like
them, but constantly repeated to herself: "Later
on I will study, I will find out."

What remote ancestress faithful to her rosary,
what forbears of robust and sincere faith, still
influenced this lonely mind? This intellectual
loneliness did not, however, overshadow her daily
life nor prevent the young scholar from being gay
among her fellows, ardent at all their sports,
their walks and excursions as well as at her studies.

Birot exulted when Davidée came home.
"Father," she would say, "why do you present
me to each of your friends in turn, as if I were a
marvel? I am no such a thing, and they have all

known me from my cradle!" But in spite of her protests, he never failed, at each home-coming, to assemble his cronies in the grand new dining-room. "Comrades," he would say, "here is the Flower of Blandes, a girl who knows everything. She can recite without a mistake the names of all the kings of Egypt. She knows what is in the earth, and in the stars, and in the inside of a lizard; she can count up to any number without using her fingers, quicker than I can strike a blow. She is my pride! Comrades, you see in her what I should have been if I had had her education. All the labour of my life has served to produce that dainty tidbit there! Is she worth it? Eh!"

"Certainly she is, Birot! and your labour has also enabled you to build such a house that there is not another to equal it in Blandes."

"That's true, too, but I am not half as proud of my house as of my daughter. Come, Davidée, stand up and recite a fable to these friends."

"Oh no, papa! I am no longer the age for reciting fables. I am nineteen, you know."

"Well, verses then, by—you know who—those verses that make one want to cry when you recite them in your clear voice."

"'The Lake'?"

"'The Lake,' yes; now you shall see! And you, mother, bring along a bottle of that liqueur of the Isles."

And before these heavy mates of his, while her father cautiously poured the liqueur, Davidée stood up and recited Lamartine. They listened as they would have listened to a song, silent and a little moved, without knowing why, except that the human heart needs to be lulled by some rhythm or other.

The mother meanwhile, who was now gray-haired, stood in the door-way to listen, and retired as soon as the applause broke out, as she did not like noise; and then the careful housewife, impatient for the hour when these men would leave her clean house, which they soiled with their muddy shoes, wandered restlessly from parlour to kitchen, from chamber to chamber, and even down to the wine-cellar which her husband had confided to her vigilant care.

The mimosa on the south side of the house had become a tree, while clumps of golden spindle-tree formed pyramids on the lawn, under the planes and lindens which had been so judiciously planted.

In the month of October, 1905, Davidée was appointed assistant in a large girls' school at Rochefort-sur-Mer. She passed three years there, and at the end of that time received her pedagogic diploma with honours. But her health had given out and the physician who was called in, advised that the young girl should be removed to a milder climate where she would not be exposed to the injurious influences of the sea-air. This was a severe blow to her aged parents, but they loved their daughter. Birot, Mayor of Blandes, had but to speak the word, and Davidée received her promotion as assistant at Ardésie in the department of Maine-et-Loire.

She had been exercising her functions for three

months, and had attained her twenty-third year
on the third of the preceding January, when
Maïeul Jacquet came to hoe her garden, when
she learned of Phrosine's fault, and the secret
trouble of Anna Le Floch.

CHAPTER III.

THE HOUSE ON THE PLAINS.

On the following day, which was a Wednesday, Davidée stood watching the return of the pupils who arrived in little squads and were not visible from the court-yard until they had entered the gate. They came from the right and left, keeping close under the wall, their sabots not clicking as usual, for the ground was still soft after the night's fog and rain. She caught glimpses of them as they approached, through an opening between two pillars; first a child's slim legs thrust forward, then a knee, then the whole little figure turning the corner of the wall. Each child, before she was well inside the court, cast a comprehensive glance about her, taking in the whole scene; first her little mates, then the teacher on duty, and lastly the exact spot where she could slip in and reach the covered play-ground where her best friend was awaiting her. Some of the pupils, on catching sight of Mlle. Davidée, ran to greet her with beaming faces, eyes shining with childish affection, innocent lips raised for a kiss and a "Good-morning, Ma'm'selle!" As soon as the kiss was given they hopped away like birds, with folded wings and half-turns of the neck to see who was watching them, and mingled with the rest of the flock. Others passed with a rapid half-curtsy, bending only one knee; a few, in haste to resume their games and chatter, took no notice of the teacher; others still, who had inherited a spirit of insubordination, observed her slyly out of the corners of their eyes, and skirted the wall to avoid greeting her, pretending to look for a ball or to call to some distant companion, and when they were well out of her sight assuming a self-satisfied, impertinent air. All played unconsciously the game of their sex, their family, and the passions they had inherited.

Davidée standing motionless, with her feet on the wet sand, and a white woollen scarf thrown over her head, was looking eagerly, not for a child but a woman. Her heart was beating fast as each new figure appeared in the angle of the wall.

"Why has she not come yet? She is not often late! The fire will not be lighted in time; this woman is neglecting her work and it is not surprising." She mentally spoke of "this woman" with an accent of irritation and contempt. She tried to command her features, to assume in advance a fitting expression of dignified but not harsh reproof. Images passed before her mind which she strove to banish and the effort half unnerved her. The children in the background rattled their sabots, as they chased each other round the court, or leaned listlessly against the pillars awaiting the signal for opening school.

Suddenly a cry arose. "Anna Le Floch! Anna Le Floch! There she is!" And with exclamations of joy and astonishment twenty little girls rushed to surround a child who was just entering, and who turned paler than before at this tumult, responding merely by a frightened and pathetic smile. Anna Le Floch, with her faded tangled locks, her startled greenish eyes, clad in a gray woollen dress which fell as straight and scant over her chest and hips as the cotta of a choirboy, stood shyly with her hands hanging unresponsively at her sides as her companions attempted to grasp them, and clinging closer to her mother, the tall Phrosine, who held her by the shoulders and gently urged her forward.

"Go child; you see they are glad to see you again! Let her alone, the rest of you; she is weak still. Go in little one; go!" For this Phrosine was a mother after all.

"Good-morning, Mademoiselle," she pursued; "I'm afraid I'm a bit late, but *she* wanted to come. You are displeased, I see, but faith! I had no carriage to bring her in." Davidée had only replied by a slight nod, and this was why Phrosine had suddenly assumed a defiant tone; why she pushed her child into the teacher's arms crying, "I had no carriage to bring her in," and hurried away toward the school-room.

The children were sorry for Anna Le Floch, but they knew no way of showing it save by embracing this little companion, who had not been able to join in their games all winter. One or two rose on their tiptoes to kiss her pale cheeks. The others drew back because "Mademoiselle" had already passed one arm around Anna's waist and was bending over her, as they moved slowly

toward the school-room, murmuring what seemed
to be words of pity, though they could not hear
them.   Anna with hard eyes, eyes veiled by the
shadow of her suffering, looked before her without seeing and made no answer.   The smoke
was already pouring through the iron pipe, which
protruded from the school-room window.

When Phrosine came out again, half-past
eight had just struck, and the children drew back
and looked up at her, with her crown of bright
chestnut hair raised high above her forehead, and
the strong, grave, maternal face, which grew incredibly soft when she addressed a good-day to
one of her child's playmates, and took on the
expression of a Mater Dolorosa when she turned
to gaze at the pale face of the child herself amidst
her ruddy companions.   She had no aptitude for
feigning and her look continued sad, as if she still
saw the little face, when she turned to Davidée
Birot and said:

"Mademoiselle, take care of her, will you?
Give her some breakfast here.   She can only eat
a few mouthfuls of bread; she is very ill."

The assistant replied: "Certainly I will take
care of her."   Then, clapping her hands, she gave
the signal for the children to enter the school-
room.   The sun meanwhile had risen higher yet
above the roof which sheltered the two class-
rooms, above the garden, and the three ancient
hyacinths which, hid in a warm corner of the yard,
raised their pulpy stalks of pallid green matching
the shutters, and flecked with sand from the play-
ground.

At noon Anna Le Floch had breakfast in the kitchen, with two other pupils who paid Mlle. Renée for their daily board. She barely tasted the hot soup which Davidée poured into her plate. "Eat some; it will do you good," said her little neighbours, joggling her with their elbows.

She shook her head, as one who knows that her complaint is past remedy, but turned thankfully toward the fire which was blazing on the hearth and held out her transparent hands to warm them. The head-mistress and her assistant at the further end of the table were breakfasting hurriedly.

"What ails the child?" asked Davidée.

"She is tuberculous and rickety," murmured Mlle. Renée. "One of those children who suffer for the sins of their fathers."

"And who is the father?"

"I don't know."

"What! you have never found out, in the six years you have been here?"

"No."

"For my part I think she has trouble greater than she has strength to bear. Have you noticed her eyes, that never look straight at you, as if for fear you should read her heart?"

"I have always thought she was a sly little thing."

"Her being unhappy would be reason enough for hiding her feelings. I am very, very sorry for her!"

"Tell me, Mademoiselle, will you look after the recess for me, as I have some letters to write?"

Davidée often took charge during the recrea-

tion hour when the children returned before the
afternoon lessons, and as many of them hurried
back to play, she sometimes took part in their
games. But to-day she merely watched them
from a distance as one by one, at a half-hour past
noon, they again turned the bend in the road and
entered the court-yard. She had gone into the
garden with Anna Le Floch, and with her arm
around the child's waist, was pacing slowly up and
down the mossy alley between the box-bordered
beds.

It was one of the first mild days of spring when
in the shelter of the wall which cut off the wind,
the sun had power to penetrate the limbs and
warm the chilled blood.

In spite of their gentle pace, poor little Anna's
hair was moist from the slight exertion and clung
damply to the child's thin temples, in straggling
faded locks. At first she tried to draw away her
arm and go off by herself, but a few gentle words
and the sympathy which she began to divine
were gradually taming her. It felt good to her
after all: the warmth of the garden and this gentle
companion all to herself.

Anna Le Floch began to realize fully that the
heart of the young teacher was not occupied for
the moment by any other affection or thought or
interest than hers, and that she, the sick child,
reigned there alone. How this thought inclined
her to confidences! how it relaxed the strong will
and broke through the long habit of silence!
Leaning one against the other and talking of
school and village matters, they turned once more

at the end of the alley and retraced their steps, with the sun shining now on their right cheeks. The laughter of the children at their games reached them more faintly on the breeze, and they felt the more alone for these distant sounds. Tears had risen to the child's eyes, but she felt almost happy.

"Tell me if you love me a little, Anna?"

"Oh, yes, dearly."

"Tell me why you are so sad? I would like to help you. Is it your illness that makes you so?"

"Oh, no!"

"What then?"

The little one stopped and hung her head. "I am grieved," she said.

"And what about, Anna?"

"I do not know—about living, I think."

Anna felt Davidée's arm press hers more closely as she spoke again.

"It is perhaps because you are longing to see your papa?"

A trembling shook the frail little body first, then the hoarse, panting voice whispered:

"He went away and never came back."

"Was it long ago?"

"Not this year, nor last, nor the year before that. I think it was when I was two or three months old, perhaps even less, and now I am twelve."

"Twelve years seem long when one has suffered, my poor child."

"Oh, yes, but I only wish that I had no other papa; and mamma has given me one."

"Does he live with you?"

"Yes, mornings and nights—always. It is only at noon that he does not come home. He is a workman at the quarries up there."

"Yes, I know."

"He wants me to love him, but I do not love him." The startled green eyes were raised to hers and Davidée read in them a deep instinctive childish aversion. The man's name was not uttered. The little girl closed her eyes and the corners of her lips were drawn down as she murmured: __

"I want to kill myself."

"What are you saying, Anna? You have no right to take your own life. No one has the right."

"Why not?"

The teacher drew herself up to listen to a sudden uproar among the children as they chased a poor terrified mouse; then as she resumed her walk she noticed that the box-bordered bed near which Anna was standing was the one which had been dug most recently. She drew the lonely, wretched child further away, saying:

"I will be your friend if you will let me. I will go to see you when you cannot come to school. Whenever you want to weep away your troubles you shall weep on my heart. It knows trouble, too."

Anna's face had resumed its wild, shy, distrustful look, and as they were now approaching the court-yard, Davidée turned toward the school with her.

The afternoon passed like so many others, but

toward its close an incident disturbed the daily routine.

Each day, when the lessons were over, Mlle. Renée was in the habit of repeating and expounding to the older girls some moral maxim; an exercise which she called, as she had heard it called in other schools, the lay-prayer. She submitted a list of subjects beforehand to the Primary Inspector and inscribed them in her school diary. On the previous day she had enlarged, with a verbal facility which had brought her credit with her superiors, upon the maxim "Time is money." The note-book bore for to-day's text: "Lay-prayer: Alcoholism is slow suicide." The five and twenty pupils were listening, as they listened to the last stroke of the clock at closing hour; putting away their pen-holders meanwhile, closing their books, and folding up their papers with a continuous rustling noise. Two or three among the more intelligent, however, were paying strict attention, and Anna Le Floch, the last on the rear bench, directly under a ray of light from the window, was listening with passionate interest. Bending forward, with her elbows spread apart, her hands supporting her cheeks and her chin almost touching the desk, she showed merely a face pale as wax, with wide staring eyes surrounded by dark circles. What was it that excited her and kept her wide-awake at the close of this exhausting day? Did Mlle. Renée suspect the breathless interest with which her words were being followed by one hearer there, under the declining light from the long window? No, the head-teacher was near-sighted, and having taken off her eye-glasses, could not distinguish Anna's face and the anguish in the childish eyes.

"The children of alcoholic parents," she pursued, "are often degenerates, infirm and ill, mere useless waifs, and sometimes criminals. We can only pity them, but what responsibility rests on the parents! To die young through the sins of those who have given us life! I hope that I may never witness the death of any pupil from any such inherited taint. It would cause me too keen a pang of grief. I have often asked myself what I should do if I had the misfortune to lose one of my pupils by death; for, as you know, I do not believe in the immortality of the soul, only in the transformation of matter. If a child of my own were to die, instead of praying for her soul, which would be an idle task, I should plant flowers on her grave and inhale their perfume."

At this moment a shrill cry arose: "Mademoiselle! Mademoiselle! Anna is dying!"

The whole class were on their feet.

"Mademoiselle, her eyes are closed! Mademoiselle, how white she looks!" Some of the children pulled wildly at the sleeve of their companion who did not stir and whose face, no longer supported by her hands, lay forward on her desk, her forehead resting on the hard wood. "She is dead! oh, she is dead! She does not hear us." Piercing cries echoed through the school-room, as the head-mistress rapidly crossed it, and laid Anna's motionless figure at full length on a bench, while she said in a tone of authority:

"She has only fainted; it is nothing! I can feel her heart beat. Do not be frightened, children, but go away quickly and make no noise! Only call Mademoiselle Davidée! I promise you that by to-morrow you shall see your little schoolmate again."

The children rapidly dispersed, but each one on reaching the door paused a minute and looked back to see if Anna had moved. No, she had not stirred, the eyes were closed and the lips parted, revealing her teeth which showed the same bluish tint as the hollows around her eyes. Davidée had come and, seating herself on a stool, had taken the child in her arms and was holding her across her knees as mothers do an infant. The little head, which had fallen back, rested on the shoulder of the girl who, with her left hand, was unfastening the neck of the gray frock.

"A little water, Mademoiselle; quickly, please."

Mlle. Renée hastened to dip her handkerchief at the pump in the court-yard and sponge the child's brow, but did not succeed in restoring consciousness.

"Carry her up and lay her on my bed," she said.

"Or on mine, if you will allow me," said Davidée. "She has grown used to me now and may be glad to see me there when she revives!"

She weighed less than a child of six, the little Le Floch. Davidée lifted her without effort, but with a feeling of anxiety and of almost maternal possession, as she carried her across the court and up the stairs. Before they had reached the chamber, Anna opened her eyes and said with dry, scarcely parted lips:

"It is over; let me be! I want to go home, I want to see mamma!"

The head-mistress was following, with the child's forgotten sabots in her hand.

"Carry her into the kitchen," she said, "and set her down in a chair; she cannot go home like that."

The child, seated beside the hearth where the brands were still burning, refused to eat or drink— the two popular remedies—or even to answer when they spoke to her. She merely repeated, moving her feet mechanically on the hearth amid the warm ashes:

"I want to go home. I don't want to die here!"

"You want to go home?—Can you walk?" asked Mlle. Renée.

For the first time the child answered directly, saying "Yes" in so firm a tone that the directress replied at once:

"Since you wish me to leave her to you, Mademoiselle, you may take charge of her and lead her home. I do not think there will be any danger. It is not far."

Oh, how slowly and silently they moved, Davidée and little Anna, but quite happily, crossing the court and emerging on the highway! It was half-past five. The sweetness of the close of such a day in early spring none can foretell; the wind must have ceased blowing, so that the sun gives forth a gentle warmth, and gnats and May-flies begin to float in the long unaccustomed air; the leafless branches laden with buds do not stir, for the harsh gales are over and the boughs drink in the gold of the sunset, while tufts of new grass spring up amidst the stones. The Ardésie landscape had now a pale charm of its own, such as a secret joy sometimes gives to a young girl without beauty.

They were alone, the teacher and the sick child; their slow steps raised a cloud of dust which turned to gold in the sunset light, but before long there were three together on the road to the village of Éclaterie, the first of the hamlets called the Justices. How did Jeannie Fête-Dieu chance to be there, at the junction of the two roads? Who had sent her? What was she waiting for, leaning against the wall of slate, her basket hanging on her arm, her apron pockets stuffed with books, her round cheeks very rosy, her round eyes very tranquil, her braids crowned with a blue and white knitted béret, and her hands thrust into darned woollen mittens? No one will ever know. She advanced to meet her poor little playmate, who was treading her Via Dolorosa, and said, addressing Davidée:

"Mademoiselle, grandma Fête-Dieu would be very glad if you would come and see her sometime; she has scalded herself." Then she took Anna by the right arm as Mlle. Birot was holding her by the left, and assuming that leave was granted to her—the best scholar, the best girl in her class—she accompanied the sick child home.

Her two companions occupied the middle of

the narrow road and she walked beside them in
the wheel ruts, taking care not to stumble lest
she should jar little Anna's arm. An occasional
whitewashed wall pierced by windows, which
were never opened, broke the long ribbon of stone
fence which bordered the road, and here and
there a peach-tree showed, above the jagged edges
of the wall, its clusters of purpling stalks.

"Do you not want to rest, my child?"

"No, Mademoiselle; I can walk on."

She said no more, but her eyes now sought the
long low roof, which almost touched the ground
in a fine curve like the hull of a ship. Soon one
could see it plainly, the great roof of Phrosine's
poor cottage. A hedge bordered one side, and an
ancient fence of chestnut wood the other three
sides of the small plot of bare ground on which
the house stood, and this shelter of the poor was
enclosed in the vast domain of a market gardener
whose house, with its barn and hedge-rows, could
be seen in the distance.

"I have never been here before," said Davidée
as she opened the wicket gate. She had approached so quietly with the two children that
even the mother had not noticed their coming.
A last breath of warm soft air was bending the
new wheat as it gleamed in the rays of the sun
about to set.

The sick child, with a sudden stiff movement,
disengaged her left arm, threw it around Mlle.
Davidée's neck and, with the tenderness of a
heart completely won, kissed the cheek turned
toward her.

Jeannie Fête-Dieu had already vanished, as Phrosine stepped out of her door and walked along the grassy path beneath the plum-trees to the garden-gate. The anxious expression of her face, as of one continually questioning and answering herself, softened as she caught sight of Anna in her gray frock, who cried out quickly:

"I am better, mamma; do not scold me."

"I will wager that she has been fainting again, hasn't she, Mademoiselle? Oh, naughty, naughty girl, come at once and be put to bed. I have just put on fresh sheets for you."

So saying, Phrosine took in her arms the small frail body, as Davidée had done in the school-room, and carried her into the house. But her head was bent tenderly over the child, whose little head she supported with one hand, as she murmured words of love and grief, this wild Phrosine of the evil life.

"I have put fresh sheets in your little bed. You will go to sleep soon, promise me! Look there at the fresh jonquils that have bloomed for you; don't you think them pretty?" But between their eyes which looked into each other, between their souls which had dwelt so long together, there passed a secret dialogue, an habitual one perhaps, for the mother understood fully what her child's sad eyes were asking of her; she knew why it was that her tenderness never succeeded in consoling or melting the heart of the sick child, who did not smile back at her now, nor at the fresh jonquils, nor yield herself to the caressing words.

The pale, drawn face of little Anna merely turned toward the open door with an expression of terror; so that the mother faltered:

"No, he is not there; do not put on that look that grieves me. He has gone to a meeting of his mates near Bel-Air; they are planning a strike, so you see he is not here! I give you my word."

The little face relaxed, an expression of gratitude, of imploring hope, dawned in the eyes. Anna looked at her mother with the look she had just given her teacher. The mother entered the house with her little burden clasped to her breast, and Davidée followed her into a small room at the left of the entrance.

"There, lie down for a while. You have promised me to try to go to sleep. I am going to make you a bowl of linden tea, very sweet, and that will surely put you to sleep."

It would have seemed to any one hearing these words that a young mother was lulling her baby to rest.

Davidée meanwhile was glancing around the large outer room which served as Phrosine's dwelling-place, at its smoky ceiling with heavy beams, above which the steep roof rose in an immense peak; at its yellowish walls on which hung a looking-glass and two or three old calendars, such as are sent as advertisements, adorned with smiling heads of women in gaudy colours and very low-necked gowns. Davidée recalled similar chromos in the white house at Blandes, hanging over her father's writing-table. A large black-walnut bedstead stood in one corner; the

wide chimney-place, with its hood standing far
out into the room, must have warmed and cheered
numerous generations. In a niche hollowed out of
the thick walls, where formerly must have been
kept the stock of rush-lights and the stalks to
replenish them, hung a man's cap. Davidée
turned away her head, and at that moment
Phrosine re-entered.

"The child is going to sleep. She refuses her
tisane and everything I offer her." Then carefully closing the heavy oak door she added:

"Yes, everything. She is very ill. I thank you,
Mademoiselle, for having brought her home. It
isn't every one who would have done it."

"Oh, it's nothing. I should have reproached
myself if I had not come. She is my pupil, ours
at least."

"And one who loves you, I can truly say
that. . . ."

"Poor child!"

The young girl recalled vividly every word that
Mlle. Renée had told her about Phrosine, and the
story rose between them like a third person, whose
presence embarrassed them both, equally conscious as they were of this hostile witness.

They exchanged formal words of gratitude and
sympathy, feeling their hollowness as they uttered
them. Davidée's hand was not held out and her
glance avoided encountering Phrosine's because
of the evil thought that stood between them.

"Some one has been talking to you about me,
Mademoiselle. I can see that, and I saw it
already this morning." This time their glances

met and clashed.   Davidée raised her head like
a brave girl conscious of a pure motive, and said:
"It is true.   I have known of your ill-conduct
since last evening."

"Well, let us talk of it then, if you are willing.
You need have no fear of meeting him.   I have
already told the child that he is not here; he will
not be back before seven.   You are in the house of
a woman who lives with a man who is not her husband.   I had no other means of living.   Why do
you look at me like that, as if you were going to
drop?   For we have hidden nothing.   If you will
consent to sit down a few moments I will explain
certain things to you which you ought to know
before judging me."

Davidée hesitated a moment, then seated herself near the hearth, facing the window.   Phrosine
was in the half-light, but a gleam, nevertheless,
lighted up the vibrating green of her eyes and the
flush on her cheeks.   What passion, what power
of will, what defiance had sounded as those words
flashed out: "We have hidden nothing."   Yet
she spoke in a restrained voice so as not to be
audible in the adjoining room.

"I seem to you a worthless creature, no doubt,
one who sweeps your rooms and lights your fires."

"No, I assure you, you are mistaken."

"One who scrubs the floors and does the dirty
work for you, the dainty and learned.   I am not
of your world and you make me see it."

"Since I am bringing up your daughter and the
daughters of all the women in Ardésie, what have
you to reproach me with?"

"Your manner, which is not the same toward all."

The young girl coloured and answered with spirit.

"Until last evening I had only the friendliest feeling toward you. At this moment all that is changed. What would you have? I cannot control my inmost feelings.

"One can see that."

"Why do you not marry this man?"

"I should have to be free to do that."

"Are you not free?"

"I am married already."

"Then it is still worse. Let me go now. I came to do you a service, not to discuss your conduct."

But Phrosine wished to speak again; there was one avowal she was bent on making.

"No, you have no right to despise me," she said; "you do not know what misery I have been through. I lived three years with my husband, a workman in the quarries, a carpenter who made the beams to support the galleries. He deserted me; he did worse, for he robbed me of my boy, whom I never saw again, and I have learned since that he abandoned him to the Board of Charity in Paris. That was twelve years ago. Where is my son now? Where is my husband? He left me just before the birth of my baby-girl, the child you have just brought back to me. I was left alone to support us both. Well, I waited three years for his return, my husband's! Ah, I have tasted want, I promise you! I have worked

for a few sous a day while nursing the little one.
When that time was over I could no longer live
alone. I had no money and no courage left. I
gave myself to some one and it was not Maïeul,
you understand. Who was there to forbid it?"

"But—the law."

"Does it feed me, the law?"

"But customs, morals—you could——"

"What could I do?"

"You could be divorced."

"What difference would that make? One does
without *their* permission. Has not every one the
right to dispose of themselves?"

"Oh, no!"

"You believe it is the mayor who can permit
such things? You tell that to the children! But
look you, Mademoiselle, the law is like customs,
morals, and all the rest. You can pay attention
to them when you are rich, and have the time, and
some one in the world who cares about you. But
as for me, no one cared about me. I could do
what I liked—die even—without its troubling my
neighbours. In fact, I had no neighbours. I was
living in the Fête-Dieu house, just below La
Gravelle—where he lodges now. Oh, I see that
I offend you in speaking as I do. But I am not
trying to appear better than I am. You have
the morals that you wish to have—I have what
morals I can have. Do not be so hard on others;
you will find many like me when you know Ardésie. However, that is not what I want to explain
to you."

Davidée found no answer ready for these moral

paradoxes, uttered with such assurance by this woman, and her irritation increased at finding herself so unready in defending a cause she knew to be right.

"The worst of it is," resumed Phrosine, "that the little one hates him. He does not know what to do to please her; she will not look at him nor speak to him, and I will tell you truly how I feel: this makes me angry with her."

"Your misconduct is killing her. Such things have happened before."

"What! because I love Maïeul Jacquet, and because I cannot live without him? She is dying for that? Mademoiselle, you are hard on us poor people, but at least you do not hide what you think. I do not believe a child could die of that."

"I, on the other hand, am sure of it, and I can understand it."

"It is true she suffers and so do I, and he, too, as much as we. Look here, I want to tell you this! You were astonished the other day when Maïeul offered to dig your garden."

"Partly so, but I thought it was a kindness he wanted to show me."

"Oh, no! It was a kindness to her. You do not know him. He has a heart as tender as a woman's, although he never laughs. He knew that she was fond of you, the child, and he thought, 'If I give pleasure to the teacher, Anna will be pleased.' And he told her about it when he came home at night."

"What did she say?"

"As always, nothing—not one word. She ate
her three spoonfuls of soup and asked to go back
to bed. When she is in there," and Phrosine
pointed to the door of the child's chamber, "she
is happier; she coughs, she is feverish, she is hungry and thirsty, but she never calls me; she does
not live with us. I assure you our life is not gay,
and I have had enough of it."

The young teacher felt a longing to open that
door again, to bend over the little bed, to embrace
her pupil, and to whisper very low in her ear:
"Little child, so touching in your purity, I am
near you; you have a true friend." But she
dared not; swift and spontaneous as were her
impulses, habits of discipline had already tem-
pered her eager spirit. She asked herself: "Would
it not be an imprudence?" and she left the house
with merely a glance in the direction which her
heart had taken.

Outside, the twilight held sway over all things;
all began to grow alike in colour—the shrubs in
the yard, the currant bushes, the manure heaps
and piles of stones were similar vague rounded
masses a little paler along the edges. The young
girl had passed before Phrosine, down the mossy
path, and out of the gate. An infinite silence
brooded in the sky, over the bare fields and the
quarry mounds. Only along the diverging roads,
faint sounds dropped one by one into the darkness,
the echo of footsteps, the rumble of wheels, and
far-off, indistinct, dying voices. Phrosine had accompanied Mlle. Birot half-way through the little
avenue of plum-trees.

"If she were to die—" she now faltered; "do you believe it?"

"No one can tell. I spoke too hastily, in a moment of agitation."

"But you think it *could* happen? That my little girl, my Anna——?"

Davidée realized that what she was about to say was a serious thing, that if she were to repeat the words, "Yes, I believe this grief might cause her death," what remained to this woman of an obscured conscience might turn to remorse and pursue its work, who knew how far? With an effort she answered: "Yes." And with this word on her lips she hurried away into the twilight. She was naturally timid. The silence of this road, which she now pursued alone, terrified her. She caught sight here and there of a great clump of ivy, looking like the head and shoulders of a man leaning over the low wall. She dreaded hearing the sound of footsteps behind her. Why might not this Maïeul Jacquet have returned at the very moment she had parted from Phrosine? He would need no long explanation to learn what had occurred; Phrosine would only have to repeat a few phrases uttered by the school-mistress. Then anger would seize him, he would rush from the house and down the path between the plum-trees, shutting the gate behind him with a clang, and breaking into a run as he reached the highway.

She had gone as far as the summit of the first abandoned quarry of Champ-Robert when she heard, in fact, rapid steps behind her, now loud, now muffled by the dust, but coming always nearer. There was still a lingering light in the sky; it was impossible, even by leaning straight and motionless against the slate wall, to escape the notice of the man who was approaching. And this man was Maïeul. She was sure of it. Who else would hasten thus, at this late hour on a March evening, when the fatigue of the day's work and the weight of the foggy atmosphere made the limbs drag? He was approaching with long strides and suddenly he began to cry out: "Hold on there, lady! You, Mademoiselle the school-mistress!"

She left the middle of the road and running toward the right stood in the shelter of the wall, with her arms hanging at her sides, and her face turned toward the figure just emerging from the mist and shadow which hung low above the earth; her heart was beating violently.

"Here, Mademoiselle! There is no use in hurrying. I can soon catch up with you!"

She did not stir; only the tips of her fingers clutched the stones to find support. She fancied that her white collar would betray her at once, even her pale face and the gleam of her eyes, which she felt to be dilating in the darkness, and she said to herself: "Since I cannot escape, I will not cry out; I will not fly, I will face him."

He was already close upon her, between two ruts in the road, swaying on his long legs, his hat on the back of his head, his head rising high above the edge of the opposite wall. He was supporting himself with a staff, and did not see the girl at once, but as he came to a stand-still ten paces away, cursing and crying out: "Ho, there, young lady!" she crossed the road and stood before him saying: "What do you want of me, Monsieur Maïeul Jacquet?"

He turned toward her.

"What do you mean by calling out my name? I thought you more civil. You must have been drinking, no doubt." And as this accusation was true, he took off his hat saying.

"Excuse me!"

Then for a moment he stood speechless, surprise having arrested the torrent of reproaches which he had repeated to himself as he ran. The words surged back upon his mind one by one, and the hand which held his hat began to tremble with anger.

"I was passing by the house just now," he began.

"Not your house," she replied.

"The house I choose to call mine. I learned that you had brought the child back."

"Not your child either. Did I not do well?"

"Oh, yes, that was well! I am not reproaching you for that, but you talked too much. Why need you meddle with our affairs? Why did you tell Phrosine that the little one might die?"

"Because she asked me."

"You wish her to drive me away then? It will be your doing if she drives me away!" At this the school-teacher forgot all conventions and let her heart speak, as she, the maiden, answered:

"So much the better!"

"Ah, you wish her to throw me off! You shall repent saying that!"

"It is for you to repent, not for me. You are living an evil life, you are the lover of a married woman!"

"Who would have died of hunger without me."

"Give her the wherewithal to live, and stay in your own house, then you can talk of your charity. You are driving a child to despair, Maïeul Jacquet! you are killing her because she has a sensitive heart which is worth a thousand times more than yours; and it is I, a woman, who tell you this out here on the highway, because I do not fear you. You are a coward! you know well what your duty is; it is to live honourably, it is to sacrifice yourself, and you will not do it! You have not even pity. You say you love the child——"

"I surely do!"

"And yet you do everything except what her poor aching heart asks of you. You will not part from the mother, yourself, and you are afraid of being driven away. Giant though you are, you seem to me a poor creature, destitute of will. I forbid you to follow me. Good-night."

And so saying she stopped to rearrange the knitted scarf which she wore over her shoulders; carefully lifted her skirt although it was short, passed calmly by Maïeul, and resumed her way along the middle of the road to Ardésie.

The man, in spite of his state of semi-intoxication, had understood everything. The words were obliged to make a journey through his brain

to reach that part of it which was still clear, but
before the assistant had walked ten paces, he
called out:

"There's a little woman for you!" And as she
was about to disappear in the darkness, he called
again:

"Tell me, young lady, where did you learn your
morality?"

She heard, but she was already far away, and
there was no sound of footsteps behind her on
the road. The houses near the school, on the
right hand, formed a darker mass amid the twilight shadows, like a rounded cloud, similar to
those above, which, heavy with rain and darkness,
showed scarcely a star between their overlapping
folds as they were borne up the valley of the
Loire, driven by a wind from the ocean. The
road dipped a little as it neared the school and
there in the door-way stood the shadow of a human
form. It detached itself from the wall, hesitated,
came toward Davidée.

"Ah, is that you at last, Mademoiselle? How
late you are! I was growing anxious!" And
Mlle. Renée embraced her assistant.

"You are heated and trembling," she said;
"what has happened to you?"

The two school-mistresses closed the court-
yard door and entered the kitchen, where Davidée proceeded to relate her visit to the house
on the Plain; but she said nothing of Maïeul
Jacquet's pursuit of her, nor of their interview
on the highway. When she had repeated some of
the words she had spoken to Phrosine:

"Mademoiselle," said Mlle. Renée, "this is a

more serious story than you are aware of. If you wish for peace, keep silent. See everything and say nothing. Take your morals as a lesson to be given in class, but outside your classes appear to forget them."

"I shall find that very hard."

"You must take my advice. I shall be surprised if this affair of yours has no consequences."

"What! because I took pity on a child? Because I told a woman she was doing wrong to live unlawfully with one man while married to another?"

"What an expression! How you go ahead! What difference does it make to you?"

"And does it make none to you?"

"None whatever. It's a matter of words. Morality is something I teach in school, according to a changing programme; a lesson, like the geography of marine sand-banks. That is what the Inspector wants, and the Minister of Instruction. They are the guardians of religion. It concerns them, not me. My function is merely to say amen. But I think just as I please on these questions; I live as I think best, and let other people live as they think best. My poor little assistant, if you set up to have moral convictions for those who have none, if you have principles, hide them well or you will be lost!"

She laughed as she said this, pleased to have her companion back again. Davidée was busy boiling water over the alcohol lamp, and made no reply beyond uttering a few assenting phrases, suitable to a subordinate.

"Do you think so? It would be hard for me

to show complete indifference; it will take time, I fear, but I will try. If you could only have seen little Anna, so ill and even more unhappy!"

When she had hastily swallowed a cup of tea, she wiped her eyes, moistened by the chilly air and some lingering emotion, and said:

"I shall want no dinner to-night."

"What a great child you are!"

"It is true that I am unnerved by all this; I need to be alone."

Mlle. Renée gazed at her attentively, with her chin lowered, which was a habit with her, as she added:

"Alone! you have just experienced how terribly alone you are. Well, good-night! Have you any idea how pretty you look when you are moved and excited like that?"

The girl silently nodded good-night and went upstairs.

Her room was in perfect order; it gave her pleasure to see that the counterpane was spread smoothly over her cot-bed, the chair drawn up close to her ink-stained writing-table, the two other chairs ranged along the wall on the garden side, the two crystal vases standing on either end of the chimney-piece with her alarm-clock between them, a neat bookcase holding all her books on the lower shelves, and her little ornaments on an upper shelf with a copper balustrade. She did not ask herself why she rejoiced to see all her possessions in place and forming a sort of harmony. She had a vague sensation of rescue, as she set down her lamp beside the inkstand, stretched her arms, and unwound the scarf on her head, but did not take it off, for the window on the garden let in, at all seasons whether warm or cold, a draught of air which whistled or moaned, caressing or cutting her cheeks.

"I am content here," she thought; "this is my refuge. Everywhere else I encounter opposition and feel my helplessness. Above all what corruption! I am enveloped by it; the farther I advance in life, the more I discover. That is all I gain by growing older. And there are things I do not know, but seem to divine, which terrify me." Davidée looked at herself in the glass hanging over her clock; she saw an image of youth, the ardent wilful face of one who was far from having attained peace. Her thoughts turned to her mother, whom no general ideas, no theories of life formulated by her husband, the quarryman, ever sufficed to move or even to interest. "I am the opposite of that," she murmured. "I believe that it is moral suffering more than any other which stirs my heart and would destroy all happiness for me if I felt it near me and could not at least try to heal it."

Her heavy masses of black hair, loosened by the wind and by her rapid motion, hung low over her brows; she wound them more closely round her head, so that they too might be in order, as she wished everything about her to be, and seating herself at her writing-table, she opened a drawer by the key which she wore attached to her watch-chain, and drew out a green note-book to which it was her habit to confide her thoughts whenever she needed a friend.

This green note-book was tied up with others like it, which she had brought with her from the school at La Rochelle, and with a few letters and pictures and a spray of withered flowers fastened by a ribbon. She began to write:

"I fear that this life I have chosen is not suited to me. I feel myself ill-fitted for the self-effacement which is prescribed for me. Why may I not follow the impulse which prompts me to help wounded souls, and why may I not judge them when they implore me to do so? How little of what I do here is done with all my heart, with my whole self! They wish to curb me. Just now, when by chance I spoke out freely, I was told that I had overstepped my province. I did not go to this Phrosine's house to surprise her secrets; I did not question her. It was she who appealed to me and I answered her as my conscience bade me. I felt myself like a sister to little Anna; in her place I should suffer as the child does. To see her mother living an evil life, not to respect her, and yet be forced to go on loving her; to be placed in the mother's heart lower than this man who has no right to come and share it, to eat one's daily bread at such a price! ah, I too should die of it as she is doing! I can never keep silent before a grief so natural and so touching. The incredible thing is Phrosine's assurance. It seems as though for her duty did not exist; that she submits to no authority; that in her eyes poverty and her selfish love free her from all the obligations of an honest woman and a good mother."

Having written these words, the young girl laid aside her pen and took from the drawer a thick blank book containing the notes she had taken from the lectures of Mlle. Hacquin, professor of psychology at the normal school. "I must review my ethics a little," she said to herself, "since I find myself consulted on moral questions and my views opposed;" and turning one page after another, written in a clear handwriting, strong and full of individuality, she read:

"There are four classes of moral problems: (1) *Metaphysical*, such as the existence of God and a future life; (2) *formal* and *abstract*, such as the question of human happiness; (3) *actual* and *social;* (4) problems in casuistics. (1) Does there exist a Supreme Being? What is His Nature? This is an infinitely abstract question remote from human conduct. Let us eliminate all hypotheses. Why should we confound true and necessary ideas, such as relate to morals, with purely hypothetical ones? Why establish a connection between subjects not conjoined by reason? This would tend to compromise morality. If we wish our ethics to be sound we must dissociate them from metaphysics."

"Ah, here is what I am looking for: Duty— morality in society is what the social order exacts —How am I to recognize that society exacts this or that? By the sanctions attaching to it, whatever these may be, from public opinion to effective penalties. Duty is the form common to all activities, whether industrial, economic, or hygienic, which does not undertake to reconsider indefinitely the reasoning on points of conduct verified once for all by experience. Our duty is merely our will disengaged from emotion—Morality, in its origins, constitutes a social phenomenon. It is dependent on society, which may decide to reject certain of its ancient ordinances."

Here Davidée paused with a sudden mental pang. What! was this all? Had she ruled her life by such doctrines as these? To do as every one about her did: was this all that was enjoined upon her! And she had called this morality, and had believed herself to have a moral system? No, it was not so; she had lived according to examples of uprightness and of honour set her by her mother, by her father even, by those about her whom she regarded as good. But whence had they, her secret patterns, drawn their inspiration? They were better than others only because, in perplexing situations, they had raised themselves above ordinary human baseness. With what an insufficient and unreasonable doctrine had her teachers armed her! To follow the weaknesses, the uncertainties of others, of her fellow beings who groped blindly, contradicting each other, and too often yielding to counsels which tempted them! To have popular opinion on one side to-day and against one to-morrow, and to find the same act approved yesterday and blamable to-day! What morality was this? It seemed to the girl as if she had opened a casket where she had stored all her fortune and had found that her treasure was gone.

She threw the blank book back into the drawer and buried her face in her hands. Mlle. Renée was mounting the stairs, the steps midway creaking, as usual, beneath her weight. Davidée feared for an instant that the directress was about to enter and would perceive how greatly her anxiety, fatigue, and trouble had increased. She heard her pause for a moment on the landing, evidently surprised that Davidee's light was still burning; then the opposite door closed and the house was wrapped in the peace and harmony of night.

Davidée, bending over the table, took up her pen again and wrote: "And what a guide the opinion of society would be for one's inner life! What a judge to which to appeal when one's inmost purity was wounded! What certainty of conviction or what consolation could it give to me or to little Anna? What! submit all my thoughts, my sadness, my dreams to the opinion of others! How could their judgment fortify me against temptation, ignorant as they must be of the force of that temptation, of the motives of the sin or the victory? What! each soul to be at the mercy of all! Oh, no, I refuse to be subject to the opinion of Ardésie, of the town, of the world; to the habits, prejudices, passions of beings like myself; all they can say to me is: 'We who are dust, whirlwind and empty sound, we approve you to-day, free to condemn when we will!' I can no longer understand how Mlle. Hacquin's lessons could have influenced me. Have I ever directed a single act of my life in accordance with them? I ask myself this to-night for the first time, and I do not find that

I have ever accorded them anything beyond the assent of a scholar, whom the search preoccupied more than the result. It is chance which brought me face to face with the most absolute unmorality. When I looked into the depths of my own soul, that which is my real principle of action, of light and energy, protested and took possession of me. And to-night I discover how sadly unprovided with weapons I should have been if Phrosine on her side had been capable of reasoning. But indeed her manner of life is in itself a form of reasoning: she eludes the duties which would fetter her, because she sees no sufficient sanction for them. *She* is not a teacher; she is poor, she loves this man, and she lives with him and is supported by him. What matters to her the opinion of others; and is not the opinion of the community partly on her side? Her neighbours do not all condemn her, and according to the doctrines of Mlle. Hacquin this serves to justify her morally. And alas! I who thought to instruct others, what assurance can I give them? Mlle. Renée is right; I must be prudent. I ought to be so—But I cannot! I shall continue as I have done, though I feel myself so alone. I have no confidence in her who should be my directress. Hers is a supple, imitative mind; a receiver of ready-made ideas; all are alike to her provided they have received the official stamp. And alas! I cannot believe her sincere; when she kissed me to-night I was conscious of an exaggerated warmth on her part which was displeasing to me. I am thrown into the midst of perplexities such as I could not foresee. To make my way through them, or to conquer them, I have no guide but instinct and the examples of my early childhood. I have no other lantern in the darkness, but I shall go on all the same. I shall not change. I will not be silent, though it is very hard."

For a while longer she lingered at her desk under the light of her lamp, lost in thought. The little incidents of the day rose before her to be judged one by one. She had no regrets, though her mind was troubled. How should she make her way through this drama which she saw opening before her? Where was her support? She realized fully that she, Davidée, Phrosine, Anna, and Maïeul Jacquet would meet again, that other words would pass between them, and that fate was about to try, lightly it might be or harshly, the solitary soul, keeping its vigils on the blue mounds of Ardésie, now wrapped in darkness.

CHAPTER IV.

"FLOWER O' THE BROOM."

ONLY trifling events occurred for the next few weeks, if the coming of spring can be called a trifling event.

Anna Le Floch returned to school the following Monday, but there was no improvement in the malady from which she was suffering. She sat on the playground during recess, some of her little school-mates bringing out a chair for her and setting her in it as carefully as if she had been a doll, all chattering at once in order to divert— as they thought—the child who could not play; then, seizing the pretext of a ball that was rolling away, or a call from the playground, they bounded off and took pains to frolic more noisily than ever, as if they felt that they were entitled to some compensation.

The sick child was used to solitude; it neither surprised nor grieved her to be left alone; but her wild, melancholy eyes, which formerly avoided meeting those of the teachers, now sought Davidée's and seemed to be trying to fill themselves with her image, far or near. An outsider might have thought it mere curiosity which kept her glances always directed toward the young girl who was walking with the older children or joining in their games. Then of a sudden the child's look melted and grew tender, revealing the secret of her silent heart.

Davidée suspected little of this. She saw Phrosine daily; they were obliged to greet each other because they both served under the same superior, and in the same school, but they never exchanged a word.

Mlle. Renée, on the contrary, had grown so expansive as to appear benevolent. She was now entertaining hopes of advancement, having heard rumours, at a teacher's reunion, leading her to anticipate a speedy change of residence, even a possible post in town.

The Primary Inspector had not pronounced the word "town," but it was easy thus to interpret the flattering allusions he had made to Mlle. Desforges. To leave Ardésie, no longer to vegetate, as she expressed it, no longer to teach the children of the poor, or of "savages"—this was another of her favourite expressions—but to live in the society of small functionaries and shopkeepers, to pay and receive visits, to walk once more on pavements; these were the joys to which she aspired with an intensity of longing as to eternal bliss. To obtain them there was nothing she was not prepared to do. She had persuaded herself, moreover, that her merits had long overflowed the measure, and no longer opened a letter without expecting it to contain the looked-for promotion.

"I will not forget *you*," she said to her assistant; "I consider you far too intelligent and, let me add, too pretty and attractive to be banished forever to this desert."

"I assure you," replied Davidée, "that I am a very home-keeping person. I have already taken root here in Ardésie."

Maïeul Jacquet had not taken his revenge as he had threatened to do. He had never been seen again at the school or even passing its door. A countrywoman, who brought her little girl to school each day, said to Davidée one morning:

"It is queer, I used to meet that big Rit-Dur so often, on his way to his work, and now I never see him. He must have changed his hours or his road."

This was the last day before the spring vacation. On the following morning Davidée started for Blandes to spend her Easter holidays there, as had been her unfailing custom for the past five years. She found her father grown feebler, but more imperious and fuller of whims than ever; her mother was aging too, but the fine new house, which was the envy of the entire village, bore no other mark of the winters it had already passed through than the streaks of greenish mould, like slender swords or iris-stalks, now staining its white foundation-stones. For the first time Davidée talked with her mother on other subjects than the weather, the house-keeping, the difficulty of finding a servant, or the unceasing rivalries which were now springing up against Birot's fortune, his power and his rude authority, rivalries which Birot, with a turn of his hand, crushed one by one. Her mother had no longer any scruples about relating to her daughter the latest scandal current in Blandes. This time it was the story of a young wife deserted by her husband who had eloped with another woman.

"How ugly it all is!" exclaimed Madame Birot.

"There are plenty of others who do the same!"

"What are you saying, child? Do you countenance such actions? If all Blandes were to justify that woman I should blame her all the more—I say she is a hussy!"

"It pleases me to hear you say that, mamma; it is a very big word for you."

"Yes, a hussy!—and I may tell you that I was once pretty and young too, and of a fine slim figure like her," and as she spoke Madame Birot complacently smoothed out the folds of her skirt. "I was looked at, too, and listened to the music of words like those in the verses you recite. But, thank Heaven! I have not a single lawless thought to reproach myself with."

"Because you are the best of women, and perhaps because you never were in love."

"Oh, yes, child, I was in love with your father, as much as any one could be in love with a man who is disputing all the time!"

"I mean to say you never loved any one else."

"Are you crazy? That would have been a nice business indeed!"

"But what deterred you, mamma, without religion as you profess to be?"

"Without religion, child! But I have a little, as much as your father permits me to have.

That is not much to be sure! But one does not need to be pious in order to be faithful to one's duties. There is——"

"What is there, mother?"

"There is honour, child."

"Oh, poor mamma! I have seen people who thought that honour commanded them not to give up the woman they loved, whether it were a lawful love or not. We can always make words serve our wishes, you see. The important, the vital thing is to know their true meaning. Men put into them whatever they wish, and so do women."

Madame Birot, who did not feel herself equipped for abstract discussions, folded her daughter in her arms, exclaiming passionately:

"You see many wretched things in your profession, my poor child! I suspected it, and longed to keep you near me, but you would not stay. Tell me the truth, is your heart so sore?"

"No, mamma; I fear it is my mind."

Madame Birot did not seek far for an answer to this; it sprang at once from her mother's heart, from that dream which they all cherish for their daughters, as she said softly:

"Why do you not marry?"

After that there was no longer any discussion between them of general ideas or theories of morality.

Spring had come at last. When Davidée returned to Ardésie, it had already tinged the sky, which is always first to catch the radiance, and was now spreading its verdure over the poorest

clods of earth. Even the slate had felt a touch
of spring, and warmed in the sun, which set the
air dancing along the mounds, it flung back the
rays as they fell, till the slopes appeared like cas-
cades of slate; such life did the sun give to
them, that scales of every colour of the rain-
bow shimmered along the stone. From out of
the banks of moss, which had swelled in the winter's rain, sprang tall, slender stalks, gilded at
their tips. The willows raised their tufts of
green in the old quarry-pits. In the hollows
where the soil had not been buried under the
débris of the quarries, the little cottage gardens,
encircled by their blue walls, spread out to the
light their neatly raked beds, their well-pruned
trees and rows of currant bushes, the tulips and
gillyflowers before the doors. There was no
morning without the song of the blackbird nor
night without the nightingale. But above all,
the broom blossoms had burst the bud and sprinkled the whole blue landscape with gold, so that
the very stones seemed to rejoice. The broom
was triumphant everywhere, over slopes and pla-
teaus and bramble patches, over all the waste
places where the soil was buried beneath heaps
of shattered stone. It sprang in the thinnest
layer of dust, and was wrapt in the warm incense from the earth. Its hour came early for
bearing pale buds on its brushlike stems, spreading yellow sails along its branches, and opening
to the air all the treasures of its fragrance. How
generously it responded to the spring breezes
that embalmed it! With primroses and a little

hawthorn and the spearmint stems still tender and half-hidden in the grass, it composed the divine perfume of early spring. The broom was hiding the desert which man had made—it was around the most ancient quarry-pits, between the enormous hollows, half-filled with water, that the golden gorse flourished most profusely, and there it was that Maïeul Jacquet dwelt.

His house, La Gravelle, built along the edge of an embankment, was flanked on the right by a pavilion, crowned with a belvedere; or to speak more accurately, the old master-mason, who built the pavilion, in order to divide it into two stories, had added to the eastern façade an outside staircase, winding around the building, and terminating on the south front in an aerial loggia with a projecting roof. Had the dwelling once belonged to some noble family? So the tradition ran, among the quarrymen. It was now occupied by humble tenants only—a couple of Breton families who shared the lower floor and the slate-cutter, Maïeul Rit-Dur, to whom belonged the stone staircase and two rooms in the pavilion, with long wide windows. All the windows and doors of La Gravelle opened toward the south and commanded a broad view. It dominated, like a light-house, the whole slate-country and the sloping shores of the Loire, where the smoke from the workshops sweeps down with the morning fogs. A few feet further back, on an embankment of the same period, stood another house, far less imposing, which was inhabited by grandmother Fête-Dieu, and further still were the pits of La Gravelle and La Grenadière.

Nowhere in the commune of Ardésie had nature resumed such complete sway as over the abandoned mounds around La Gravelle. Between Maïeul's house and that of good Mère Fête-Dieu, it was all one golden garden. The steep slopes leading up to La Gravelle, the footpath below, the billowy mounds where the traces of man's labour were still discernible, were all clothed in broom and its sprays were all of living gold. The edges of the twin pits of "The Rabbits" also wore a golden fringe, and shafts of broom buried themselves like rockets amidst the reviving verdure of thorn and thicket. All this soil, so excavated and overturned that it rang hollow beneath the tread, displayed its glory before the richer, deeper earth, hardly mellowed yet by the sun's rays, and the traveller through these paths breathed an atmosphere of joy.

It was thus that Davidée felt on a late Thursday in April, the second after Easter, as she approached the hollow of La Grenadière, where a woman was busy washing, bending over the edge of a plank set amidst the reeds. She followed the shore of the pond, listening to the sound of water gurgling through the sluice-ways and losing itself beneath low branches; then she climbed a steep incline and beheld before her the pavilion of La Gravelle, rising in the light a few hundred yards ahead, and the carpet of golden broom sloping down from the spot where she stood; and at that moment the breeze, which at times seemed to swing and sway its perfumes like incense, enveloped her in its languid breath.

"Ah, what a delight!" she said; "all spring

is in the air! If only it could blow like this through the school and through my heart!"

She was on her way to see old Mère Fête-Dieu as she had promised to do before the vacation. But her thoughts turned for a moment to Maïeul Jacquet.

"He passes for a maker of songs and a fine singer. He would do far better to live decently and speak civilly to those he meets! What conduct, to pursue me along the road, shouting my name! I have met Phrosine twenty times since then and she has never spoken to me; he has changed his road home from his work; and that is all the influence I have gained over either of them."

She remembered that it was a week since she had seen little Anna and she only knew, as every one did, that the child had grown worse and no longer left the garden.

Following the track, which wound across a pasture, at times well-trodden and then losing itself in the high grass, she was soon in the midst of a sea of broom. Turning to the right and climbing a steep bank through the blossoming stalks, which brushed her face as she advanced, she caught sight of a long spreading roof above low walls. She knocked at the door and a youthful voice bade her enter. Coming toward her in the dim light of the room, she saw little Jeannie of the round eyes, who beamed at her and said:

"Oh, how kind of you to come! Grandmamma is there. She is better, you know."

"One always grows better as one gets near

the end of the road!" said a feeble voice from
the back of the room, where, under the green
baize curtains of the bed, lay the old half-
paralyzed grandmother. One of her eyes was
still bright and keen, while the other was partly
clouded. With her good eye she gazed at Davidée Birot and seemed to take pleasure in the
sight, as if she were gazing at a spray of broom,
a rose geranium opening to the sun in the cottage
window, or a sunbeam entering the poor room.
Her look was equally kind, whether turned on her
beloved Jeannie or raised to the young teacher,
who bent over her with a smile and said:

"The spring is so fine, you will soon be better,
Mère Fête-Dieu!"

But the good woman was pursuing another
train of thought:

"Are you, then, the new school-mistress?"

"Yes, I have been here only seven months."

"*She* has told me already how kind you are.
They are sharp-sighted, these little ones, they
can read the heart."

"But I assure you, Mère Fête-Dieu, that my
heart is no better than others."

"Oh, yes, it is! Your eyes answer for that—
they look so young and so eager to do right.
Sit down, Mademoiselle. What are you thinking of, you naughty little Jeannie, that you do
not bring a chair for the young lady?" and the old
woman began to talk, telling her story, to which
the younger one listened, at first out of kindness,
then with greater interest, for Mère Fête-Dieu,
after retailing a string of dates and names, of

births and deaths, and the details of her latest
trial, the stroke which had rendered her helpless
for months, began to return thanks for her seventy
years of life, while permitting herself only the
slightest lament over her present sufferings.

"I am not over and above patient," the good
woman said. "Time hangs heavily when Jeannie is in school, but luckily the Breton women
from La Gravelle come to see me sometimes,
as you have done. I am completing my time
and winning my reward. God is the end of all
my pains." Then, growing a trifle weary, she
closed her eyes, and seemed to lose all notion
of time. On feeling a keener pang of suffering,
she opened them again, but without seeing her
visitor, whom she had already forgotten. Gazing up at the smoky rafters above her head and
clasping her one serviceable hand in the other
which no longer obeyed her will, she murmured:

"My God, I suffer much, but if thou willest,
I can suffer more," adding below her breath,
"just a little more."

The young teacher turned pale, feeling the
thrill she had often experienced on repeating to
her pupils the noble words of some heroic man or
woman. She cast a long gaze at the old grandmother, who was now dozing, and stole away
softly, accompanied by Jeannie, and with the
cat rubbing against her skirts.

La Gravelle was directly opposite, standing
high on its mound, plunging the jagged outline
of its roofs and chimneys, its walls and loggia
into the splendours of the late afternoon. But

it was only the back of the house which was in
view, and the façade, with all its windows and vine-
trellises, its Breton tenants and their children,
the whole teeming life of the place, was suspended
along the other terrace above the Loire. Here
no sound was to be heard save the humming of
gnats, drunk with the odours of the broom; even
little Jeannie's farewell was lost in their murmur,
though this served only to emphasize the silence.

"I should be nicely caught," thought Davidée,
"if Maïeul Jacquet were suddenly to descend
the mound toward me! This time I think I
should be frightened." As her plan was to return by the village of La Martinellerie, she took
the right-hand track through the broom, and was
about to emerge upon a little-frequented road,
which led in that direction, when she saw con-
fronting her, a little way off, motionless, and
evidently awaiting her, the figure of Maïeul
Jacquet.

The quarryman was in his Sunday clothes:
a well-brushed coat, shoes without nails, a double
chain across his waistcoat and a new green tie,
and his moustache twisted and curled proudly
upward, as if he were on his way to a wedding.
On catching sight of Davidée, he took off his hat
with such an intimidated air that she no longer
feared him; she merely thought: "I will pass
him with a slight nod and he will perceive that I
have a distinct remembrance of our last encounter.
How does he happen to be here? Did he see me
leave the school? His workshop is not far distant, and by climbing a wall or a heap of stones

it might be possible for the sharp eyes of a look-out man like him to see the school-house door. He must have made haste, taking the shortest road while I was loitering along by La Grena-dière, and he would have had time to change his clothes while I was visiting Mère Fête-Dieu. But what can he have to say to me? Does he think it sufficient to plant himself in my path to make me forget his disrespectful conduct of the other day?"

She had time for these reflections, as she had relaxed her steps in order not to appear alarmed. She advanced slowly with eyes partly lowered to escape the dazzling light, but on glancing up to scan the road before her, she saw the work-ingman standing beside the last stalk of broom, holding his hat before him with both his hands. He looked so droll in this humble attitude that she smiled involuntarily, and as she resumed her somewhat studied air of dignity, Maïeul ad-dressed her:

"Mademoiselle," he said, "I have not behaved well toward you!"

"That is true," she replied, without pausing in her walk.

"I was ill-mannered. I did not know what I was doing, and I am ashamed of myself."

"I thank you for telling me so, Monsieur Maïeul," and as she spoke she continued to walk on, past the fields of broom and the man stand-ing there.

"And yet there is not a single person in the whole parish," he used the old-fashioned word because he was speaking from his heart, "not one whom I should be so sorry to give pain to."

Davidée stopped at this.

"Why so, Monsieur Maïeul?" she asked.

"Because you gave me a piece of your mind and right soundly too."

"And I have been thinking that I made a mistake in being so frank with you."

"Oh, no, far from it!"

"But of what good was it, since nothing is changed?" And as she spoke she looked straight into his eyes, with flushed cheeks and a slightly haughty air.

He reflected a moment before replying. "To change is harder than to speak and to confess that you were right. But, all the same, if I *were* to change——?"

He did not end his sentence, but for the first time he ventured to look directly into the face of the slight proud girl for whom he had been waiting for the last half-hour amidst the broom. And she knew well what he was trying to say.

"Then I should respect you more," she said. And on the strength of these words which, though severe enough, were not an actual condemnation, he began to walk beside her, but a little in the rear; and while she descended the slope, turning her head away slightly so that she might not appear to be paying too much attention to this man's words, he said, lifting his eyes above her head and above Ardésie as it lay before them, as if he were addressing the whole valley:

"I have not had an education like you, Mademoiselle. I have had no mother, nor sister, nor any one to speak to me as you have done, of my salvation and my paradise."

"Did I speak of paradise?"

"No, but no one could mistake what you said. I have friends who live as I do, and neighbours who do not care. The inspector at the quarry does not trouble his head about my doings nor the director either. There's none but the curé who would speak to me like you, and him I do not know."

Davidée made no reply, and as they had now reached the cross-roads where several old houses stood, Maïeul hastened to add:

"I see plainly that it displeases you to talk with me. I did not mean to offend you. You are not so talkative as the other day. But I wanted to tell you also that little Anna cries for you. Do go and see her, Mademoiselle! It would be better for you not to go in, but you can talk to her over the hedge."

They walked on a few steps, then he added:

"Good-by, for the present, Mademoiselle!"

"Adieu, Monsieur Maïeul."

He descended the road to the left toward the quarry, while she turned to the right. Without saying so to him, she had made up her mind to go at once to the house on the Plains.

"Oh!" she thought, as she pursued her way, "how full of consequences is every one of our acts! How far each word we speak may reach! Because of the indignation I felt, I assumed the rôle of a judge between a mother and child and

that mother's lover, between a tender heart like
Anna's, a troubled conscience like Maïeul's, and
a hostile spirit like Phrosine's.   Even if I wished
it, I could not arrest the changes I have caused,
the sources perhaps of good, perhaps of mere
useless trouble, which I have opened up. And
I do not know why I showed such severity. I
have acted as my mother would have done, and
I can only defend myself by saying: 'It is my
instinct which acted, something in me, stronger
than the lessons of my teachers. Those whom
I have ventured to reprove know better than I
in what name I have spoken: that of the one and
only Judge.'"

She felt herself a poor, helpless girl. She
watched, as she passed the low, broken wall of
the quarry, the slate-cutters at work behind the
shelter of their wind-breaks. They turned their
heads as she passed, the younger men at least,
and those nearest her, and followed her with
their eyes, exchanging bantering words which
she could not hear. The old men were as indifferent to the sight of her youth as they were
to the soft spring breezes blowing through the
quarry from the heights above. With her alert
step the girl went her way, past the line of wind-
breaks rising against a background of blue, where
the slate lay in piles as far as the eye could reach,
and amidst them, the gangs of men moving
mechanically, without haste, every motion regu-
lated by daily habits of labour. Some of them
had harsh faces, but for the most part, they were
merely serious, few of them reflecting that glow

of health, peace, and gayety which mocks at toil.
"I should like to bring up your children for you,"
thought the girl, "so that they might carry into
your poor homes a breath of spring, such as we
inhale so gladly and without thought. I can
teach them to read, but that is for themselves;
and to write, and that is for themselves too; but
when I teach them to be good, that is for you.
But pleasure speaks too, and how many of them
could I persuade to give up a new hat or a ribbon for their parents' sake?"

When she had passed the sign-board of La
Martinellerie, Davidée met several of her younger
pupils, who gathered around her for a moment.

Some of the mothers, too, nodded a good-day
to her through their closed windows, but she kept
on her way through the village, then across several fields, until she reached the yard in which
Phrosine's house stood. She softly approached
the hedge-row, now in leaf, and showing here
and there, amid its dense shining foliage, a cluster
of white blossoms. The market-gardeners were
no longer at work; a flock of magpies were cir-
cling around an owl perched upon a heap of clods,
the only moving things on the steeply rising
slope, except for the tall ears of wheat which
tossed and swayed at every breath of wind, with
little shiverings and changing reflections, as if
to mimic the movement of flowing waters. The
door of the house was closed. Davidée wondered for a moment if Anna would appear leaning on Phrosine's arm, returning home from a
walk; but as she approached the wicket gate she

found the sick child on the other side of the hedge,
half-reclining upon two chairs, under the shade
of a plum-tree, with her head resting on a pillow
and a warm comforter thrown over her knees.
She was sleeping; her face so pale that one might
have thought her dead; her respiration hardly
stirring the worn bodice, while both little arms
fell limply at her sides, touching the grass. All
appearance of life had quitted the frail form of
this innocent victim of the sins of others. And
yet, as if through the mazes of sleep souls could
signal to one another and make themselves
known in no uncertain fashion, Anna suddenly
opened her eyes, her face lighted up, and life
and joy reappeared there together. Lifting her
hands slowly, with the movement of one bearing
a sheaf, and then clasping them together, the
child said:

"I was thinking of you."

"It was the spring day that brought me,"
Davidée said.

The little girl replied, as if indifferent to all
which interrupted her pæan of love:

"Yes, the day is fine," then resumed in a tone
of rapture:

"You have come at last! For days I have
been expecting you. It was not very comfort-
able on these chairs, but you could not come
inside the house; no, it was better that you
should not enter mamma's house. I thought you
would not want to come in again, so I begged
to be carried outside. The first day, I did not
see you, nor the second, nor the third, but now

you are here! Don't be afraid, Mademoiselle!
Mamma cannot hear what I am saying to you,
and besides, she is very good to me, now. Let
me look at your hat, please."

"Yes, look! Is this the way you would like
me to turn my head? If I were nearer, I would
try it on you."

"Oh, no, *you* are pretty—for me it is not worth
while—" she did not continue, but spoke as if
in a dream.

Davidée in the hope of diverting her, began
to talk of the school, but at the first words Anna's
brow darkened, the inner light withdrew from
her eyes, the clasped hands trembled. It seemed
as if youth vanished from the childish face, and
the soul of a sensitive, anxious woman informed
the tiny features.

"Mademoiselle," said the pleading voice.

"What is it, little one?"

"I want to know from you, because you are
good, because you come to see me——"

She hesitated as if oppressed, the green of her
eyes turning deep as the green of sea waves.

"Must I pray?" she murmured.

"Yes, child."

"Mademoiselle, is there not a good God?"

The girl felt a shudder pass through her, shaking the blackthorn hedge on which she leaned,
as she thought: "Can I say no? Have I the
right to drive her to despair? Do I know, I, who
have voluntarily neglected all these things?" At
last she replied, using the tender "thou" unconsciously because the intimate words she spoke

seemed to require it, and all inequalities of age and condition had vanished between them.

"Anna, dear little one, I love you dearly." She felt herself cowardly and cruel for giving no direct answer. The child only replied:

"I, too, Mademoiselle, love you dearly."

Davidée hastened to add: "I will come back. You shall see me soon again. But you must promise me to sleep as soundly as if I were not to come."

The pale face was lifted a little, then fell back amid the thin braids of hair.

"Promise not even to think of me."

The little head tossed upon the pillow as if to say "no." And at the same time the lips parted in a childish smile so pure, so tender, in its refusal not to think of her, that Davidée turned away to hide her tears.

"Good-by, for the present, darling."

The hedge soon hid her from the sick child's sight; the row of plum-trees and the low roof disappeared behind the wall bordering the road. Davidée was soon in Ardésie; she found the schoolhouse deserted, Mlle. Desforges having gone to spend her half-holiday in town.

From the Green Diary.—"Here I am alone in the house! My window is open upon the courtyard and the perfume of the invisible broom is brought in on the breeze. It blows from the mounds of La Gravelle and La Grenadière. It brings with it the dust of the roads and of the court-yard trodden by children's feet, and the perfume loses half its sweetness, as life does. I am troubled at finding myself so unequal to the task I have not undertaken voluntarily, and which grows constantly harder and more complex, driving me to form resolutions and to utter words for which I am ill-prepared. I no longer fear the vengeance of Maïeul Jacquet, but I fear something worse: a passion which I have unwillingly aroused and which repels me. I perceived it in his look and gestures, in the care he had taken to dress himself in his best, in the spot he chose to meet me in—far from witnesses—in the tone of his voice. What an insult! To speak as he dared to do, to me who knew the life he leads and with whom! And yet I did not show him fully the indignation I felt. Why did I allow him to go on? How weak I have shown myself, in spite of an outward show of strength! How Mlle. Renée would scorn me if she could know or guess all! But alas, I was far more a coward when little Anna questioned me. What she asked included everything—the whole enigma of her life and mine. Her reason has grown in suffering and solitude, she was seeking some support —a consoler, a to-morrow to this life which she feels fleeting from her—and she chose me to answer her. I was her teacher. Could it be possible for the teacher not to know if there be a Heaven? The child wished to believe in order to bear her sufferings better. She had prepared her question; she was thinking of it while I talked to her of other things, and she received no answer. I feared to say no, I was not brave enough nor

pitiful enough to say yes. I told her to pray
because that committed me to nothing. But
pray to whom? Before the great trouble I gave
half the answer of the Christian which I am not.
How pitiful, how contradictory! but how pitiful
above all! Poor sick child, who thought you
had come to a fountain and found it dry! I am
a fountain without water, with only mire and
dust to offer, like these dried-up pools about us,
drained of all hope, of all that slakes the world's
thirst. I have only a little draught for myself
which will soon be dried. And since I have
mingled with actual life, I see that there is no
knowledge to equal that; all is there: to know
whence we come and whither we are going.

"I do not know. My little friend will leave
me; her wild green eyes will close, and I shall
have given no answer to the question she had
prepared for me. And for three years I have
been teaching children! These little ones, when
they have passed through my classes and Mlle.
Renée's, will in a few years become the wives
of labourers, artisans, or farmers. With what
strength shall I have fortified them? I do not
know; I doubt everything to-night, myself and
them. I ask myself whether I shall not have
made heavy hearts heavier and added moral poverty to the lot of the poor."

During the following ten days, Davidée returned twice to the house on the Plains. She
longed to go oftener, but her duties, the papers
to correct, the visits of parents, as well as the

warnings of Mlle. Renée that she was away too much, all kept her at the school. No one spoke of the child any longer, now that she had ceased coming to the play-ground. In the morning Phrosine, avoiding the assistant, would say to Mlle. Renée: "Things are going worse with us all the time. We have no luck." She almost always arrived early, before the teachers had come down, and having done her morning's work, sweeping and airing the rooms and sprinkling the floors with a watering-pot to lay the dust, she disappeared, leaving the court-yard gate open for the children to enter.

On her next visit to the Plains, Davidée had no expectation of finding her little friend out-of-doors. Warm spring showers were falling at times, over a few fields only, driven across the clear sky by distant thunder-clouds.

But Anna was there, sheltered by an umbrella which Phrosine had hung above her head among the branches. She was breathing more easily and a tinge of colour had come to her cheeks.

The child had barely greeted her friend when she said eagerly:

"Tell me, I beg of you, what I asked! You did not answer my question the other day."

Davidée, who had anticipated this persistence on the child's part, replied:

"Have you made your first communion?"

"Oh, surely!"

"So have I. Pray then to Him, since the desire moves you."

"Oh, Mademoiselle, what are you doing? Take care!"

For Davidée, with a sudden movement, had thrown open the gate and was crossing the grass, holding up her skirt with both hands to avoid making a rustling sound among the leaves. She came close to the child and kissed her on the cheek, and in doing so she inhaled her feverish breath. She involuntarily drew back and as she did this the thought crossed her mind with wonder: "If I had faith, I should bend over her again with a smile." But she only said very gently: "It is you, Anna, who do *me* good!"

The sick child in her joy had closed her eyes, she now opened them again, and made a sign that her friend must not stay, that there was danger there.

"I had to beg very hard to be allowed to come out in the rain. But I am happy, oh, so happy!"

"At what I have just said to you, Anna?"

"Yes, but above all at what you said before. As happy as a queen!"

"As a queen!"

The little one murmured as Davidée turned to leave her:

"My beloved Mademoiselle Davidée!"

A moment longer above the hedge her teacher's eyes met hers and saw that they were beaming and that the lips still murmured: "Beloved! Beloved!"

Davidée long treasured these words in her heart and many thoughts sprang from them.

She went back once more, on the 2d of May, which was a Sunday. Vespers had just finished ringing from the church tower of Ardésie, the sun was still warm. Anna lay with her body bent double between the two chairs, and her face, only half-raised, had lost all trace of colour in the cheeks, all light from the eyes. At the moment when Davidée arrived, Phrosine, having perhaps caught the sound of approaching steps, half-opened the door of the house at the end of the alley of plum-trees and peered out, her face, habitually hard, now wearing a hostile expression. She did not wish that the child's teacher should lean over the hedge; she was about to speak rudely to her, to drive her away, to catch up the child in her arms and carry her inside the house, where no stranger could speak to her of her mother. But the little one, though unable to turn round, or to utter a cry, had perceived, from the look in her friend's eyes, that her mother was behind her, and feared that if Davidée were driven away she might not return. And knowing this, she raised one arm above her head like a little ivory sceptre, and made a sign to her mother, several times repeated, which plainly said: "Go back; leave me my only joy!" and Phrosine obeyed without a word. Without laying aside the expression of hostility and defiance which she wished should be seen and understood, she drew herself up and retired within the house.

Anna, realizing that all danger was over, that she should not be carried in against her will, closed her eyes and seemed lost in thought. Davidée, fearing to weary her, withdrew a little from the gate, but the child at once beckoned to her to return. Pressing both hands to her lips and throwing her whole soul in a kiss to this half-

unknown friend, who was about to disappear,
she murmured very tenderly, like a prayer or a
last wish:

"I give mamma to you."

The young girl threw open the gate and ran
to the child, kneeling beside her in the grass and
embracing her. This time she did not draw back,
she felt beating against her breast the tired heart
which revived a little at the sweetness of her
words:

"I accept, Anna; I give you my promise, and I
will love you forever."

When she returned from the house on the
Plains, on that 2d of May, she felt her heart
crushed and emptied of joy as a bunch of grapes
crushed in the wine-press. She looked at the
blossoming hedge-rows, at the branches peeping
over the wall, at the tender blue of the sky, with
no sense of pleasure in them. In the road close
to the school, she was enveloped in a sudden breath
of warm air laden with the scent of broom, and
she said: "Pass on! my child is dying; pass on
to others, you have no power over those who
are really suffering. A heart must be half happy
to expand at your touch." She saw men and
women coming out from the church, where they
had attended vespers. Their faces wore a firm,
tranquil expression. Most of them belonged to
a colony of slate-cutters settled for generations
on the borders of the valley, people of worth
and dignity, and of ancient race; and mingling
with them were a few Bretons who remained
loyal to their faith, though far from the country

of the open spires. As they passed the assistant teacher, a few bowed to her, others glanced at her distrustfully, because she was not one whom they met at religious services, and of her personally they knew nothing, as her family were strangers, and the school was a closed and forbidden spot to them. Davidée understood all this, she had the gift of divining sympathies and antipathies. She opened the door of the schoolhouse, of her "home," and, as Mlle. Renée, on hearing the click of the latch, appeared on the threshold, she cried out to her:

"Ah, Mademoiselle, I am very unhappy!"

The blonde Mlle. Renée, who still had her best hat on, and was removing the glittering hat-pins, rejoined, with her mind full of other thoughts:

"Really?"

"We are going to lose little Anna Le Floch. I have just seen her, she cannot live."

"I was expecting it."

"You are not grieved over it as I am then? It does not matter to you?"

"What a state you are in, my poor Mademoiselle Davidée! You are not at all reasonable! Come in."

The directress took the young girl's hand and led her into the parlour, where she seated her in a chair, and sat down near her in the solitary armchair, which was usually reserved for the inspector, when he made his rounds two or three times a year.

"You are much too soft-hearted!"

"But the child is dying, I tell you."

"In the first place, you cannot be sure of it. She is young! And then, you cannot be the teacher of twenty or thirty children without one of them dying some time. Death comes to all ages."

She spoke in an amiable tone of voice, as one who wished to please, but not to express sympathy. For sole answer Davidée burst into tears, and instinctively laid her head on the shoulder of the one human being who might possibly comfort her. Mlle. Renée kissed her and patted her hair, and there was in her caress an evident admiration for these soft dark tresses and an extreme complaisance of manner.

"Do not weep, child. It is bad for you. You will wear yourself out, and no one will thank you for it. At your age one should not weep too much, one should try to enjoy life. Drive away these sad thoughts; let us talk of other things. By the way, tell me the first steps in your love-affair with Maïeul Rit-Dur."

Davidée rose to her feet and pushing away the directress, cried:

"What are you saying, Mademoiselle? I cannot permit you—you insult me—I am in love with no one, and least of all with that man. But if I should ever have a confidence to make, I swear to you——"

The directress had risen also.

"Go on, Mademoiselle; go on, I beg of you!"

The assistant had already reached the door, and as she opened it she heard a burst of mocking laughter following her.

"You are prostrated, are you, Mademoiselle? Ah, you strike me as utterly ridiculous! Look me in the face, I insist upon it. I have the right to give orders here."

Davidée turned her head and saw a face pale and convulsed with passion, with deep lines furrowed in it, and eyes blazing with hatred; while this woman, standing there in her fine attire, clenched her hands, calling out in accents broken by rage:

"It is all over, I tell you—I have been too indulgent. Ah, you dare to treat me in this fashion! You shall pay for it, I promise you! For the moment I merely give you warning that your intimacy with that Phrosine is regarded as absolutely disgraceful. Your virtue, Mademoiselle, stands in need of lessons. It prefers to give them, but will have to receive them too. You are compromising yourself. And you would do well not to converse on the road with Maïeul Jacquet, your gardener while awaiting something better. But you think I know nothing; I know everything you do; take care!"

The assistant made no reply; she turned and went up to her chamber, no longer weeping. Standing before her window, her eyes fixed on the distant prospect, a fever in her blood, she reviewed the incidents of the past few weeks. They poured through her mind tumultuously; fear had no part in the emotion which, while it held her trembling and oppressed, left her completely mistress of her reason and her will. The girl was striving to recognize the motives which had in-

spired her actions, to recall the impulses of her
soul at each meeting with Phrosine, with Maïeul,
and with Anna, and the fancies which had filled
it. She would have been glad of some external
aid, some witness who could assure her that she
had not yielded to an excess of irritation, perhaps
to a secret and hitherto disguised antipathy,
when she had broken just now with Mlle. Renée.
Henceforth the hostility of the directress was
declared; it would be open and implacable; and
yet Davidee regretted nothing, neither her words
nor her indignant gesture; for what had caused
them but her wounded sense of honour, over-
sensitive perhaps, but which she could not dis-
avow. She would never yield, cost what it
might; in utter solitude though it were, she
would maintain her right to live as she thought
best, and to act, outside the school, as she had
done hitherto. More than all her reasonings,
it was the memory of Anna Le Floch which
helped her through this moral and physical crisis.

It was often the custom at nightfall for the
village children to wander from one hamlet to
another, by twos or in little groups. On Sunday especially, those who had been spending
the day with a friend rarely failed to return home
for supper. Remembering this, Davidée now
descended the stairs and seated herself on a
stone at some little distance from the school-
house door. The evening sky was cold and
pure; the wind which had been spring-like all
day, light and warm, now blew in sudden gusts
which made the late strollers along the country

road shiver. The broom flowers had doubtless
withdrawn their perfume into the depths of their
golden calyxes, for the wind bore upon it only
the odours of upturned earth and fresh sods.
What stubble fields, high upon the plateau; what
fields of young wheat were sending their message to the world below, that bread should not
fail? The young girl wrapped her arms closer
within the folds of a cape she had thrown over
her shoulders. She raised her head and showed
the worn and weary face of one emerging from
a sorrow of which the anguish is a little spent,
but without strength and without consolation.
She looked toward the west where the sky was
darkening, and thought of little Anna. She was
like a mother parted from her child, who still
sees her everywhere.

One or two stars began to twinkle between
two gnarled old willows in the pasture opposite.
Suddenly she heard a clattering sound which
seemed to come from the direction of the quarries; now nearer, now further, to the right, to
the left of the old houses; one could not tell
whence came this noise, which approached, then
died away, then returned again, sounding like
the clapper of a great millwheel. But those
wheels belonged to her own country, where the
water sets the mills singing on the plain of Charente, and where the sea pours her torn sea-weed
in through so many streams and channels to be
swept out again by the tide. There, in her fine
new dwelling far too large and too white for her,
sat an aged woman, who, having dusted, brushed,

waxed and set her house in order all the week, was now waiting until the day should be quite spent, and she, grown one day older, could forget in slumber her only daughter, this Davidée, who, seated by the roadside of Ardésie, was sighing as she used to sigh when a tiny child, a long while after having wept.

Three quaint little figures, three shadows holding each other by the hand, were approaching from the direction of the mounds, their sabots clicking all together as they hesitated half-way between the school-house wall and the straggling hedge, terrified at the sight of that crouching immovable figure, with a white drapery about its head. But a well-known voice called to them so softly that not a bird fluttered in the bushes near by.

"Louise Tastour, Lucienne Gorget, Jeannie Fête-Dieu." Then the dance of the wooden shoes set in again, and fear fled across the embankment of La Fresnais, while the three children rushed forward as boldly as if in broad daylight, and surrounded their teacher where she sat. Louise Tastour wore in her hat an enormous feather, evidently picked up in the barnyard; Lucienne Gorget's felt toque was encircled with a wreath of flowers; little Jeannie was bareheaded, but her brush of hair stood as usual erect upon her forehead. The three children were so happy at meeting a friend on the deserted road where they had feared to pass but now it was a sad disappointment to find that their teacher had been weeping. What! Weep-

ing when one can command others! when one
has no lessons to learn! What could ail her?
They could not ask except with their eyes, which
did not half speak in the darkness, even though
they bent over her and were quite, quite near.

"Your school-mate Anna Le Floch is very
ill, children."

They understood now why Mademoiselle had
been crying and they became a little sad too,
but much less so than she.

"Yes, Mademoiselle."

"I fear that you may never see her again."
A little sob broke from one of the listeners, but
no one could have told which it was who was so
grieved, for all three were hanging their heads,
with their chins on their breasts.

Their teacher longed to say, "Pray for your
little friend," but she dared not; she never spoke
that word before her pupils, nor elsewhere, even
in her own heart. If it came to her mind that
evening it was because the sick child herself had
spoken it.

"You love her very much, do you not?"

The three little heads nodded all at once. "Yes,
Mademoiselle."

"Think of her then, will you not?"

One of them alone understood what Mademoiselle meant; this was Jeannie Fête-Dieu,
whose round eyes glittered in the darkness like
those of a little gray owl. She alone repeated,
more gravely this time: "Yes, Mademoiselle."

Davidée put out both hands and softly—as she
would have pushed away two pet lambs, with

her hand buried in their wool—she pushed aside
Louise Tastour and Lucienne Gorget, while she
drew Jeannie closer to her.

"Bend down so that I can whisper in your
ear; lower still! I want you to deliver a message
for me, but you must tell no one whom it is from
—no one!"

"No, Mademoiselle."

"You promise me? Then listen."

She murmured a few words in the child's ear.
Jeannie drew herself up, making little signs to
show she understood, and so pleased that her
grief for Anna Le Floch was quite forgotten.

"Now, children," the teacher said aloud, "run
home quickly; I shall hear your sabots clicking
till you have turned the corner. By the way,
Jeannie, how does it happen that you have left
your grandmother alone so long?"

"Some one is taking care of her, you see!"
said the child looking up; "if it were not for
that——"

"Who is it?"

The little one laughed as she answered. "It
is a man, a neighbour, Monsieur Maïeul!" And
she hastened to add: "For more than a week
he has never left the hill. Sunday, Monday,
he was there—we have never seen so much of
him! He passes all his evenings on the hill now.
So he promised the Breton women, those, you
know, who live at La Gravelle, that he would go
down twice at least while they were away, and I
too—and see how grandmamma was. It was kind
of him, wasn't it? Good-night, Mademoiselle!"

The three children ran off with a sound of sabots clattering, now louder, now softer, as on their approach. The young girl had leaned her head back against the wall; she realized that a feeling of joy had entered her sad heart. Was it possible? In return for her little effort of courage in throwing aside her apathy, in being the maiden who dares to speak for purity in the name of eternal laws—for had she not said some such thing, hardly conscious in her agitation what words she spoke?—here were ruined souls rising and obeying those laws—one of them at least had obeyed. What a struggle with themselves! And what secret strength must have aided them! What mysterious power had intervened, by which the word of a mere girl, the grief of a child, had triumphed—even once, even for a time— over passion, over habit, over the pity for a shattered tie? It was not to be explained, but it was beautiful. It was the same power which had given to little Anna's face that look of inward joy and ecstacy. The child had said no word. Who had implanted such purity in her soul that bad examples, heredity, neglect, the absence of all higher teaching, had been powerless to corrupt it or to harden and render it insensible? What compassion had listened to the prayers of the dying child? Could there be in the universe a watchful tenderness which listens to the poorest souls and aids the feeblest impulses of charity, repentance, doubt, desire for purification, or even the mere weariness of being bad and a burden to oneself? Davidée meditated, her heart penetrated with the sense of obscure destiny, and mysteriously, on this night, she felt growing within her that store of hope which each of us needs to carry us through this human life.

The stars had risen above the branches of the old willows—the earliest ones visible—and shone upon the lonely road. "All his evenings now he passes on the hill." Davidée looked up to where La Gravelle and Mère Fête-Dieu's house were sleeping together under the same shred of sky in the vast darkness.

She entered the house, where Mlle. Renée had left a lamp burning for her on the kitchen table, and a little bowl of soup on the smouldering ashes of the hearth.

CHAPTER V.

ANNA'S FUNERAL.

ON the three following days of May there was
bad news from the house on the Plains. On the
sixth, Mlle. Birot was busy distributing books
from the school library. Several of the pupils
and a few village girls who had left school, had
arrived at eleven o'clock on this first Thursday
in the month to bring back the books they had
read, and ask for others. The young teacher
was standing before the varnished pine bookcase
in which were ranged a couple of hundred volumes, bound in cloth, and protected by a wire
netting and green baize curtains.

She knew most of these books by heart, and
could lay her hand at once on any she sought,
as the pupil entered and, bowing to her, said: "I
would like a novel, something a little jolly!"
How often she had heard that word and how she
detested it! She had just heard it again from
the stout Lucienne Géboin. Davidée watched
the older girls who walked away, reading as they
went, and the little ones who trotted off with a
book stuffed into the pocket of their apron or
tucked under their arm.

She was about to close the library and return
to the house, when Ursule Morin entered, Ursule,

slim as a sheaf of oats, indolent and shy, who blushed and bridled at the smallest compliment; at this moment she was looking sad.

"What! you, Ursule? You have taken to reading, then? What shall I give you—a fashion book?"

The teacher had spoken before looking at Ursule Morin's long thin face, always bent to one side like that of a stubborn young goat; it was now stained with newly shed tears. Stepping quickly toward her, Davidée exclaimed: "What ails you, child? Is Anna Le Floch worse?"

Ursule, with her lips tightly closed, merely bowed her head.

"Is she very ill, then?"

The child bowed her head once more.

"She is dying? I must see her again; I must go to her at once."

"No, Mademoiselle, it is not worth while to go; it would be too sad; she is dead."

It was a long and cruel afternoon for Davidée, such as are hours of grief when there is none to share it. Mlle. Renée, on hearing the news, began immediately to plan for the funeral.

"What would you have, Mademoiselle? It was to be expected, was it not? It must be a relief to the mother."

"Oh, Mademoiselle, say rather a remorse, a terrible blow which will change everything in life for her."

"How little you know these people! But it does not matter—I shall leave it to you to look after the children on the day of the funeral. You

must see that every child in the upper class wears
a white dress, if she has one. To-day I must
remain at home for I have a headache; moreover,
it is not fitting that you or I should go inside
Phrosine's house. If you chance to be walking
in the direction of the town——"

"I hardly know. I have no plan."

"I merely suggest that if you go that way you
had better order a wreath of flowers. My children will contribute enough for that and I suppose
yours will do as much. Something suitable, without extravagance; no excess of sentiment, you
understand?"

Davidée made no reply. As soon as she was
free to leave the school she went out, and to make
it evident that she was not on her way to Phrosine's, she started in the opposite direction, toward
the village of Malaquais, where she intended to
take the tramway. The thought of Anna was
constantly with her; the child was more present
to her than the landscape around her or the men
and women she passed, who were working in
their gardens, or beating their clothes beside the
pond, or walking along the same white ribbon of
road with her. The child had vanished from
amidst these visible sights, but was it possible
that she was gone forever? Not to have bloomed
for a single hour and to die, thus! What injustice, if compensation were not granted her at
once and forever—assured, eternal! These brief
unhappy lives, how they seem to call for an after-
life! The thoughts which filled Davidée's mind
were not cruel ones; there was consolation mingled with them, an intimate persuasion, hidden

in the depths of her soul, which formed itself
into words—into a voice which spoke to the girl
with no conscious will on her part. "I have not
lived in vain," it seemed to say; "my suffering
is over and it has been fruitful suffering. I was
placed near souls in peril, my mother's, yours,
others' perhaps. The whole meaning of my life
has been in its purity. I was filled with a mysterious love for laws of right which I hardly knew;
I have suffered for that love. I have died for
it, and through it I am a conqueror—a conqueror
for her who formed my body and whose soul I
may save, if you will help me, my beloved teacher.
I have given her to you. Do not look upon her
as others do through her sin, but through my
suffering. Try to raise her! She is weeping to-
day; continue the work which I alone could
begin. Do not listen to your aversion, let nothing repel you!" And Davidée's soul overflowed
with a sudden tenderness, which was her answer.

On reaching the suburbs of the town she
stopped at a shop where they sold funeral wreaths.
A stout man behind the counter addressed her
with effusive politeness. "If Madame will examine our latest novelties, I am sure she will be
satisfied." Behind him, in cases, were suspended
rows of wreaths made of beads or artificial flowers, as well as zinc medals, cast-iron crosses, and
marble tablets with inscriptions.

"It is for a child," she said.

"Of what age? The age is a very important
element. This year, for instance, for the new-born
what we use most is——"

"You may make," Davidée broke in, "a

wreath of white flowers and tie it with a ribbon bearing the name of the school. Make the wreath large for it will be the only one, as the mother is poor."

On the morning of the second day following, the assistant was leading a band of forty little girls between the sun-steeped walls along the road to the house on the Plains. There were but forty in line when she left Ardésie, but at every cross-road, at the gate of every field, at every house door they passed, stood a child clad in white, or black and white, or blue, who joined the procession. For fear of creating a scandal, the two teachers had agreed that they would not go to the house, which was, moreover, one of the farthest away from the village. It would be unfortunate if they should have to encounter Maïeul at the house on the Plains, giving orders as if at home. The evening before, a woman had passed through the cluster of hamlets, bearing a paper on which were these words in an unformed handwriting: "The burial of my child will take place to-morrow at ten o'clock. You are asked to be present—Mother Le Floch."

Who would answer this summons? What consideration or pity would be shown toward this woman, who was rarely seen now outside the school-house or her own doors? At the second cross-road, where the children, with Davidée leading them, were drawn up beneath the wall, which afforded just shade enough for their height, the breathless chant of the Ardésie chorister arose

and floated over the glowing fields. The tall
white cross, borne by a choir-boy, appeared at a
turn of the road, flashing as it turned; then came
the curé preceded by his chorister, and lastly the
black horse drawing a small hearse, without fringe
or ornament or initial letters, but richly adorned,
all the same.

All the little girls peered out from the shadow
of the wall into the sunny road, murmuring:
"What is it? There are showers of it everywhere, to right and left, dropping and shining
on all sides. Oh, how pretty it is! When it
comes nearer we can see what they have placed
around her."

To the slow steps of the one horse, the car
drew nearer, the jolting and rumbling of its
wheels audible between the words intoned by
the chorister, and soon they could plainly discern
the flower-decked casket of little Anna. Scattered over the white cloth were great sprays of
broom, the most profusely blossoming of the
golden spindles forming a garland more sumptu-
ous than any that could be bought, more dazzling than the wreath hanging below them tied
with its white ribbon. How marvellously spring
had adorned the dead child! Some hand must
have been busy all day ransacking the thickets,
choosing only the sprays without one faded
blossom. Some one doubtless had paid the
authorities for leave to surround the child with
the flowers she loved.

Behind the car walked a woman, her head
covered with a long black veil, and leaning on

the arm of an older woman, one of her neighbours; beside them walked a man who had known the child's father, wearing his Sunday suit and tall silk hat; there was no one else. The school-children formed in a double file behind the two women and the man. They were scarcely think-ing now of the little companion who had played with them, laughed with them, recited the same lessons; mourning lasts but a moment at their age. They no longer spoke of Anna, but, softly among themselves, knowing that they must be on their best behaviour, they whispered the names of the quarrymen who stood outside their straw shelters as the procession passed, raising their caps respectfully and with feeling—both young and old—while some of the women looking out of their windows crossed themselves—but not all—and thought of more things than the men, es-pecially of the stricken mother.

The children whispered too: "There are the bells tolling; they have caught sight of us from the belfry tower." The broom swayed lightly with each turn of the wheels, and flights of mar-tins, though it was not yet their hour, circled around the church steeple. Davidée, who now walked last in the little procession, said to her-self: "To-morrow there will be only her mother and me to remember her." She felt grateful to Maïeul for not having shown himself. "What a power there is in death! How it holds in check those feelings which have no right to express themselves, or to greet its coming. I thank you, Monsieur Maïeul, in the child's name."

It was the first time since her coming to Ardésie
that Davidée had been present at a child's funeral.
Before setting out she had taken from her locked
drawer the only book of piety she had ever owned,
her little morocco-bound prayer-book. When they
entered the church she opened it, while several
of the little girls nudged each other and pointed
with a laugh to the teacher who was reading the
mass.

Davidée read very little. She lowered her head
and raised it by turns; now and then a word,
a sentence in the liturgy, brought her thoughts
back, enriched by their depth of meaning, to the
child whom she saw so plainly and who had assembled all her little playmates around her for
the last time. Who among the pupils was praying? They were so young, so unreflecting! One
or two perhaps had recited an Ave Maria at the
opening of the mass.

Phrosine, seated with bowed head in the first
row of seats, was such a stranger to the rites of
worship that her neighbour was obliged to touch
her on the arm when it was time to rise or kneel.
The man, the father's friend, was doubtless awaiting, at the tavern opposite, the conclusion of the
mass. And thus the young girl, moved by this
loneliness of the newly dead, felt herself the only
friend who was praying and joined with her
whole heart in those thoughts which seemed to
her beautiful in the unfamiliar service. Was hers
a prayer? To whom was it addressed? It was
the cry of a great pity and of a friendship which
had no longer any human means of expression

or of service, and which sought the beyond. "Deliver her not into the hands of the enemy and forget her not forever, but ordain that she may be received by thy blessed angels. . . . We would not have you ignorant concerning the dead, that ye be not as those who sorrow without hope. . . . Now is Christ risen from the dead and become the first-fruits of them that slept. . . . I am the resurrection and the life; he that believeth in Me though he were dead, yet shall he live. . . . Let the light eternal shine upon her!" The greatest words the world has heard bore upward the memory of a child and the name that was heard amidst these prayers: Anna! Anna!

When the service was over, the humble procession reformed, having but a few rods further to go. The graveyard of Ardésie was a long narrow field where, in the shelter of high walls, mosses and shrubs, broom and live-oak, flourished in profusion, taking the place of the funereal yew. The oaks with their low branches formed a wide-spreading roof through which came glimpses of the sky as through stained-glass windows. These boughs served as a shelter to the carriers of Ardésie, like those thickets which rise on the hill-sides of Provence to protect the traveller from the southern sun. Crosses rose beneath them, half hidden at this season by masses of red fumitory and golden buttercups. There were foot-paths here and there amid the dense grass, and spots worn bare by the knees of those who had knelt there.

It was here that they laid little Anna's coffin

while the priest and the chorister chanted a final
psalm.   The mother standing beside the little
grave gave one wild cry and leaned sobbing upon
the shoulder of the woman who had never left her,
and who now led her away across the fields, saying softly, "Poor soul! poor soul!" while Davidée
thought within herself, "I wish that I had been
the one to comfort her!"

She watched her pupils filing by, grown serious
for a moment, as they sprinkled holy water over
the white cloth and the open grave and then
turned away, resuming their accustomed order,
two by two, with the smallest ones ahead.   The
sound of steel hammers falling upon slate filled
the quiet air and died away.   Davidée was so
full of sorrow, she felt herself so strongly drawn
toward the childish form resting there, that, having given the signal for departure, she turned back
to gaze once more on the live-oaks, the open grave,
and the trampled grass.

At that moment the curé of Ardésie was leaving the cemetery, wearing his shovel-hat and carrying, tucked under his arm, his starched surplice,
which bent like a bow at each step.   She had
never spoken to him, though sometimes they had
exchanged bows as they met upon the road, she
taking care to show by her stiff, slight nod that
she was saluting an adversary of state education,
and he, not entirely able to hide the displeasure
he felt on meeting one of the pair of women who
were instructing the children of his Ardésie flock
without any religious belief, and probably—as
he supposed—with the secret design of turning

them aside from the path of salvation. He could
not look at Mlle. Renée or her assistant without
reflecting that he was too poor to have a free
school of his own, without regretting, envying,
and suffering. And as he had never hitherto exchanged a word with either instructress he could
not fail to hold them in equal suspicion. He was
a man past middle-age, tall and gaunt, with red
hair and eyebrows and a face furrowed by trial
and opposition, pale lips accustomed to silence
and to hard crusts, and eyes of an extraordinary
limpidity. These intensely blue eyes, in their
deeply hollowed orbits, seemingly distrustful of
themselves and habitually cast down, were like a
child's eyes in their candour and a man's in their
gravity; eyes which would have liked to see the
world all beauty, and consequently rested on the
sights around him and on humanity with precaution and with brief glances. When he spoke
of God and of heavenly things his face showed
how fidelity to ideals can transform the most
unpromising countenance. Mlle. Birot had hitherto noticed only the abbé's stiff bow and his
faded cassock; she now saw both nearer; but it
seemed to her that it would be a discourtesy not
to speak a word to the priest who had just uttered
his benediction over little Anna's grave, and who
had hastened, as she knew, on Sunday evening
to the house on the Plains.

"I thank you, Monsieur," she said.

He gave a little start on hearing this unknown
and unhoped-for voice.

"What! For administering the sacrament to

the child? But it is I who have to thank you, Mademoiselle. It was you who sent word to me on Sunday, was it not, by Jeannie Fête-Dieu? That was very well done; it was, in fact, admirable; yes, truly admirable."

"What else could I do, Monsieur? I knew Anna's sentiments and I loved her."

"She was a martyr, Mademoiselle; there are many such who are little known, many, many; they mount straight upward!"

Davidée looked at the abbé, and he at her, and each perceived that the other had a tear on their eyelashes. The girl was touched; she said quickly, wishing to rejoin the children:

"Can you do anything for the mother?"

"Humanly, nothing, Mademoiselle. She only received me on Sunday for her child's sake. But I shall pray for her to-morrow at my mass. Really it was admirable on your part—admirable!"

Davidée was tempted to smile, in spite of her grief, but at the same time she saw on the abbé's face the radiance of a thought which kept his soul as serene as the air of spring. She bowed and walked away rapidly, for her little charges had already passed the first houses beyond the church.

All that afternoon Davidée was thinking by turns of Anna, of Phrosine, and of Maïeul Jacquet. What was to become of this woman who had nothing to live upon—if she had really broken with Maïeul—beyond the paltry sum which the Municipal Council voted yearly for the sweeping of class-rooms and school premises? Davidée felt herself a novice in the rôle of counsellor which

she had assumed; she foresaw that the counsels
of poverty would soon be more potent than hers,
that the memory of the child would fade, and the
evil life be resumed with one or another. How
could this woman succeed in earning two francs,
or even a franc and a half, a day? That was the
chief problem. Could she do washing by the
day in one of the deserted quarries? No, Phrosine would never accept such heavy toil as that.
Could she do sewing for the neighbouring farmers' wives? But seamstresses were already numerous in Ardésie, each having her patrons, and
it was only young women who could secure work
as their assistants, and, besides, there were long
intervals when no such work was to be had. What
could she do? Take a place in the match-factory
or some other large factory in the neighbouring town? What a risk for a woman with her
past and her still striking beauty! These proj-
ects and others like them passed through the
assistant's mind while she sat in the school-room
till evening, having papers to correct and next
week's classes to prepare. Yet the brightness of
the spring day outside was tempting; all the facets
of the slate piles and the roofs glittered in the sun,
and the belfry was wrapped in a sheath of warm
rays; none could tell which way the wind was
blowing, for each weathercock told a different
tale. Peace descended upon the earth with the
fall of day.

In the vicarage garden, which was almost
wholly uncultivated, as the soil was poor and
thin, the curé had been reciting his breviary.

He was seated under a trellis of wild vine bearing small hairy leaves upon its enormous branches. With his thumb slipped between the pages he marked the place where, by and by, he would resume his interrupted reading. Above the aged mossy pear-trees and the crest of the wall softened by hanging weeds and grasses, he was watching the clear light gleaming over his Ardésie. Absorbed in thoughts and cares for his small and scattered flock, he sighed as he turned his eyes toward the distant chimneys or gables or the tops of the cherry-trees, which hid some invisible house whose dwellers he knew; then he murmured gently: "Oh, God, I take these cares too much to heart; I vex myself too much! In our lamentations over the wickedness of man we forget that thou art God, that thou art ever present, that thou lovest us, and that where thou art, *there* is hope. Thou hast shown it to me. The child thou hast taken to thyself was a dove of innocence and purity. Who could have looked for it there? Nothing had armed her against life, but thou didst provide thy grace. And thou didst touch the heart of this young girl who summoned me. Turn her soul now toward thee; and sustain mine which is too keenly alive to the extent of evil and its deep blindness. Men would rob me of my charity, didst thou not replace it by another, new at each moment. I no longer complain, I no longer seek my own will. The bell that rings the sweetest chimes has passed through fire. I shall ring my chimes some day. I must force myself not to despond. How clear the sky is!

There is heavenly seed everywhere sufficient to sow every field—even this parish of mine—even France. And have I not my consolations too, in such an one as poor Mère Fête-Dieu, that humble witness to the eternal gospel? The evening air is sweet; nature is like man, now in sin and now in grace. The blessed sleep of childhood enwraps the world. Deliverance! Deliverance! The wind, that tired wagoner, has finished his daily work; we hear no longer the voice of the north and west, but the sounds of life close around us, and the weary labourers returning home. The air is sweet; the day is dying well. Magnificat."

CHAPTER VI.

A TALK WITH PHROSINE.

THE day after the funeral Phrosine came as usual
to do her daily work at the school. She was no
longer in mourning, but wearing the dust-coloured
livery of every day. Davidée, who saw her as
she entered the school-rooms and as she came out
again, was touched by the look on her face, so
livid and furrowed by grief that the children,
mistaking suffering for anger, drew away from
her, without their customary "Good-morning,
Madame Phrosine!" She never ceased to think
of her while hearing her classes. It seemed to
her that it was cowardly not to speak comfort
to this misery for which no one cared, and she
was concerned how best to do it. Meanwhile
the children were restless and inattentive and she
herself very weary. At the moment of leaving
the school-room she saw Mlle. Renée coming
toward her, surrounded by a buzzing swarm of
children. The directress said:

"Your friend, Madame Phrosine, wishes to
speak to you, Mademoiselle."

The pupils tittered at these words, without
fully comprehending the emphasis thrown by
Mlle. Renée on the words "your friend."

The assistant crossed the court-yard, opened

the garden-gate, and at the end of the box-
bordered alley saw the woman whom Maïeul had
left, the mother who had lost her child; she turned
pale and strove not to show that she was trembling, for Phrosine was staring at her fixedly, her
body bending forward, her elbows on her knees,
her chin supported on her two hands; and there
was something in those staring eyes, in that immovable figure, a sort of madness of grief and also
a hatred going straight to its aim, which wounded
the young and timid heart of the girl. She had
approached close to Phrosine before the latter
stirred or spoke or ceased to fix her with her eyes.
Davidée seated herself beside her on the bench
and said:

"You wish to speak to me, Phrosine?"

"Yes, I wish to tell you how I hate you and
your bigotries. You have done me such injuries
that I ought——"

"What ought you to have done?"

"To have burned your house over your head!"

"But I have no house."

"The school-house, then! Do you think I
could not have found two or three sturdy lads to
help me if I had wished! But I care nothing for
men now, only for my misery. I hate you, do
you hear?"

"Say it, if such words soothe you; repeat it,
if you will. It is enough for me that I have not
deserved your insults, Phrosine."

"Do not call me Phrosine. I am no longer
the drudge who sweeps your school-rooms. That
trade is done with; all is done with between us.

I am Madame Le Floch, deserted by her husband and, through your doing, deserted by her lover. I am, above all, a mother whom you robbed of her child's love, and then of her child's joy and her life."

"Who—I?"

"You, no one but you! Look here! it is all very well for the priests to despise and condemn a woman like me. They have their gospel, their God, their prayers. But you! how does it concern you? Where did you learn that we cannot lead our lives as we will?"

"From the laws."

"What laws? Those that can be made and unmade? I know who they are who make those laws; much they trouble themselves if these same laws stand in *their* way! You are all hypocrites, you and those like you. It was not your place to judge me and it was you who taught my child to judge me."

"No, she judged you herself."

"But you encouraged her in it, you, Mademoiselle Birot, and she is dead, dead, dead! And for a long while I have only held her body in my arms when I embraced her. I hate you for all the hollow kisses she gave me, for all the tears she shed—which wet my cheeks! Without your lessons she would be living now."

"Alas! she had other reasons for dying."

"What were they then?"

"The blood in her veins. But if I helped to make her soul purer I do not regret it, even if she suffered; even now, when you reproach me for it. I wish all my children in the school were like her."

"You see! You upheld her in it! Besides, you told me, beneath my own roof, that I was sinning. You must change your ways, lay-teacher as you are, or else——"

"Or else——?"

"There are fellows who are afraid of nothing here; they will report to your chiefs and you will march!" She said this without moving, in a low sinister tone, without ceasing to stare at the courtyard, whence came the cries of Anna's living playmates. It was by a visible effort that she restrained the sobs which shook from time to time the head propped on her hands and the loosened masses of her hair which glistened in the sunshine.

Davidée, in order to restrain her impulse of indignation, spoke as few words as possible. She felt all there was of bitter grief, but also of revolt against everything, and of moral perversion, in this anger and these threats of Phrosine's. These two women appeared to any one watching them from a distance, as Mlle. Renée did, to be talking calmly enough, one of them bending over wearily, the other sitting erect beside her in the brilliant morning light. Davidée, on hearing herself threatened—what mysterious feeling of generosity was it that had taken possession of her?—was moved only to pity. She bent over the woman and said:

"Madame Le Floch, since you do not wish me to call you Phrosine, I am only a poor girl who is trying to teach others. I know little, I doubt many things. What I teach is perhaps Christianity, though I am little of a Christian myself, but I am very sure that there can be no happiness in a life of disorder, and that, you see, is what made me speak. I loved your child, I guessed why she suffered, though it was not I who planted those seeds of suffering in her heart. But no one can make me say that she was wrong. I may have to 'march,' as you say, but nothing can prevent my justifying my little friend, who wished her mother not to have a lover."

Phrosine broke in: "You will give me a living, then?"

"I would gladly, if I could. I would willingly share what I have with you."

The green eyes opened wider as they turned upon Davidée, and one could see in them the ignoble spirit, suspicious of all good in others and confident only in itself. Phrosine shrugged her shoulders with a scornful laugh.

"Innocence! I am not one to be led by you. You need not try to do me good, it was enough for you to preach to the child. I am of harder stuff, I don't believe in words and I did not come here to ask alms of you. But I wish you to know something besides what I have already told you. You have succeeded in separating Maïeul Jacquet from me. You think that a fine victory?"

"For him perhaps."

"You are mightily mistaken; he loves me still. It was he who wished to leave me, I won't deny that. As for me, I let him go on account of the child who was so ill. But if I had chosen to keep him he never would have left me. He had me in his blood!"

"I have no wish to hear your secrets."

"And what if I want to tell them to you? This very day I need only make a sign to him. If I come back some day——"

"You are going away then?"

"If I come back, and if I wish it, I need not even make a sign. I have only to throw him one glance across the old pit of La Grenadière, and he will come back to me as a dog runs back when you call him."

"Why do you tell me this?"

"You are warned, that's all!"

"I have no need of a warning."

"I know what I am saying! Yes, I am going away. You will hear no more of me for many a long day, perhaps never. I cannot do without a child; my daughter is dead, I must have my son. I shall go until I find Le Floch and make him tell me what he has done with Maurice."

"What will you live upon meanwhile?"

"I can surely earn ten sous a day, anywhere, by sweeping houses as I did here, can't I? Don't begin again giving me moral lessons. It is a good riddance for you when a woman like me goes away. I shall hunt for my first child, the one his father robbed me of. Good-by, Mademoiselle."

She rose to her feet as she spoke and Davidée took her hand. "You have not succeeded in wounding me," she said. "Tell me where you are going?"

"Straight before me!"

She did not draw away her hand as she spoke, however, but left it in the young girl's. The children were at that moment forming in line to enter the school-room.

"Have you at least some reason, Madame Le Floch, for believing that your husband is alive, and if so, where he is likely to be working?"

"I heard something about him from the man who was at the child's funeral."

"Have you any money for your journey? Is it far from here?"

"I shall work my way."

"But you will not know any one. When shall you start?"

Phrosine made no answer.

"I must see you again; when do you go?"

Without turning her head the woman replied: "To-morrow at sunrise"; and saying this, she turned to go, and Davidée entered her class-room at the same moment that the servant, in her working clothes, but with a sunbeam falling on her hair, opened the gate leading into the highway and disappeared.

From the Green Diary.—"How hard this day has been for me! If I could only have had leisure and freedom to think over what I should say to Phrosine, this morning, and decide what I had best do. But the rest of the morning was spent in suppressing noise and chatter in the class, in punishing some of the girls, and listening to answers which showed clearly how little interested the parents are in their children's work, and how it is

left to me to deal unaided with these undisciplined
minds and untrained impulses. When I said this
to Mlle. Renée, whom I scarcely speak to now,
she merely laughed at me. What coarse natures
there are among these children! And when I
reprove them, I am conscious that I do not reach
them. They fear me, that is all. My words
have no influence, they are met only by sullen
indifference or a spirit of irony and defiance, which
seems born in them, which they breathe in with
the air around them and which is like Phrosine's
laugh. And yet some of them show affection as
they gather about me after the lessons. But,
alas, what will their affection for me weigh ten
years, or two years hence? Even if I succeed in
making them really love me, what shall I have
given them to make them better? I have dreamt,
like so many others, of surviving in my scholars. I used to say in myself: 'My thoughts, my
strength, my judgment, will live in the minds of
these girls and these mothers.' What thought?
What strength? What real authority will Davidée Birot's judgment have over them, when self-
interest is involved or passion carries them away?

"It is growing late. I find it hard to collect
my thoughts after the emotions and tumult of
the day. I still hear the sound of the children's
voices, as I sit alone here in my room, and Phrosine's voice as she spoke to me this morning.
What did she mean when she boasted of possess-
ing a power over Maïeul which no one could shake?
'I have only to look at him,' she said, 'across the
pit of the Grenadière, and he will come to me as

a dog to its master.' Why did she say that to me? It must be that gossip has been active here, among the quarry-pits, and that my name has been mixed up with their wretched slanders. Ah! how base it all is! And yet I must see Phrosine again. What do *his* threats matter to me? I cannot let her go without some proof of interest on my part. I have given her my promise, and now that she has been deserted, she is even more alone in the world than I. I have twenty francs here in my drawer, I will give them to her, and I can beg mamma for more. To-morrow morning —at what hour? I will leave my shutters open so that the sun pouring in may wake me."

CHAPTER VII.

A CLANDESTINE DEPARTURE.

At dawn of a clear bright morning, Davidée had risen and left the school. No one was stirring yet, among the mounds, nor along the roads. The only sound that recalled men's labour was the whistle of an exhaust pump, throwing off its puffs of white steam, at regular intervals, at the entrance to a quarry-well at Trélazé. The fields lay wrapped in slumber and the grass was heavy with dew and sleep. The girl walked onward rapidly. Should she meet Phrosine? She barely glanced at the scene around her, her heart was heavy at the thought of this woman setting out alone, without help of any sort, leaving behind her the house where little Anna had lived. Had Phrosine given notice to any one of her departure, she wondered? Perhaps some neighbour was helping her at this moment to tie up her bundle of clothing and close the house. Here was the long roof and the hedge! The market-gardeners were not yet at work; a sparrow was twittering on the roof, but there was no smoke rising this morning from Phrosine's chimney. What silence seemed to surround the departing woman! The morning mists were melting away, overhead,

and blue sky peering through, as the sun was
about to rise. Davidée heard no sound but the
neighing of a horse turned out to pasture and the
distant slamming of some housewife's shutters.
As she pushed open the little gate and took a step
or two along the mossy path, Phrosine appeared
on the threshold, closed the door and turned the
key. She had no longer any hold upon her poor
dwelling except this key which she turned slowly,
slowly, standing motionless for a moment as if
she could look through the closed door. Then
she turned away, holding the key in one hand and
carrying on her arm a large white wicker basket
whose double lid was gaping; for everything she
owned was in that basket—her clothing and food
for the journey, a pair of shoes and a few memen-
tos of her dead child. As she caught sight of the
assistant teacher her face, which had been merely
sad, grew suddenly hard. After casting a last
glance around the silent garden she approached
her, saying:

"Don't make any noise! I haven't given the
landlord notice. He can sell whatever he finds;
I have nothing to pay him with, but I will write
and ask him to have patience." She had on her
black dress, the collar of which was fastened with
a gold pin, the sole remnant of her wedding
fineries. She always went bareheaded along the
Ardésie roads, and to-day as usual she wore no
cap nor bonnet. She was well aware how beautiful her hair looked in the sunlight. Davidée
could not restrain her admiration as she gazed
at her.

"How young she looks!" she said to herself; "what a pity it all is!"

"I will walk part way with you," she said in a low voice. "Let me help you carry your basket." She took hold of the handle as she spoke, and walking a little apart, with their burden swinging between them, the two women took the road toward the town. The houses they passed, standing amid their gardens, were some of them old and fine, with pointed turrets and mullioned windows commanding a wide view over the valley. Phrosine turned her face away to avoid being recognized by the farmers' wives who dwelt in these old houses. As the road made a bend among the orchards, Davidée asked: "Are you sure of finding your husband?"

"No!"

"Nor your son?"

"Just as little. But I *will* find them. If I have to make the tour of France and enter every house where there is a boy fourteen years old, I will see my son again."

"You may not recognize him!"

"He was the image of me. Do I look like other people?"

"You are on your way to the station, are you not? How far do you expect to go to-night?"

Phrosine walked on a while without replying. Just then they heard a sound of wheels behind them. It was a peasant woman driving her small cart laden with milk-pails.

"Shall I give you a lift," she cried, "you, Mère Le Floch, and your companion?"

"Thank you," answered Phrosine. "I am not going far." And turning toward Davidée she began to address her volubly:

"Two years ago, he took our son away from the Board of Charity Home where he had left him. He went to Paris for him, he can't deny that; no, for those who manage the home sent for information about him and me to Père Moine, the man you saw at my child's funeral. My husband was at Orléans then, or in the neighbourhood. I shall take a ticket for Orléans and hunt for him there; but you must tell this to no one."

"I give you my word, Madame Le Floch."

The woman shrugged her shoulders. "Oh, come! You might as well call me Phrosine, you won't have long to say it."

They had reached a height, in their steady climb, where the air, blowing across the hills, fanned their faces. And on feeling this keen air from the slopes beyond the Loire, where broader roads cross the wide valley and lead into the wider world beyond, the two women paused with a sudden sense of weariness. They set the basket down in the dust by the roadside.

"Ah!" exclaimed Davidée, "we are far enough now from Ardésie."

"The wind no longer smells of the broom," Phrosine answered. "It is all over. I have set off this morning on the longest journey I ever took."

She raised her hard, resolute eyes toward the valley, but she no longer saw it clearly.

"Come, come!" she said, "I mustn't flag now.

I think it must be the air of this new country which makes the basket so heavy. My arm is like wool. If only I could leave it all behind."

"Yes, all the evil of the past, Phrosine."

"All the poverty, to be sure!"

"But not all the sorrow. Take that along with you, Phrosine; it will protect you on your way. The sun is already high; only look!"

The tiled roof of a cottage by the roadside was flushed with pink like a newly opened rose. The two women stooped and set off again, keeping step, as they swung the basket between them on their out-stretched arms. They walked on thus for a couple of hundred paces till they reached the rusty gate of an old brick château, closely shuttered now, but which had formerly looked far out across the valley. Here they paused again and turned their heads with one accord to the left, whence came the breeze and the morning light. Under their feet was the last plateau of that vein of slate which here sinks into the depths of the earth; before their eyes was a deserted knoll, clothed with a thin herbage already scorched by the heat, which dipped downward to mingle with the light soil of the plain. Below them rose long lines of poplars, showing where the clay and ooze of the stream fed their roots. Farther still could be discerned another curve of the valley, now veiled in mist, where white houses rose amid the joyous landscape, with its wide highways and rich pastures interspersed with budding boughs on the hedge-rows bordering the fields, on grove and woodland, and

with sharper pinnacles of foliage emerging here
and there. The wide expanse was half-swathed
in a veil of mist, as far as the line of hills which
follow the windings of the Loire and the pale
blue circle of the horizon. The two women experienced, perhaps, a kindred emotion, as they
breathed in the air of this wide landscape and
followed with their glance the sweep of the valley curving toward the east, and the river flowing
through it from the farthest borders of France.
They could see the hill of St. Saturnin, which
alone loomed mountain-like in the scene, its
wooded slopes rising like faint blue smoke above
the dazzling mists of the valley. Phrosine asked:
"Is Orléans over yonder?"

Davidée gave an affirmative nod.

"If I could only find my boy!"

"Oh, yes!" cried Davidée fervently; "only to
find him!"

"And take him away from my husband. He
shall not have him! And yet to think that I
cannot see my Maurice except by means of that
man!" She said this with a smouldering rage,
long nursed in solitude, and ready to break out
at any moment. Her eyes followed the line of
the valley and the houses dotted along the highway, seeing, perhaps, nothing of it all, absorbed
as she was in her bitter thoughts and the uncertainty of her future; nothing save the far-off villages which she would enter, seeking her faith-
less husband and a son who might be dead or
lost to her. There were no witnesses near them
now, and her heart spoke out.

"Mustn't he have been a wicked man! To snatch my little boy away from me, when he was barely three years old. To carry him off at night, when I was coming home late from a hard day's washing and my baby was so soon to be born!"

"He had not even threatened you? There had been no quarrel beforehand?"

"No—as to quarrels, one can't be married without them—but he had made no threats. He had only said when I told him my news: 'What! two brats! No, not for me.' And when I came in that night, dead tired, I found the house dark and empty—as it is now—with only a cold hearth awaiting me."

"What a coward!"

"Just as they all are, a bit more or a bit less." And Phrosine laughed aloud, showing her white teeth and tossing back her masses of golden hair. "And yet I was a handsome girl, I can tell you. He had courted me and spent money for our wedding, as though I had been a queen. But there are plenty of such two-year queens about the world! I don't know why I tell you this, but it seems to me as if I should see him there, at the end of that lane, and as if we should kill each other when we meet. How I have cursed him! He was the cause of all!—of all!"

Davidée stretched out her hand toward the hills across the Loire.

"Who knows, Phrosine? He may be quite changed now!"

"Oh, no! not he!"

"What if you were to find him sick or in poverty?"

"That man, never! He is having his sport with some other woman. I am as sure of it as that I am alive."

"What if he should be touched at meeting you? If you could win him back? Only try."

"My poor young lady! we should need to have fresher hearts than ours for that. We hate each other now, he and I, with a bitter hatred."

"But even if you come back with your child only, it will be the saving of you. You will begin a new life, with your boy to aid you; even with a little help from me if you are willing. They forbid my seeing you, but I shall manage to see you all the same. You will not be lonely and desperate then as you are now. There will be friendly people around you."

Phrosine listened to these words with her lips contracted by the old, bitter mockery. She scarcely knew the sound of words of pity. She did not want it, she distrusted it. Was she being laughed at? she wondered.

"Look here, Mademoiselle Davidée; do not play the innocent. It's not for your interest to look after me, quite the contrary."

"I do not understand you."

"Enough! you would do much better to look after yourself."

"I shall have time to think of that after you are gone."

"You had better be seeing about your position in the school or you will lose it. You have been denounced."

"Denounced? For what reason?"

"I am merely warning you. You *have* been,
I know it."

"Very well then, I will defend myself."

"Look out for that, in the first place. And in
the next place, do not wish me to come back. It
will be far better for you if I never come."

"Why so, Phrosine?"

The woman stooped, seized the handle of her
basket, and began to walk on, with her eyes fixed
straight before her on the first houses outside the
town; then she spoke without turning round: "I
am not worth much. Beware of me, I tell you; I
am not your kind. If I were ever to come back
you would be sorry you had known me; do not
doubt it! Now let us talk of something else.
There is the high-road, over yonder."

The answer did not come at once.

"You do not like me, Phrosine; I know that
now. But if you ever need me, call on me all
the same."

Phrosine merely shrugged her shoulders. They
had reached the spot where the road joined the
high-road from Angers to Briare. The tram-car
was approaching, rumbling and snorting along the
rails like a huge bumblebee caught in a spider's
web.

"I thank you," said Phrosine. "What you
have done was in memory of the little one. I
know that well." And with these words she stopped
the passing car, boarded it, and, having set her
basket on the rear platform, she called back over
the railing:

"It will be better for you if I never come back. Good-by."

A cloud of dust and steam followed the car, but through it Davidée could see the gleam of Phrosine's eyes, still full of Ardésie.

CHAPTER VIII.

LYING IN WAIT.

DENOUNCED! The word is quickly spoken, but the sensation of anxicty it arouses lingers long in the mind. Nothing happened, however, to confirm the warning given by Phrosine on the morning of her departure. A spell of oppressive heat had succeeded to a week of cold rains and hail showers. Thunderous clouds hung in the sky and cast a tawny light all day long, wearying to the eyes. All living atoms seemed to vibrate more keenly. The air was filled with the humming and buzzing of gnats and flies, the children could not study, and even the teachers had to suppress their yawns and struggle to keep awake.

"If the inspector were to arrive on one of these exasperating afternoons," Davidée said to herself, "I should be lost. He would grow impaticnt and I should respond with a burst of tears, which, from an official point of view, is the worst of answers."

Mlle. Renée no longer addressed a word to her assistant and showed in every look and gesture an unappeasable irritation. Rural guards were patrolling the shores of La Grenadière, where troops of young workmen plunged into the pond at all hours without bathing suits. Gossip was rife at evening, among the neighbours, gathered on their slate door-steps, all along those bits of road rambling across the fields which constitute the hamlet of Ardésie. Rumours of a strike began to fill the air. In his house of La Gravelle, one evening about this time, Maïeul Jacquet sat wrapt in thought with his elbows on the stone rails of his belvedere, hanging high above that torn and cloven earth which is never suffered to rest. Maïeul had little taste for the taverns. Not that he was never seen entering the Little Poland or the Père Pompette on the general pay-day which, occurring only twice a year, must be fitly celebrated; or even sometimes on a Saturday, after he and his mates had received their weekly instalment of pay at the office. But a certain dislike of expense, a canny desire to amass a few sous in order to purchase a garden, with a small lodging at one end of it where he could live by himself, had survived in this grandson of peasants. He had neither the bearing nor the speech of a rustic, but rather resembled in his carriage, his glance, and his words some dismounted cavalier of former days. Yet he had in his blood this streak of the peasant; and so at this mid-May season, when an electric current seemed to flow through men's veins and arouse them to a feverish pitch, instead of sitting with his comrades on a tavern bench, Maïeul was perched at the top of his winding stair. Having no house-keeper and being careful of his apparel, he often busied himself with sewing on buttons or mending a torn vest or jacket—a slow and difficult operation, to be struggled with on his return from work—or else he fastened fish-hooks to his lines, stooping behind the parapet, so that the neighbours should not see him preparing his fishing tackle for the evening and night of the Feast of the Ascension: excellent nights for fishing—as every one knows—since then the fish always rise to the surface of the water. From time to time, his neighbours in the main building called out to him, in the silence of these stifling evenings: "Ho, there, Monsieur Maïeul! is it cooler up where you are?"

"None too cool," he would answer.

"You say nothing, then?"

"It must be because I have nothing to say." And so the colloquy was soon broken off. The women all said of Maïeul Rit-Dur: "There is one who does not waste his words, nor his money, nor his time! What a husband he would make if he chose, but he does not choose!"

Nine o'clock, half after nine, ten struck; one could hear all over La Gravelle the sound of suppressed yawns, scraps of talk and the light foot-steps of mothers and children moving about the house, while in the sky daylight lingered as if reluctant to depart.

On Wednesday evening, the vigil of Ascension, the women having called out as usual to the lodger in the pavilion, and received no answer, a small boy climbed cautiously up the outer flight of steps, in his bare feet, for fear of a cuffing from Maïeul, who had no mercy on spies; but he was soon down again, capering and shouting: "No-

body at home, and the door locked awful tight."
Whereupon the women said: "He must have
gone to set his lines, as the night is so fine."

As it happened, however, he was much nearer
home, in that hollow, filled with fading broom,
which nearly concealed the house of Mère Fête-
Dieu. He was seated before the entrance on
a bowlder, with his hat off on account of the heat
and also out of respect for the infirm old woman,
whom he had helped drag herself as far as
the door-way and who was seated beside him,
enveloped in a strange assortment of petticoats
and shawls which he had caught up hastily. The
little gray eyes of the old woman never ceased to
wander over the fields of sky above her, which
were the only landscape visible from where she
sat, and where a few pale stars were twinkling.
Yet the eyes smiled as they looked up, for they
had emerged from the darkness inside and, on
feeling the light strike them, assumed an expression of curiosity as regards all visible things, and
at the same time of a sort of repose and beatitude
such as is rarely seen save in the eyes of children.
Three steps away from her, poised beneath the
grape-vine on a low chair, which she had tilted
back so that her head rested against the wall,
while her feet dangled without touching the
ground, was little Jeannie Fête-Dieu, intently
watching Maïeul and her grandmother, the sombre cluster of broom along the edge of the hollow,
the three tufts of gillyflowers on the wall and the
prowling cat, but rarely glancing at the sky. In
the last few weeks Jeannie had grown taller

and her colour brighter. She blushed more readily and put on little airs of archness and coquetry, together with a self-consciousness which was quite new to her. Maïeul paid no attention to the child, which was the cause of her seeming indifference. He talked, with little pauses between his sentences, to the old woman, for whom this was a moment of rare pleasure.

"This is the time to set the bees to swarming," said Mère Fête-Dieu. "In my youth we used to watch for them in the heat of the day, and as soon as they had flown, it was I who ran the fastest after the swarm, clicking my sabots together between my two hands; you should have seen me! At Ascension time everything stirs; in the air, in the water, and I may even say in men's hearts."

"You may well say that," responded Maïeul.

"Even the little beasts have a way of their own of keeping the feast of our Lord's ascension to paradise. They do it better than many a Christian!" And so saying the good woman cast a little glance at the slate-cutter, who laughed as she proceeded:

"And so Monsieur Maïeul will be setting his lines in the pond of La Grenadière?"

"No, Mère Fête-Dieu."

"In the Authion, then? No? As far as the Loire? Oh! it's many a long day since my goodman used to go and set his, on the eve of Ascension Day, where the brook of Belle-Poule flows into the river."

"You've not hit it yet, mother. I am not out

with my lines, that will come later. I am out
with my gun to-night."

At the same moment he gave a significant nod
toward little Jeannie, who was still tilting back
and forward in her chair.

The grandmother spoke at once. "Jeannie, my
pretty one, will you go just for a moment or two
up the hill and see if the neighbours are in bed yet?"

The child rose with a sulky air and began as-
cending the little paved path that led up the hill.
"You don't want me to hear what you are going
to say," she muttered, "but if you think I can't
guess!"

"Run along! run along! Did ever one see such
a rogue! The truth is, Monsieur Maïeul, that
she's far sharper than I if she can guess what you
want to tell me."

"The little maids begin to be sly at her age,
Mère Fête-Dieu."

"They are not dull, it is true. She is a good
child, with no mischief in her, only a few little
airs; such a short while ago she was as simple as
a little lamb or a young chick, and now she is
more like a lapwing with a new crest! What
was it you were going to tell me?"

"Mère Fête-Dieu, I want to shoot a hare to
send as a present to Mademoiselle Birot, the assistant teacher here! It's easy enough to shoot
the hare, but when it's shot, how am I to get her
to accept it?"

"She will never accept it in the world!"

"Ah, you feel as I do! You think her a young
lady?"

"Better than that, Maïeul Jacquet; she is a girl of a high spirit. Ah, look here! Is it about her you have come to speak to me?"

"Yes, it is."

"Oh, my poor lad!" And, so saying, the old woman clasped her hands over her many wrappings, as if to quiet the beating of her heart. Then she was silent for a long minute, and the world about her kept silence too. There were stars in the sky that appeared to be listening, and Jeannie listened behind the fringe of broom.

"Maïeul, it is a good thing, all the same, if you are off with that other!"

He made no reply, but sat as one who is hearing his sentence pronounced, with eyes fixed and lips parted. What had she still to say—she who had the right to judge, being so near the boundary of this life and already above it?

"You have sinned, Maïeul, and given a bad example to others."

"That is true, mother."

"It may be that God will pardon you, when you ask him, but she, this Davidée, who is only a woman, will she pardon?"

"I had not known her, and besides, Mère Fête-Dieu, I am young, you know, and weak—and that other is like a fate, one can't escape her."

"That is always easy to say. Do you renounce her in your heart, that Phrosine?"

"I don't renounce her. No one could do that but a sort of saint. I can only say that all is over."

"Because you have left her?"

"No."

"Merely because she has gone away? Oh, my poor boy, you are young indeed! What if she were to come back? Our poor human hearts are so weak!"

"No, Mère Fête-Dieu; there is the dead child between us. I see her every night."

"Little Anna, yes, yes! I see her too, with that look of hers which was beyond her years."

"Don't speak of her! She is my regret. I tell you that it's over forever."

"So be it! Listen, Maïeul, it is a sacred thing what one says to a young girl who has kept her heart pure, like that one at the school."

"So I think, Mère Fête-Dieu."

"She is pure-hearted; that can be guessed. There is the promise of great goodness in her; that can be read in her eyes."

The man added very low as if dreaming:

"And in her hands too!"

The old woman gave a short laugh, for she could not understand how any one could admire a hand. She thought this Maïeul very deep in love, and something tender and maternal in her urged her to praise Davidée still more and to assure herself that the young man meant honestly.

"I have known several of her profession here in Ardésie, but not one who could hold a candle to her. She is so good, too, in the words she knows how to invent; to one, one thing, and to another something quite different!"

"Yes, even when she's scolding you; I know something about that."

"Yes, there's a something in her voice and her air which makes those who have seen her enter their home regret her when she goes." And the poor old woman shook her aching head slowly from side to side.

"You would like to have her friendship, would you?" she went on. "Well, you are not worthy of it."

"I had thought of that before you said it."

"What then?"

"I can become so," he said proudly. But she made no reply.

"Don't you believe that I can become so, Mère Fête-Dieu?"

He bent his ardent gaze upon her as he spoke; he had half risen and she saw the pupils of his eyes quiver in the midst of their light blue iris. A sigh of the wind was wafted down the hollow and stirred the young leaves on the trellis, which rustled against the wall, while the old woman, her hands trembling with the inward dread she felt at what she was about to say, reflected for a moment longer. Then she spoke gravely:

"I think it would require a good many things."

"I will do them all. I have even thought of several already."

An observer might have fancied that Maïeul had just been asking for Davidée's hand, and that she had not positively refused him. He had risen, and all his youth glowed in his face. And yet the woman who had spoken was merely a stranger, with no rights in the matter; who had only seen for one short hour out of her whole life the girl whom she was defending thus. The very old have sometimes this mysterious authority. At this moment a clear distinct voice reached them:

"Grandmamma, they are all going to sleep. I am back again!" and a sound like the scampering of a young doe rang along the hollow mound, as, bounding over the tufts of broom and heather, Jeannie reappeared in sight.

"I cannot tell you what I shall do," pursued Maïeul. "I have more than one plan which I mean to carry out by myself, without aid or counsel from any one, because it is my own idea. You will see! For to-night, if I should catch a hare, have you any one who can do my errand for me?" The old woman pointed toward Jeannie who was approaching, stepping now with precaution, in the hope of overhearing the end of the conversation. Her grandmother's gesture signified that Jeannie would be ready to do his errand and, to show that she had a basket, the old woman's shaking hand formed in the air the rounded curve of the handle.

"Yes, yes, it's understood," the child cried; "I have a basket, but Monsieur Maïeul will have to fill it. Where shall I carry your game?"

"Hush, my child, you shall know presently. The gendarmes may be making their rounds. It's as well not to mention names."

Jeannie laughed below her breath at this poor pretext. Her grandmother made an effort to rise and go back to her bed, but Maïeul cried:

"Lean on me; my arm is strong." And having

led her inside the house, he soon emerged alone, passing lightly and rapidly along the bank without a sound. For greater precaution on leaving his room at nightfall, he had put a pair of sandals on. From out of a clump of heather, on the edge of the path winding around the mound, he picked up his gun, an old-fashioned fowling-piece, long and slender, with a single barrel, which had long served one or more slate-cutters of Trélazé, before becoming the property of Maïeul Rit-Dur for the sum of twenty francs.

He turned sharply to the left and, skirting a woody plateau above the pit of La Gravelle, to avoid a sleeping farm-house, he descended into a triangular meadow, the point of which was held, as in a vice, between the last rocks of an old quarry and the embankment, rising black in the darkness, of the Orléans Railway. Maïeul climbed with some difficulty through dense thickets and over high banks, until, having crossed the railway tracks, he found himself in the open country where he was entirely at home.

The fields, surrounded by lines of trees and hedge-rows, sloped upward toward the north. It was in that direction that the young man was bound, as leaving on his right the village of St. Barthélemy and crossing the highway, he soon struck into a densely wooded region which grew constantly wilder and more lonely, and where he was sure that a gunshot would not arouse any watch-dog nor a farm-hand jealous of an intruder poaching on his preserves.

Dense forests once clothed this deep soil, pierced

by veins of clay and iron, where the oaks swell
with sap, and ferns, mosses, and mulleins spring
up in their shadow and preserve the moisture
round their roots. The woods which form the
parks of Pignerolle and La Marmitière are sur-
vivals of this primeval forest; they must formerly
have been connected with the woods of Echar-
bot, and between these two belts of woodland,
like a peninsula between tilled lands, stretch
the birchen copses of Bouleaux. As Maïeul was
skirting these copses, partridges, hidden in the
stubble, flew across his path. He perceived in
the distance the great farm of Haye-le-Roy, and
finally sprang down into the road which passes
behind this farm, and forks, at the extremity of
the woodland, into several branch roads of equal
antiquity, contemporary with the oldest cathe-
drals in France, and which go their way like winding streams across these solitudes.

Are they hollow ways, these ancient roads?
No, they have no side banks, but are rather like
avenues connecting peasants' houses, long dis-
tances apart. Lofty trees, oaks especially, abound
along their edges; they have never been levelled
and are grass-grown, being less often trodden
by the feet of men than by those of animals, such
as flocks of sheep and cattle, which, having exhausted their pasturage, are making their way to
new meadows, stray dogs bent on marauding ex-
peditions, and game of every kind. It was here,
at this crossing of the ways, that Maïeul knew
an excellent hiding-place where he could lie in
wait; this was the inside of a hollow stump, the

opening of which was just wide enough for a man to slip in and keep himself half hidden, to one side. Bushes rose around it, completing the shelter without masking the view. Before climbing the bank and gaining his post of observation, the young man plucked a sprig of holly from a hedge and stuck it upright in an open spot where the grass was cropped close, near the centre of the road. Then he slipped into his hiding-place, loaded his fowling-piece, and waited.

He began to recall words which Mère Fête-Dieu had spoken to him; one sentence above all came back to him in the solitude and darkness: "I think many things would be required for that!" Poor fellow, he had invented a very singular proof of affection; a strange token to offer her of whom he was afraid and whose gentle hands he so loved. He shrugged his shoulders involuntarily as he thought of the contrast between her and a poacher such as he, in hiding on the outskirts of the copse of Bouleaux on Ascension night. "What a fool I must be!" he thought. "With her it is necessary to know how to talk, and that I dare not. I only know how to make songs, and I have no heart to sing them now. She has already passed judgment on me. She despises me because I lived with Phrosine. She is right. It is not the gift of a hare which will change her toward me. I was indeed a fool to come, I was better off under the roof of La Gravelle." And yet he did not issue from his hiding-place, and took care not to move the barrel of his gun; he had already denied himself the pleasure of smoking, by the simple device

of leaving his tobacco at home. Suddenly a long
black shape bounded noiselessly along the grassy
road. The leaves about him quivered, as he instinctively lowered his weapon, but he raised it again
immediately, sure that the flying shape could only
have been a watch-dog from one of the farms, one
of that dangerous sort which pursues its prey in
silence. A sudden rebound of bent brambles and
a noise of twigs lashing the air without visible
cause, showed Maïeul that the dog had hurled
himself into the wood and started the game. "I
might as well be off," he thought; "my chance
of sport is over!" But the slight noise died away;
not a breath of air stirred. The night was growing cooler; the grass was heavy with dew-drops;
he could discern, a short distance away, the outline of field and hedge-row like two shadows of
differing values, the one densely black, the other
gray and without the slightest gloss. Beyond
the road was a lighter line where the dew was
lying, or the grass had been worn away by passing
feet. But the sky above gleamed like a night-lamp.
High up in the zenith a veil of diffused light
seemed to hang beneath the stars, transparent
as water lying in the hollows of the sand when
the tide is low. This light was leading the passing day into the coming dawn; it cast no deep
shadows like the moon; it was not the aurora;
but its radiance dominated the land, from west
to east, and paled the stars. All nature was
sleeping; it was that hour without fear, the mid-
hour of the brief summer night.

Maïeul, who had been peering at the sky be-

tween the branches, on lowering his eyes toward
that part of the road which was enveloped in
mist, saw emerging from it a little shadow, which
made one bound, then stopped. He softly raised
the barrel of his gun, and as he did so, the hare
lifted its head and pricked up its ears; then, re-
assured by the stillness, took three more leaps to
the summit of a little green mound, where it sat
erect with its fore paws as stiff as rods, amazed
at encountering that unknown tuft of holly
which Maïeul had planted there. And as it
paused, a sudden flash rent the night air. The
shot resounded as far as the woods of L'Hopital,
where it was deadened by the foliage, and up to
the farm of Haut-Moulinet, at the top of the
hill, where it was lost in the distance. Maïeul
Jacquet, with limbs stiffened by the cool night
air and his motionless watch, descended the bank
slowly and, having scanned the road to right and
left, came out into the open. The hare lay on
its side with its nose against the spray of holly;
its white breast, touching the grass, still stirred
with a faint breath. Maïeul, with one turn of
his hand, drew the four paws together and lifted
the little creature, head downward, its supple
body swinging at each step as he walked away.
By two o'clock in the morning the young quarryman was back at La Gravelle, having met no
one on his way, save at the entrance of a wood-
road, where he caught sight of a doubtful shadow
resembling the form of a seated man which
dropped suddenly into the ditch.

At eight in the morning, as the sun rose high,
little Jeannie climbed the steep pitch behind her

grandmother's house which led to the summit of the broom-clad mound. She looked more serious than usual. On her arm—instead of the small black satchel in which she usually carried her lunch, consisting of a sandwich, a couple of apples or a handful of cherries—hung a huge and heavy basket; one of those wicker baskets, without a cover, in which the peasants gather potatoes. It was full of clover and lucern which dangled over the edges. Jeannie hastened her steps and had already reached the high-road and passed the church when a school-mate called out to her:

"Where are you going so fast? It is not school-time yet."

"But I am in a hurry."

"What are you carrying there?"

"Grass and clover for the rabbits."

She went so fast that her little mates had not time to slip on their sabots and hurry after her, before she was out of sight. She was as red as her clover blossoms before reaching the play-ground, where only three little girls had arrived before her. All three rushed up to her with hands out-stretched, crying:

"What are you bringing to the *demoiselles?* Let me see!"

With a half turn of her shoulder which brought her basket round in front, so that they could not peep into it, Jeannie hurried on. She nearly ran into Mlle. Renée who was standing in the middle of the yard, looking amused and amiable and a little curious; and who, quite sure of her power, cried out:

"Come, child, show me the basket!"

The little one turned on her heel, shaking her
head vigorously, and ran toward the porch. "It
is not for you," she cried, with the tears starting to her eyes.

And now she is calling in the corridor, calling
with all her might for Mlle. Davidée, whom she
does not yet see. She is there, however, half-
way down the stairs, fresh and bright, fastening
her bodice as she descends.

"You need not call so loud, dear child; the
house is not ten stories high. One would think
you were a chickweed seller. What have you
there?"

"A present for you, Mademoiselle!"

"Who sent it?"

"I am not to tell."

"Let me see too," said the blond Mlle. Renée,
suddenly entering the room. "It seems that it
is not for me, but I suppose you have no secrets,
Mademoiselle."

The assistant shook her head to signify "no
secrets whatever." Jeannie looked from one
teacher to the other, blushed a deeper red, then
set down the basket on the table, from which
Mlle. Renée hastily slipped off the blue-braided
cover, and all three stood, with the basket before
them, appearing equally embarrassed.

"You might venture to open it, Mademoiselle,
since it is for you," said the elder one; "the school
bell will soon ring."

With the tips of her fingers, as if she were
turning over the pages of a book, Davidée tossed
aside the sprays of lucern and clover, revealing

tufts of white hair, a drop of blood, then a glimpse of tawny hairs. There was no longer any doubt, both had guessed who the poacher was. Davidée turned pale and bit her lips.

Mlle. Renée laughed below her breath, murmuring, "Very pretty! Very pretty, indeed!"

"It's a handsome hare, isn't it, Mademoiselle?" said Jeannie, who had recovered her spirits. "It was grandmamma who arranged him in the basket, but I picked all the clover."

Mlle. Renée, taking infinite precautions to avoid blood-stains, and spreading out her fingers like a rake, uncovered the hare completely. She was quivering with malicious triumph, but on account of the child, she contrived to modulate her voice to an amiable pitch as she said:

"I congratulate you, Mademoiselle Davidée. You are the object of attentions which leave no doubt as to the sentiments you inspire, and doubtless share."

"I beg of you——"

"But why not? Nothing could be more honourable, only this happens not to be the open season for game; so I must ask you to have your little feast cooked elsewhere, will you not? Being a state servant, I have not the right— Listen to me, Jeannie! Do not breathe this, nor tell any one what you have been doing. Do not speak of what you had in the basket, nor mention the name of the—gentleman."

Jeannie raised both hands with palms upward.

"Oh, no, Mademoiselle!"

Davidée, who did not choose to reply to Mlle.

Renée's sneers, took a five-franc piece from her
purse and put it into the child's hands. It was
evident that her mind was firmly made up.

"Here, little one," she said, "you may give
this to the person who sent you."

Jeannie, being a rustic, understood the full
gravity of this affront: to pay any one who has
made you a present! She hesitated and did not
even venture to close her fingers over the silver
piece.

"Do as I tell you, and go straight into school."

The child raised her skirt and let the five-franc
piece slip into a black pocket she wore under-
neath, then hurried away. The two mistresses
passed out behind her, Davidée, who came last,
locking the door and taking out the key.

From the Green Diary.—"I can no longer
doubt that Maïeul Jacquet has raised his eyes
to me. The thought made me shudder this
morning. I felt insulted by this love which does
not even choose at first, and then chooses far too
suddenly. It is not his being a workman that
shames me, nor his lack of culture. I see too
plainly what the other sort are often worth. But
I am not a Phrosine. I am not moved by having
compliments paid me or presents like this offered
me. What could he have thought? How could
he believe that I would accept his gift? And
what recklessness! In a village like this where
scandal is the only news! Jeannie, I am sure,
has not spoken of the errand she was sent on;
Mlle. Renée has said nothing; Mère Fête-Dieu

receives no visits, and yet the whole village, or
cluster of villages, will be entertaining themselves to-night with the story of the slate-cutter's
game; and my name will be pronounced. Words
and plans and adventures will be attributed to
me such as will fully justify Mlle. Renée's ill-
treatment, in spite of her having nothing she can
truly reproach me with. The answer I have made
has irritated this young man who was so self-
confident. This is not a suspicion on my part;
I am sure of it. At six o'clock, the hour when
the men go home from the quarry, we were sitting, Mlle. Renée and I, in the parlour, not for the
pleasure of each other's society, but to correct
papers together—or rather I was helping her to
correct her older girls' themes, for I try to give
her reasons for not detesting me. As it was very
warm, we had left the windows open, but had
shut the door on the road. I had shut it myself.
Suddenly we heard a sharp sound, and a pane of
glass was shattered to atoms. I sprang up, crying: 'This is frightful, they are throwing stones
at us!' But the directress took me by the arm
and pointed out an object which had rolled along
the floor and hit the wainscot. 'No, Mademoiselle; it is your five-franc piece come back to you,'
she cried. 'You have a very polite admirer.' I
could not refrain from replying: 'At any rate,
he has a certain sense of honour about him; I
have humiliated him and he refuses to submit
to it. I like him the better for that; as to the
rest, you know that Monsieur Maïeul Jacquet
is nothing to me, absolutely nothing. I have

not the power, unfortunately, to prevent people from paying me unwelcome attentions or from persecuting me.'

"'And what would you do if you had that power?'

"'I should beg them all not to trouble themselves about me, and to leave your assistant in peace.'

"Yes, that is what I answered, and yet I think, in spite of myself, of that poor Maïeul and the pain I have given him. I was obliged to do it, I could not help myself. But what of him who had passed the night out-of-doors, lying in wait for his hare; who had thought of me, uttering my name in his heart, hoping I know not what; perhaps a little beginning of friendship, perhaps less, merely a little confidence in him. And I have made him suffer! Why is it so hard for me to feel this? I am sure that of us two, it is I who suffer the most, I who do not care for him. How absurd it is! When shall I cure myself of this excess of feeling? The cloud has passed and still the rain is falling. Oh, heart that loves to weep!"

CHAPTER IX.

TROUBLED SOULS.

From the Green Diary.—"June 6, Trinity Sunday. I could no longer endure that life of perpetual hostility. We had a little holiday at Whitsuntide and I ran away to spend it at home. My brother was there. He was full of complaints of the ill-temper of his chiefs, and of the injustices he has had to endure at their hands. My mother lamented the solitude in which she had lived for months and in which she would have to live once more after we had left her. She complained also of my father, who now passes half of his days at the tavern. *He* was complaining of his health, which is, I fear, greatly undermined, and of his political friends who are relaxing their attentions toward him, and, what my father cannot pardon, no longer stand in fear of him, now that their former master is growing old. I should have liked to bring my troubles too, into that fine new house which is so far from gay; fainthearted grumbling is so natural to all of us. But no, I found myself a child again. I forgot everything that had come since. I was the one they all turned to. 'Won't you come to walk with me?' said one. 'No, stay at home with me,' said the other. 'Look at me, console me,

192

will you not? or at least sit beside me while I work, even if you say nothing!' So I taxed all my energies to keep peace and tranquillity among these weary, dissatisfied souls. They all long desperately for happiness, but do not know where to look for it. This made me think deeply. I was their happiness once, but for how short a time, and with what effort on my part! How sure I felt that I could not long fill that rôle which required more strength and greater reserve power than I have. I felt myself so poor for such an arduous life, requiring a constant giving out of oneself. The ardour and the impulse are there and the will, but it is soon exhausted, and when it is not weariness that conquers, it is the clear, too clear, sense of how poor a thing I am. I can make myself loved, but to induce my little folk or others to do as I wish, through love for me, is not to guide them! Whenever I have won the race against egotism, dulness, moral apathy among those I have lived with, there or here, I have won it by maintaining noble truths which I could not support by reasoning, but which were instinctive in my soul, or implanted there I know not how.

"To-day the Ardésie children communed, or renewed their communion. I was present at the ceremony, seated in the background with the parents, and on their account. I saw my children, the very smallest ones of ten or less, coming back with clasped hands, and downcast eyes filled with a joy which we cannot give them, and which has no resemblance to that we can give.

Not all of them wore this look of ecstasy, of bodies which are mere shells over the flame of their adoration, shades above a lighted lamp, but it was the greater number. I was deeply moved. 'Catholics!' I thought, 'you will soon have to lower the communion table to the stature of these little ones, whose lips sometimes scarcely reached above the white cloth, while the priest had to bend very low. If I were one of you, how beautiful this would seem to me; to lower all barriers, to multiply the divine visits, to pour love into the prison-house newly built and still undefiled!'

"I thought: 'There is an undeniable relation between these budding souls and the mystery offered to their faith. They so weak, with such wretched inheritances, who have meditated so little and received so little religious teaching, have to-day taken the same flight, and to what heights?'

"I thought: 'And I? What part have I in that which raises them thus? I have not destroyed faith like Barrentier, who cannot see a crucifix without foaming; like Judémil, who makes his pupils sing "To the gutter with Christ!" like some of my own colleagues, who nourish a secret, dry, erudite hatred of religion. No, I have not led my little ones astray, but I have done nothing to help them to believe; I have not led them into regions nearer to belief, where I might have guided them; I have spoken vain words. I feel myself a sower of empty seed which cannot spring up in joy.'

"And yet these children love me because they still have hope. They had been told that, like all their teachers, I possess the secret of happiness. They believe, they must believe, that what I teach them suffices for their life. Their mothers believe it also, and their fathers and some among my chiefs. Mlle. Renée believes it too, with her poor narrow mind, a garden shut in by high walls. Oh, no, it all suffices merely for the material commerce of life: I am not making women. I have not caught the whole secret. There is something else, which is the chief thing of all, and which I have not grasped, either for them or for myself, which I only divine. For a long time I was fully persuaded that the name of peace could be truly applied to the state in which I lived, absorbed in my professional duties, living for my classes, a life of text-books and manuals, with no thought of what it all leads to. But I have been thrown, all at once, into the conflict of good and evil; it is around me, pressing upon me, urging me to take sides, and I do so; but when the moment for action comes I realize my poverty. Mère Fête-Dieu is rich, some of my children were evidently rich to-day, and I am not like them. Phrosine, whom I feel to be guilty, whom I see to be morally so destitute and adrift, had only to remind me that my morality was founded on human conventions, for me to be sure that she was in the right as against me, but that we were both wrong in face of a higher morality: that which has the right to command this ever-rebellious world, that which can oppose another power to our cruel and insatiable self-love, that which alone can dare to speak of purity. I have seen pure faces and the sight has troubled me. To be morally clean is so far, so very far, from that marvel: perfect purity!

"I ask myself whether true happiness has not its roots in this secret force? That would help us to understand why it is so rare. And for me, how can I protect mine? What shall I say to Maïeul Jacquet if he comes to offer me a real love? I am not one of those—and I have proved it!—who hardly wait for the end of the first tender speech to answer: 'Yes.' But if I sought to demand from him some proof of regret for the past, something better than mere words, what could I ask which would give me assurance? Would he not still have his heart of yesterday, the heart he gave Phrosine? Where can I find help outside myself, beyond that of the eyes and cheeks and lips which will soon fade, I who wish to be loved forever. I think of all this and find no answer.

"Mlle. Renée declares that I have compromised myself. I believe that she would gladly do the same.—No, I am like one who is on the watch in a time of disquiet. I am like those sailors' wives in Blandes who come out of their houses and walk up and down the shore, treading the mussel shells with their bare feet, looking up to the sky heavy with clouds and crying: 'And yet it is dawn! What will become of us? There is no daylight left! What storm is about to burst? What gale will follow the storm?'

"On Monday, Tuesday, and Wednesday, as the heat was intense and my throat was parched by reading, dictation, and reprimands in the exhausted air of the school-room, I walked home

with a group of children beyond the church. I even
went a little further and entered for the first time,
alone, the graveyard, where the Spanish-broom beside the gate was in bloom. I sat there, my back
against the low wall and my arms stretched out
along the warm stones. Anna's grave was just before me, like a tiny bit of stubble amid a wilder-
ness of tall grass, funeral crosses, and live-oaks.
I sat gazing at it quite alone. The one among my
little charges who lived farthest from school had
entered her mother's door and I had heard the
latch fall as it closed behind her; there was no
sound to warn me that any one was near, and
yet I felt certain that I was being watched. I
turned my head very slightly, and there *he* stood,
just across the road. He was in his working
clothes, and bareheaded; even now I can see his
look of passionate reproach. He did not speak,
but when I turned back toward the little grave,
I could still feel his eyes fixed upon my hair and
upon my hands; then I heard the sound of his
retreating steps. The following day I descried
Maïeul again on the farther side of the deep
green pool near the church, and on the next day
also. He was sitting on a rock with his feet
hanging over the water. He did not stir on my
approach, but his whole heart spoke to me. I
did not return that way. I believe that this
sombre, passionate Maïeul has almost ceased to
work, and that it is on my account."

At the same hour that Davidée was inscribing
these words in her diary, Maïeul was returning

from a working men's meeting at Trélazé, where he, with the others, had insulted and threatened a foreman who had been accused of trampling and crushing to atoms several rows of slate piled up outside the wind-break of one of the workmen. No one knew positively who had committed this spiteful deed. At early dawn one of the mechanics, on his way to the machine-shop, had passed the hut and noticed the havoc which had been wrought there in the night. There were no positive proofs against any one, but this particular foreman was detested because some five years before he had openly trampled on several hundreds of slates which he pronounced to be rotten, and which the workman was obliged to replace. In the tenacious memory of the slate-cutters nothing is forgotten; the man was accused of this new misdeed as a punishment for his former act. He denied the charge. For two long hours he had stood with his back to the wall in the long low hall where two hundred of his comrades held him prisoner striving to defend the position he had earned by fifteen years' labour, and, with it, his daily bread, his family, his right to reside among the blue villages where he had a garden and a little group of friends, and which was endeared to him by habit. Meanwhile the crowd facing him had not remained seated ten minutes, but after listening to a few brief words from the leader, who had first said: "This is he!" they had risen, all together, and formed themselves into a compact howling mass, bristling with uplifted hands, advancing and receding like waves beating upon their victim, who stood on a chair, his arms crossed on his breast, his mouth open, shrieking out words to which no one listened. A shower of blows rained upon him, some stealthily, some directly, but he made no attempt to return them, nor to hold on his clothes which were dropping off him. The buttons had been torn from his vest and his hairy chest showed between the opening of his shirt. His trousers were falling off his hips, his necktie was gone, and rags of shirt-sleeves hung from his shaking arms as he poured forth his hoarse cries: "It was not I, cowards! it was not I!" After two hours of this torture, as he had not yielded, they decided to declare a strike in order to force the slate company to dismiss this man who refused to resign. He had then crawled out between two lines of his tormentors, who struck at him as he passed. Finally he had plunged into the night, with the free air and open space before him, and groping painfully along the wall with his hands, he had passed down the street—a forlorn shape recognized by the women at their windows where they were watching wearily for the return of their husbands—and seeing his bent, crushed, lamentable figure, they threw their windows open, leaned out, and spat after him, crying, "Scab! Traitor!"

Maïeul also was returning at this hour; he had left the town behind, and was crossing the mounds where the scales of slate crackled under his feet with a sound like the faint chirp of crickets. He walked slowly, and when the full moon emerged from clouds which looked heavy and hot as stones in the glare of sunlight, his glance sought the portal and roofs of the school-house, the class-rooms extending along the road, and the gable overlooking the neighbouring house on the left, where Mlle. Renée's room was. He thought of the woman who had rejected his gift; he imagined Davidée sleeping, as she must be at that hour. An intensity of feeling, stronger than was habitual with him, filled his soul this evening. He was dissatisfied with himself. Toward the end of the meeting, he had experienced a sensation deeper than pity when the foreman had turned pale, and on that corpse-like face a few drops of blood had trickled slowly, as if the veins were wrung dry. At that moment he had ceased to join in the cries; shame and remorse had swelled within him. It was the memory of his base and sluggish life which rose from the turbid depths of his soul and overflowed it. "How fine it is—what you are doing here!" he thought. "You have joined two hundred men against this one, and you have half murdered him; he has but one thought and one cry left, and you look on and see him suffer because you have not the courage to kill him outright. What will-power have you of your own? what energy? You make no resistance when your mates call on you. They say you have character; yes, because you are quickly angered, but for what reasons do you get angry oftenest? Are they creditable ones?" And the thought of Davidée came to mingle with his self-reproach over his past life. "You pretend to be astonished when the *demoiselle* from the school despises you. But she is right. What

are you beside her, Maïeul! you, who made love
to her servant? She has a heart like little Jeannie
Fête-Dieu's; it is proud, and you are not much
compared with her." Pausing in the great
bramble patch close to La Gravelle, Rit-Dur reflected first on what a worthless being he was;
then he thought how he felt for this woman—
who was not even from his part of the country—
a friendship so strong, so strong, that it roused a
fever in him. He saw, with the eyes of his love,
those dark eyes, that pale, firm face; he saw her
hands. If he had known how to put his dream
into words he would have said—and such ideas
did pass vaguely through his mind: "Your
hands take of themselves the gentle curves of
pity; when you clasp them together it is as if
they held a lighted lamp. Is it youth? Is it
goodness? Is it pardon which you hold in those
hands? I have never seen any others so delicate
and white and touching." But as he was a very
simple fellow he found only one small thing to
say, and he said it over and over before the distant vision of the school-house roofs: "If I held
that hand in mine I should walk straight, very
straight."

The heat was penetrating; it filtered through the
blades of grass, and even the thistles drooped their
heads. There must have been a thunder-storm in
the distance, for in the south the flashes of light-
ning were frequent; but the sound died out before reaching where he stood, and all seemed to
sleep; and yet what passions were awake amid
that silent scene! How many loves, hates, envies,

ambitions! The suburbs of the town stretched
out their sparkling lights into the night. When
Maïeul had climbed his outer staircase and had
paused at the top for one last look at the school,
a resolution which he had been turning over and
over in his mind began to rise to the surface.
He pushed the door open with his shoulder, receiving full in his face the icy air of the closed
room, lighted his spirit-lamp, opened the window,
and, amid the hum of gnats, began to compose
a letter to Davidée Birot.

CHAPTER X.

MAÏEUL'S SONG.

THE letter was not long; it was as follows:

"MADEMOISELLE:—I should be very much honoured by having a few words with you. I cannot ask to see you at the school because the other teacher would insult me. And yet I must see you. There is one thing I might do, but I should like, before venturing on it, to ask you if it will be right. Mademoiselle, at one o'clock on Thursday next, which will be the tenth of June, I shall be crossing the hill near the pit of La Gravelle. I shall have with me Jeannie Fête-Dieu and a Breton woman who comes from near my old home. If I could meet you there I should be very happy. The pain of having displeased you lies heavy on my heart. I am, Mademoiselle, with respect, your servant,

"MAÏEUL JACQUET."

"P. S.—There will probably be a strike on by that time, but that will make no difference. When I have said a thing I seldom fail to carry it out."

Davidée received this letter by the morning mail; she read it through twice—the first time with a feeling of impatience, but on the second

reading she reflected a little over the words:
"The pain of having displeased you lies heavy
on my heart." And she said to herself: "I will
go."

By Monday the strike had already begun; it
amounted to very little at first; the men gathered in groups about the wells, cursing, threaten-
ing, and attempting to gain over the unskilled
and lower-paid men.

The slate-cutters, who are the higher-class
workmen, the aristocrats of the quarry, had all
quitted work. Their huts looked as dead as the
deserted tents of an army during manœuvres.
The slate had ceased to grind under the knives;
the horses, amazed to find themselves standing
idle in their stalls, stretched their necks each
time the door opened, to see if some one was
coming to take down their harness with its blue
tassels, which was hanging over their heads, and
seemed to ask each other: "What do you
want, old boy? See! the man hasn't touched
the harness; he has only thrown a handful of hay
into the manger, and is going out again. Feast
away, stuff yourself full, lazy-bones! There's
no more work for us." Meanwhile the pot-
houses were full; the topers, who at first had all
shouted at once, were now tired of talking and
of hearing others talk; above all, of guzzling, and
breathing in that wine-reeking atmosphere. They
now sat back against the wall, with their heads
sunk on their breasts and their eyes fixed in a
vacant stare upon the indefatigable orator who
was holding forth steadily without any need of

relays, his Adam's apple rising and falling like
a weaver's shuttle, his scanty beard wagging with
the flow of his eloquence.

At home, the housewives were far from content, knowing that there would be little money
on hand when pay-day next came round. They
kept mostly out of sight and tried to find comfort in scolding the children, or in hiding in some
safe nook any stray two-franc pieces they found
lying about too conspicuously.

If they were obliged to go out to dry their husband's shirts in their small clothes yard paved
with slate, they turned an anxious ear in the
direction of the café. Was the noise growing
louder? What was that distant sound of shouting from the well of La Fresnais. "Thank
Heaven, it is dying down again! Say, neighbour;
how do you like having a husband who won't
listen to a word of reason? As for me, it makes
my blood boil."

At the same moment a troop of handsome
girls were promenading the streets, blooming
young creatures, linked arm in arm, so that they
formed a chain across the road, not pausing, but
slackening their pace a little where the groups of
working men were densest. The tall girl in the
centre wore a red scarf round her white throat;
it was she whom the men were cheering, while
their wives at home listened anxiously. Did the
sound come from the well of La Fresnais? No,
the women had been deceived by the direction
of the wind. It was from the Plains—that quarter where the town joins the country. Night

was about to fall; the twittering of sparrows and
the uneasy cries of house-martins had superseded
the usual cheerful sounds of men returning from
their day's work.

The second day was as still as death until two
in the afternoon. The rain of the morning had
ceased. A procession had formed in the village
of Justice; one group, carrying a red flag, had
terrified the peaceable spectators at first, but was
soon augmented by a number of them who had
joined the throng. Some carters had been met
at the outer limits of the quarries bringing in a
load of slate; they were surrounded and beaten,
the harnesses were cut and the horses let loose.
From far and near the rumour spread and terror
increased. The mothers began to look out anxiously for any child who had strayed from home.
The executive committees, which had been secretly in existence for a long time, began to
emerge from the masses, who awaited their
orders and had only changed masters. Reporters had been seen in Ardésie, and even a gendarme! He was not a native, however, but a
harmless visitor, taking a holiday walk with his
wife. But on being greeted with scoffs and jibes
he began to understand the situation; his wife
was alarmed, but took pains to smile whenever
any one looked at her, always with the same
forced, deliberate smile to show that she was
not afraid. At nightfall a cartridge burst here,
another there; children awoke crying with fear.
All the men who would have liked to go on working were anxious for their homes. There were

strange noises in the darkness, a heavy tramp of
feet along the road; but it was not a martial tread.
The troops had not yet arrived; these men tramping by in the darkness were civilians. Within
the tightly closed and barred houses the old men
recognized voices outside and named the strikers as they passed on their way to the meetings.
"Things are going from bad to worse," they said;
"these are the bellows that blow the fire; to-
morrow morning there will be troops in Ardésie."

And, in fact, on the morning of the third day,
there was a sprinkling of poppy-red among the
mounds: an infantry company was encamped on
the square and in the half-ruined storehouses
where, by night, owls chased the rats.

The reporters came to interrogate Mlle. Renée,
and rang the bell of the school-house door during
lessons. Mlle. Renée opened to them herself;
she was pale, but held firmly to her resolution
to tell nothing; to treat them as if they had come
on professional business. She knew nothing, absolutely nothing, she said; "my duties have kept
me with my pupils."

Thereupon the reporters proceeded to inform
her that dragoons had been patrolling the lines
of the Paris-Orléans Railroad, that soup distri-
butions had been going on since daybreak, that
funds were pouring in from Paris, from the north,
from the west. Then, when the newspaper men
were gone, it was the children's turn to relate
what they had heard at home. As soon as the
teacher re-entered the school-room, they all
raised their hands, as they were in the habit of

doing when asked a question they could answer,
and the legend began to form. How was it possible to oppose it? How punish them for this
partisan spirit which the youngest have in their
blood? They all in turn hastened to contradict
or to confirm each other, to mingle with this
opening drama the voices of their homes. How
ardent they were already for or against the strike!
How one could read their hearts! These inno-
cents said: "Yes, Mademoiselle, they have
sworn that if a single workman is hurt there will
be soldiers killed. The slate-cutters will join
hands; they will push the soldiers into the great
pits which no one ever comes out of alive. It is
true, Mademoiselle; my father said so. On the
edge of the ancient pit near our house the earth
is all undermined, ready to sink into the pool
at the bottom. That is where they will push
them, and then they will throw stones; there
are plenty about—and bricks too! And there
are wires to trip up their horses if they march
on us—and dynamite bombs."

"And there are men too, who don't want harm
done to any one," replies a fresh young voice,
vibrating with emotion. "My father voted for
the strike, like the comrades, but he says that if
they hurt a single soldier or even a gendarme,
he will beat the cowards." "Who are the cowards?" "You!" Voices are raised in protest,
there are cries, then of a sudden all is still. The
sound of horses' hoofs is heard under the windows which open on the high-road. The children stand upon the benches, they jostle each

other. Through the doors they can hear noises in the adjoining room; there, too, they are climbing on the tables. "Mademoiselle, it is the troops going by. The dragoons! There are twenty, thirty—no, thirty-two. The officer doesn't look very pleasant. He has on a pretty uniform though, and such a little moustache! Look at the rider over yonder! He is from our way: 'Francis!'" And Francis has turned his head and shown his white teeth, his hand on his horse's crupper.

At noon the teachers had decided to give the children their dinner at the school instead of sending them home to their parents. "How could one tell what might happen at such a moment?"

Davidée, who was not afraid, went out with one of the big girls to buy bread. They dined as best they could; the afternoon lessons began very late; what did it matter? The school had become merely a place of refuge for the scholars. At half past four the teachers led two bands of little girls, one toward the right, the other toward the left, for a hundred yards or so, and then allowed them to disperse among the lanes and by-paths between the mounds where, to the east, men were still gathering in throngs.

The heat had become torrid. The assistant mounted to an attic above Mlle. Renée's room, where there was a dormer-window commanding a view of the country, whence she could see the scarred blue earth, the workshops, the little orchards nestling between the slate mounds, the ruins of the old abandoned pits, and the tracks which could be divined by the paler line of turf.

Piles of stacked muskets were gleaming on the square of Ardésie, the foot-soldiers sleeping beside them. An officer could be seen standing on guard in the distance, his figure outlined against the sky, which had the tint of hot ashes. He was looking through his field-glass. Black dots, which were slate-cutters in motion, isolated or in groups, were visible mounting and descending the mounds in the direction in which the officer had turned his glass. It was that first week of June, when the grass in the mowing-lots turns rose-red at the tips. The meadows lay sleeping, ripe and warm, in the evening air.

Horny-handed lads whom the strike had turned into loafers, were trampling down the tall grain, careless of the harvest which was not for them. They stooped now and then to pluck daisies for girls who were in wait for them at the turnpike-gates.

At last the tenth of June arrived. It was a Thursday and the feast of Corpus Christi. Luckily the children had a holiday. Would they return to school on the morrow? Who could say? Without their fathers or mothers, without the reassuring tenderness of home, they would doubtless be terrified by the great uproar filling the air, the hoarse cries, the trumpet calls, the hootings which threaten some victim—no one knows whom —the imposing march of processions through the hollow roads of Ardésie. None of these noises proceeded from the immediate neighbourhood of the school, but they broke out on all sides.

The school-house, with a few cottages around it, formed a sort of island amid the rising tide. Mlle. Renée was keeping her room, under pretext of a headache, and would not be down till the mid-day breakfast. It was Davidée who went out to fetch the milk; for the farmer's wife from La Mouronnerie had not passed that morning, seated in her little cart amid her tin cans, raising her hooded head and calling: "Fresh milk! Fresh milk!" This was a bad sign. She must have taken a shorter cut to town to avoid the winding lanes among the quarries where the strikers were in force. When the assistant pushed open the gate of La Mouronnerie and entered the court-yard, holding in her hand her well-scoured earthen jug, she was roughly greeted by the farmer's maid, who was badly frightened, though she had not lost the ruddy hues which glowed equally on her cheeks, her arms, and hands.

"Shut the gate closer than that, Ma'm'selle! You must know that they have been firing around here all night. No? Did you sleep through it all?"

"Yes, pretty nearly."

"Good Lord! What! with those bombs going off, and the stones whizzing through the air? Well, don't go to sleep now! They say that the big fight is coming off this afternoon."

"Why are you trembling so, Mariette? Your fright prevents your giving me good measure."

But the girl refused to smile. "You are new to this business, Ma'm'selle," she said. "You don't know yet that in a strike it is always the women who weep."

Davidée returned to the school more agitated than she cared to show. She walked with measured steps and head cast down, apparently absorbed in contemplation of the white full-moon of milk oscillating in her jug. But in reality she was pondering intently over the rendezvous she had promised for the morrow. Was it possible that at one o'clock she would be climbing the high embankment overlooking the whole wide expanse of the slate country? To await Maïeul there would have been a daring act of charity even a week ago, now it had become the height of imprudence; and, after all, would it not be a useless risk? Maïeul might not be free, as by reason of his great physical strength, as well as of the ascendency which he exercised over his comrades, he was one who could not be spared from the strikers' battalion. They would not suffer him to go.

The young girl had reached the school-house door when the thought of Mlle. Renée, sick with terror, brought a smile to her lips, and finally decided her. "No," she said to herself, "I will not miss this meeting. I have given my promise, and Maïeul would never have written to me without some serious reason. He may have a service to ask of me. He may have received tidings of Phrosine, which might be dangerous for him, but will be so no longer when he has told me. And even if he merely intends to renew his declaration of the other day, and express his feelings toward me, I shall not regret having met him, for I shall make him understand that I am

not like some women, that I can guard myself—
for whom I know not—perhaps for a life of
solitude only, but a solitude at least free from
remorse." She pushed open the little chestnut-
wood door, framed in the great portal, and turning for a final glance over the expanse of stony,
desolate, blue-gray landscape around her, she
thought again: "What a strange destiny mine
is! I have been forced to take sides against a
pair of lovers and have made them my friends
by my very severity, or if they are not my friends,
I am their confidante, which is no less compromising."

By half-past twelve, Davidée, having washed
the breakfast dishes and set them away on the
closet shelves, had gone up to her room to put on
a straw-hat, her last summer's hat newly trimmed,
which looked like an inverted harebell. She was
on her way downstairs when she came face to
face with Mlle. Renée looking doleful and dishev-
elled, and holding a cup of tea in her hand.

"You are going out, Mademoiselle?" she cried.

"Yes, Mademoiselle."

"I thought I heard you in your room and
wished to make sure. You are actually going
out into the midst of a strike?"

"I wish to see it nearer."

"And wearing that white hat!"

"I have no red one."

"It is simple madness."

The tone was so tragic that Davidée could
hardly refrain from laughing outright. But the
inclination left her when she had once more closed

the school-house door, and was fairly on her way
to the rendezvous. She turned at first toward
Trélazé, then having crossed the square of Ardésie, which was occupied by a detachment of
troops, she bore to the left, and choosing the
short cuts through the quarries, which the strikers used, she had soon reached the region of steep,
abandoned mounds. Thus far she had encountered only a few workmen, placed as pickets
outside the workshops, a group of women here
and there, and a couple of children—for them
there was no strike—picking Easter daisies at
the foot of the hill. Now there was no longer
a being in sight and she was alone on the high
plateau, overgrown with gorse and thorn-trees,
whose seams and furrows were filled with water
from the long-abandoned quarries, and from
whose heights the new slate works were visible.
Here was the abandoned pit of La Gravelle, with
its deep sombre pool, and beyond it rose the
sparsely grown woodland to which Maïeul had
referred in his letter, saying: "At one o'clock
I will be in the thicket of La Gravelle."

Davidée had climbed so rapidly that it still
lacked ten minutes of the appointed hour. She
entered the grove, and approaching its further
edge, she peered out between the bare boughs.
Everywhere before her and beneath her lay
stretched the barren lowlands with their work-
yards and wells, their ponderous machinery and
scattered houses; the whole busy, dusty, noisy
region which was to be the scene of the approaching conflict.

Why had she met so few people on her way? She knew the reason now. The thronging masses were below her, beyond the valley, amid the deserted work-yards and neglected piles of slate; yonder where the slopes began to rise again, and where blue-gray walls and roads, and masses of débris surrounded the gaunt scaffolding of the quarry wells. Above the valley rose a confused murmur which spread over the mounds and across the fields; no words could be distinguished; the air carried only a jumble of discordant notes and disconnected fragments of speech which did not blend. All at once a great cry arose and was borne upward on the wind. Ah! this time they have all shouted the same words. Davidée can make out their meaning. "Down with Trémart! Death to traitors!" It is impossible that Maïeul should be coming, he must be one of that dark swarm, filling the road and besieging the enclosure around the quarry mine. Assembled before the door which opened each morning for the day's work, but which is tightly barred now, were the quarrymen, their wives, and a swarm of children. This living mass was moved by sudden impulses; it eddied hither and thither, advanced, recoiled, scattered, and collected again without any reason apparent to the on-looker. Even with a field-glass Davidée could not have recognized the faces, but she could recognize attitudes. There was Madeleine Bunat's father, there was Guillemotte, whose daughter was in the upper class, and those gigantic arms and shoulders over there, which hide several others,

and rise like one of the monumental stones at
the entrance to the works, must belong to Géboin
or Le Derf. On the further side of the wall, half-
way up the slope of the hill crowded by machine-
shops, a detachment of dragoons was drawn up,
motionless in their saddles, guarding the flight
of steps leading up to the works; further down,
the works were defended by squads of infantry;
officers dashed back and forth between them.
Ah! there was another cry. A handful of soldiers, making a ladder of each others' shoulders,
attempted to scale the wall; they fell back, a roar
deep and full of passion greeted their fall. Then
stones must have been flung at the troops; the
lines wavered, horses reared, a party of besiegers
filed along under the shelter of the wall, in search
of some weak spot in the long enclosure where
they could make their way into the shops. Davidée followed them with her eyes, saying to herself: "Maïeul must be somewhere in the midst
of that torrent." She saw in imagination the
carbines lowered, the first ranks of the assailants
falling, the others scaling the hill, and then flames;
a mighty column of flame rising from the rafters
steeped in petroleum, and she shivered with terror at the picture she had conjured up. She was
amazed at the stolidity of the crowd opposite her,
on the further heights, who had apparently come
as lookers-on at a show; one would have supposed
that they had hired seats for the occasion. They
thronged the orchards bordering the road, where
they formed patches of bright colour; there were
women with gay parasols and summer hats, look-

ing as if a bed of gillyflowers had suddenly sprung up on those far-away terraces. And above this scene, high into the air, rose the gaunt scaffolding of the quarry wells, with their cables, their immense pulleys, the chambers containing the windlasses, pumps, and dynamos; the wealth and power, in short, against which this whole assault is directed. The mob no longer cried "Down with Trémart!" No petty new grievance could have such power over them. This is the old leaven which has always stirred the masses; the revolt against masters, the rage to seize and to destroy, the memory, perhaps, of a cruel word spoken by a dead foreman to his workmen—all of whom are now dead—the promise of new social conditions and a new prosperity, a reversal of the whole situation, the present system of equality destroyed for the exclusive benefit of the labouring class.

Davidée, kneeling on the edge of the embankment, leaning forward beyond the shelter of the wood, exposed to wind and sun, suffered and trembled and longed to throw herself between the combatants. She reviewed hastily in her mind the names of those she knew in that mêlée. "My quarrymen are all mad with rage, the fathers and brothers of my little ones are there. If there might only be none killed among them, or among the others in that throng! for though my heart is more concerned for those I know, I pity them all. Ah, there is a shot fired! Another! They were fired outside the gate of the enclosure by some of the workmen. Now all

are in wild movement, besiegers and besieged.
The scarlet trousers are advancing upon the black
mass which has grown enormously on the right
—and to the left. Ah! there the dragoons are
descending slowly with measured steps, for the
mob has burst into the workshops. An order
has been given: 'Draw sabres!' and the troops
charge on the trot upon the band which has
turned the wall and leaped into the enclosure.
They plunge into that howling mass which flings
itself upon them, which wounds, and is wounded.
Stones are flying, I can see them from here. The
workmen take refuge behind their wind-breaks;
they are overturning carts. Ah! there are women
among them. A few years hence my old pupils
may be doing the like. They are driven back
and a cloud of dust has hidden them. There is
wild disorder in the crowd along the road and
amid the orchards—and it is the 'International'
with its assumed airs of a religion of humanity,
which presides over all these horrors! I can no
longer see what has happened, the dense clouds
of dust hide everything. But the infantry also
seem to have repulsed the assailants. The crowd
of spectators in the orchards are cheering. Whom
are they cheering?" And in order to see more
clearly, Davidée rose and stood up on the outer
edge of the grove. What had happened? Piercing
cries could be heard from the throng besieging
the entrance-gates, and all faces were now
turned in the direction of the orchard slopes
and the valley, and of Davidée where she stood
watching.

"What are they gazing at? Ah, there is a man who breaks away from the black mass of the strikers and starts down the road on a run! Three men are after him, four, five. They have caught him? No, he has sprung into a field. They are like a pack of hounds after their prey! He dashes across the stubble with his pursuers at his heels; he has gained on them; no, he is losing ground. Unhappy wretch! It must be Trémart whom they have discovered and who has made a desperate effort to escape. He has reached a hedge, he is caught in the thorns. There! he has fallen. The men have hurled themselves upon him with their sticks raised. They are beating him, they will kill him!"

At that moment the mob cries: "Rit-Dur! Rit-Dur! Seize him!" It is no longer five men who surround the fallen Maïeul; it is at least a hundred strikers who have poured down the slope. The victim could no longer be distinguished from his assailants, for the whole throng was in motion and the field was wrapt in a cloud of dust.

Davidée had fled through the wood. She ran as far as the fields of broom beyond, and thence began to descend the slopes toward Ardésie, avoiding the houses, in haste, and deadly pale.

Wild thoughts surged within her: "Is it possible? They have wounded Maïeul, killed him, perhaps? And I am the cause! I know it, I feel it; he has not betrayed his comrades, no! But he gave his promise to a village schoolteacher, saying: 'At one o'clock I will be in the

wood of La Gravelle'; and he would not fail to
keep his word. I am the cause of it all. He is
like me, this Maïeul, when he has promised no
obstacle can stop him. Who can give me news
of him? I cannot go about asking it, for they
are fighting in the streets, and the soldiers guard
the roads."

The tumult passed, as the storms of winter
pass, always, always! The girl reached the
school-house, sick with anxiety, and not wishing
to shut herself up in her chamber at the other
end of the house, she entered the lower class-
room, and, standing on a chair, supported herself
against the window railing. In that position
she could see the passers-by and ask news of
them. But the road was deserted, she could not
see the valley; she had before her only the straggling hedge, the bare pastures, and the deserted
slate mounds. A cloud of dust was floating in
the air about the mine well which was out of
sight. Fighting must still be going on. At moments all the distant country beyond the line of
vision seemed shaken as by a tempest; she could
feel beneath her feet the trembling of the earth
under the gallop of horses and the flight of immense throngs. She kept repeating to herself:
"It was for me that he took such risks, that he
ran and fell!" All at once, beyond the houses
adjoining the school, Davidée caught a glimpse of
a woman timidly crossing the place, and called
to her. But the woman motioned back that she
was in haste and did not care to linger on her

way home. About four o'clock Mariette, the
dairy-maid, passed, leading two cows from pasture and pricking them with a pitch-fork to make
them go faster.

"Are there any wounded, Mariette?"

"Yes, several."

"Are any dead?"

"So they say."

The girl had already passed the school when
she turned back to cry:

"I told you it was the women who weep! Shut
your window! Go in and pray, if you know how!"
She was angry, remembering that Davidée had
laughed at her that morning. A little later, an
ambulance passed on the trot, and the soldier
who was driving the horse, seeing a pretty face
at the window, cracked his whip.

"Have you any news of a man named Maïeul
Jacquet?"

The soldier merely shrugged his shoulders,
shouted "Gee," and lashed his horse instead of
cracking his whip in the air.

Then, as evening stole on, there came a calm.
The noise of voices, the distant sound of tumult
died away, though the dust continued to hang
over the distant prospect. Davidée realized that
the combatants had gone quietly home to their
suppers. This is the sort of thing that happens
in civil risings before actual war has broken out.
She hastened out, and ran as far as the church,
which is but a short distance from the mounds
of La Gravelle; she entered a cottage near by
where the woman of the house was terrified at

first by her entrance, but smiled on recognizing
her and asked pardon:

"I am lighting the fire to boil my soup, as you
see, Mademoiselle Davidée. I was not expecting
to see you. How flushed you are! Has there
been any disaster at your house?"

The assistant was ashamed at having shown
so much feeling. She turned toward the door
and, raising one arm above her head, rested her
hand against the wall and drew a long breath,
as children do when they have been playing on
the way home. "I have run too fast," she said;
"I am not brave enough. Tell me, Mère Jumelé,
is it true that a man has been killed?"

"You mean Rit-Dur?"

"Yes, he was wounded, I know."

"So severely, my dear, that he was brought
home on a litter. His head was bloody and his
eyes closed, and he remained three hours without opening them."

"What did the doctor say?"

"No doctor came."

"Why not?"

"None was called! The quarrymen attend
to those matters among themselves. Maïeul had
hardly regained consciousness when he asked to
speak, not to a doctor, mind you! but to the
strike-leaders; he said: 'I want justice done me.
They shall know why I threw up the game; I
was not betraying them. Am I a traitor?' That's
what he said."

"And what did the leaders do?"

"Two of them came. They held a council at

his house, you know, up there at the pavilion. It seems they answered him: 'Rit-Dur, it is you who are in the right.' But what other words were spoken, nobody knows. Now he is in a high fever, and the Breton grandmothers are watching with him; no one knows whether he will recover."

Mère Jumelé, who had succeeded in kindling her green fagots, now approached Davidée, and having assured herself that there were no listeners on the road outside, within earshot of her whisper, said:

"For my part, Mademoiselle Davidée, I believe it is some idea about a woman that has brought that poor fellow to his ruin."

Davidée looked out toward the mound of La Gravelle half lost in shadow, and at a star just rising above its slope.

"There are women who ruin and women who save," she answered.

And the housewife rejoined, as she went back to her hearth:

"All the same, if I were in that woman's place I shouldn't feel easy."

Davidée did not feel easy as she walked back through the ominous darkness. She slept badly. Troops of strikers marched along the road singing. She had but one desire; for daylight to come and bring news of Maïeul. She said to herself: "It is the suffering of others that changes one. No, I am not the cause of it; no, I have done him no wrong; no, I am not in love with him; but since they have wounded him, my heart has been full of this Maïeul and sick with pity for him."

Three days passed: It was reported that he was a little better, and that he had been seen on Sunday evening taking the air on his balcony. But the women added: "He looks like a corpse come to life." The strike was not over, but was dragging along, empty of the passion with which it started. The processions of strikers and patrols of troopers came into collision less frequently. Many of the strikers were at work in the hay-fields; their wives no longer dared to ask for credit from the bakers and sent their children in their place. On the fourth day, just before noon, Davidée, who had accompanied a party of pupils beyond the church, because the mothers feared to let them go alone, was returning along the familiar road where there were only scattered houses on one side. How many times she had tramped this dusty route, how often her eyes had scanned this dreary prospect of poor roofs and straggling bushes! She no longer noticed them, but walked along seeing nothing but her own thoughts. At that moment she was thinking of the dreary expanse of summer weeks stretching before her, when the heat sets one's blood on fire; of the silence of the mornings, noons, and evenings, in that school-house, between two teachers who were enemies. The sun was scorching, and the mud of former winters, ground to powder along the road, was turning Davidée's skirts a dingy gray. She almost gained the school when she suddenly paused:

"Mademoiselle Davidée!"

The side of the road where there were no houses was divided from the pastures and stony stubble-fields by strips of hedge connected by a rusty wire fence. It was from this direction that the call came. Davidée recognized at once the voice of Maïeul Jacquet, and turned toward him. He was standing a little below the road, and was obliged to raise his head to see who was approaching. Oh, that poor bruised and scarred face, white with suffering! Those hollow eyes, from which his ardent youth seemed to have vanished! His head was wrapped in bandages and his working-jacket showed on one shoulder a straggling, badly-mended darn, where a wound had been. He was leaning with both hands upon a stick. "I couldn't come that other day, Mademoiselle Davidée. You must forgive me!" he said.

"How they have wounded you!"

"Oh, yes, a little."

"They might have killed you."

"I don't bear them any grudge. They were within their rights; they thought I had betrayed them. But it is all made up between us. I explained to them——"

"What did you say? That you had an appointment with me?"

His face darkened at her suspicion, as he answered:

"I spoke another's name, as you may think." And they kept silence for a long moment, with the thought of Phrosine between them. Then he spoke again.

"I am leaving here on her account."

"You are going to join her?"

"Not I! Mademoiselle Davidée, do not turn from me in anger as you are doing! Do not leave me! Do not go back to school! I am wretched enough as it is." These last words had the power to arrest Davidée. She had already passed Maïeul, and her eyes were bent once more upon the schoolhouse and the daily duties awaiting her there.

"Say quickly what you have to say to me," she answered. "They are looking for me."

"It is not so with me! No one is looking for me, here, nor elsewhere. There where I am going to the Combrée region, a dozen leagues from here, I know nobody. And yet it was I who begged to be transferred to the quarry of La Fôret. I asked it, some time before the strike, because I cannot hold on here. I don't want to offend you, but you see, here in Ardésie now, all alone, I am caught in my memories as in a thicket. I cannot even do my work well. I no longer care for the slate. The mates say to me: 'You were not so gloomy, Maïeul, in the house on the Plains!'"

"And is it true?"

"Yes, it's true. You cannot understand, a girl like you. But, all the same, it's you who parted us. So I wanted to tell you that I'm going away and that I do not lay it up against you; that in the depths of my heart I am glad, after all, that I no longer love her. Oh, no, no! Only——"

"What is it then?"

"I still fear her."

At this, he thought she was going away without making him any answer; that he was going to lose her, and he added hurriedly:

"You know all now, and you must despise me." To his surprise she did not leave him. She remained standing in the middle of the road, and bending her head a little, looked, not unkindly, at the man who was thus humiliating himself. She did not wish to be hard on him; she was used to encouraging her pupils when they confessed their faults, and she now said:

"You are mistaken, I do not despise you. I believe that you are doing right."

"Since you say so, I shall have more courage, Mademoiselle Davidée, but I am a poor sort, I fear."

"I am poor, too; there are many ways of being so."

"Since I lost my father and mother no one has ever reproved me when I did wrong. You were the very first. I am more grieved over the child's death than I can ever tell you."

And as Davidée did not go away, as she was before his eyes for a short minute more and her eyes were full of the kindness which listens willingly, he grew bolder and, with a gesture to show her his wounded head, he added:

"And so I am off! But when I am quite cured in every way, may I not see you again? Mademoiselle Davidée, I have never known your equal."

"Is that so wonderful? I do not come from about here, you know."

"When you pass, the trees bend for love of you."

"Oh, no, Monsieur Maïeul; it is the wind that bends them."

"The children on the road, as far off as they can see you, send their hearts out to you."

"And I do the same in return; I belong to them."

"We all know that you love only them. You are not like other school-mistresses——"

And as she stood motionless, still bending toward him, he ventured to say once more:

"When I have shown that I am capable of living like an honest man, may I not see you again?"

She made no answer, but turned very white, and resumed her way far more slowly than she had come.

All that afternoon Davidée's time was very full: hearing lessons, receiving parents, preparing songs for a festival that was soon to come off, and getting dinner, as it was her week for keeping house. When night came, weary as she was, she could not sleep. She sat for a long time at her open window thinking of Maïeul's departure and the words he had said to her. Some of these words were new to her ears, but scarcely had she dared to take pleasure in them when others recurred to her memory—cruel words—which he had also spoken: "I still fear her." Then all the sweetness died away.

It was hard for Davidée to distinguish, in the shadows, the school-house garden from that of the next neighbour, or from a poor vineyard beyond, whose rows of vines stretched into the darkness like the furrows in a ploughed field. But this was enough to bring the whole of Ardésie before her mind's eye; all its fields and roads, its hamlets, the daily work and the familiar faces.

Some one was about to leave this corner of the earth, where peace was no longer possible to him, because of old words spoken here. How many broken lives there had been! She could not rid herself of a thought which recurred as persistently as the refrain of a song: "These are his last hours here. Like Phrosine, he will go at break of day." The earth, steeped in dew, brought to her window the odour it gives out after rain, and the silence was so deep that she could hear the drops trickle from the leaves.

It was just before daybreak—the hour when the earth was still dark beneath a paling sky—that Davidée, who had thrown herself upon her bed, rose with a start. She had recognized a voice, she heard a man singing. Quickly and noiselessly she opened her blinds. The voice was not close at hand, it was that of a traveller passing along the road and these were the words he sang:

"She to whom all my thoughts belong
  Has never had one thought for me;
  'Tis for her sake that I must flee,
As youth and joy have fled me long.

"From her I flee, with tortured breast,
  Wherein her image ever dwells,
  And clinging, tears its inmost cells
As ferrets tear the wild bird's nest."

How sad the air was, like the slow chant the

drovers sing returning from the pastures driving
their herds before them! The voice was dying
away already, perhaps in the vineyard, perhaps
in the open country beyond. It still chanted
words which did not reach her window, then
became silent. It was just daybreak.

One woman only had understood the song,
though several may have heard it. But when the
sun had risen, from the heights of La Gravelle
came another music, sounding thin upon the
wind which bore it far into the distance, and it
must have spoken from the soul, for souls were
moved by it, each after its own fashion.

The children beyond the fringe of broom,
wakened early by the sound, in the warm beds
of their low-roofed cottages, began to laugh when
they heard it, and wakened their parents. "Listen, father, that is Maïeul's flute! Oh, how
pretty! It is a long time since he has played it!"
But they did not go beyond the pleasure which
the tripping notes gave to their ears. The slate-
cutters, who made their morning toilet in the
garden, splashing half-naked in great tubs of
clear water, were the next to share the astonishment of the children, and they laughed, too, as
they cried. "That is not the music for a strike!
What is Rit-Dur thinking of?" But old Mère
Fête-Dieu clasped her hands and murmured:
"Oh, Lord! bring him back with a soul that is
saved, and a flute that no longer weeps." She alone
heard the tune aright, she and one young school-
mistress, pretty and sad, and already touched at
heart, who said: "He loves me yet; that is the

music of a sorrowful love which is going far away."

Thus the rustic flute sounded over the mounds of La Gravelle, soon so faintly that it must surely be travelling down the valley where the roads were bordered by high hedges; by the time the sunlight had grown bright, it rang no louder than the hum of a gnat; and when it was broad day all knew that the quarryman Maïeul Jacquet had gone away from Ardésie.

CHAPTER XI.

THE INSPECTOR'S VISIT.

AFTER the incidents of the tenth of June, when the shedding of a man's blood had virtually killed the strike, all the parents in Ardésie were anxious about their children. Even the most violent were heard to say: "There are all sorts of people about on the mounds. It won't do to trust them." The classes were, therefore, nearly empty on Tuesday morning. In Mlle. Renée's there were but eight scholars, Mlle. Davidée had nine. The children who were present nearly all lived in the cluster of houses surrounding the church, or in the small square to the right of the school. The moment she entered with her little girls into her class-room the assistant noticed that Mlle. Renée had made a more elaborate toilet than usual and that she was highly excited.

"Have you brought all the themes back to me corrected, Mademoiselle?" she asked.

"Yes, certainly!" Davidée replied.

"And is all the needle-work in the chest of drawers in my room, next to the mineralogy drawer?"

"Yes, Mademoiselle."

"So much the better, I must go and see if you have arranged them properly."

232

At nine o'clock there was a ring at the door. Usually when the woman who waited by the day was absent, Mlle. Renée sent one of the older pupils to open the door. This time she hastened out herself, and Davidée, a moment after, hearing a man's deep voice replying to Mlle. Renée's veiled soprano, felt certain that the directress had gone to meet the inspector. Proof was not long wanting. The sound of a gliding step and of a heavy tread crunching the gravel, the roll of a bicycle in its narrow tracks accompanied these words which were audible through the open bay-window:

"It is true, Mademoiselle. I am terribly heated. What dust! What heat! Your Ardésie is a perfect furnace."

"I should not have ventured to call it that, Monsieur, but I have been thinking so for the past six years."

"Six years! In Ardésie? You must have requested to be retained here then."

"Not at all, Monsieur. Would Monsieur partake of a little refreshment?"

"Never, Mademoiselle. I never accept. I am on duty, but it is true nevertheless that I, who am from the south, have never suffered from the temperature at home as I do here. Is this your class?"

"Pass in, I beg——"

"After you."

The voice belonged evidently to the southern type of orator, for whom a single listener is as good as the crowded forum. His entrance into

the class-room was boisterous. Davidée, all this
time, was dictating to the younger girls a page
from a manual on civic duties. It was a pleasure
to catch through the partition the slightest notes
of this paternal barytone alternately interro-
gating the pupils, whose timid answers remained
inaudible, and congratulating them and their
mistress. "Very good," he was saying, "that
distinction between lepidoptera and diptera! four
wings, two wings! Natural history makes us
learn to cherish nature. Indicate the methods
of separating the oxygen in water from the hy-
drogen. Very good! *There* is a future house-
keeper who will be able to explain, I am sure, the
phenomenon of ebullition. What is her father's
profession, Mademoiselle?"

The studied falsetto of Mlle. Renée replied:

"A pork-butcher, saving your presence, Monsieur."

"Very good! Her orthography leaves something to be desired, but her memory is excellent.
Our highest faculty, Mademoiselle!"

"Yes, Monsieur."

"One of the chief joys of life!"

"Yes, Monsieur."

"And one which you are cultivating with success. Show me the rotatory schedule of daily
studies. You do not know what that is? I
understand, I excuse you! That is the name I
proposed to the Minister of Public Instruction,
whom I knew very well, to designate what you,
perhaps, call the schedule of studies. But rotatory occurred to me, a word that vibrates. Ro-

tatory gives an added meaning, it makes a picture; rotatory was my own invention. The minister said to me afterward: 'I regret it.' Thanks, Mademoiselle, that is right." Davidée, dictating in a lowered voice, was watching to see the door-handle turn, or to hear the approaching footsteps of the inspector and the directress, and was ready to spring to her feet. But the visit, next door, was prolonged. At a quarter past nine the assistant heard their footsteps retreating, and for ten minutes more there was no sound from the upper class, save whisperings, suppressed peals of laughter, and the fall of an occasional pen-holder on the bare floor, whence the assistant inferred that the inspector and Mlle. Renée were walking in the court-yard or the garden. At half past nine they entered; the inspector came first, and opened the school-room door as cautiously as if he were venturing into a lion's cage, with a rapid movement, his head thrust forward and his eyes fixed upon those of the wild beast. The latter was represented by the assistant, who had risen from her seat to greet him. Having introduced himself, he broke the magnetic current by glancing around at the empty benches, and smiling upon the nine pupils present. Then he resumed his air of gravity as he seated himself in the chair which one of the older pupils was bringing in for him.

"Let us see this dictation!"

He took up the nearest copy and gazed at it approvingly:

"A page from Souchet-Lapervenche? One of

our best prose writers. I often recite extracts from Souchet-Lapervenche in the salons of my friends. It produces a great effect. Not enough punctuation, Mademoiselle; how do you expect a pupil to understand that which is not punctuated? Do you dictate the punctuation?"

"No, Monsieur."

"You are wrong. Listen to this extract properly punctuated, children; notice the difference between my semicolon and colon!" He proceeded to recite, while Mlle. Renée listened with admiration, Mlle. Davidée stood beside him respectful and resigned, and the pupils stared at his mouth curved in a bow whence proceeded the voice of a chorister intoning, at the full, shaven cheeks, and the chin lengthened by the pointed tuft of a blue-black beard. This inspector, who had been appointed to visit the department as a substitute during a colleague's illness, belonged to that race which never grows weary of itself. Wherever he happened to be he overplayed his part in order to prove that his talent exceeded his present functions. He carried himself with an air of conviction; with a direct, patriotic, imperious glance, which some of his intimates at the Café d'Auch even ventured to call "imperial." Having once heard this word, he pondered it incessantly; it was his "breach into the Vosges." The inspector never discussed an order, and the obedience he exacted from others was rendered sacred and beautiful in his eyes by his own example. Crafty, beneath an off-hand manner, he had the art of casting a sidelong glance at the subordinate whom he was addressing, as if to imply: "I am a good fellow, you see; I can smile on you, give you my protection, and exert in your behalf a credit which has made many jealous of me, and may perhaps make others jealous of you." In actual fact, this look rarely went further than such professional hints. Some unusually pretty assistant teachers, here and there, had discovered that the inspector was a connoisseur in beauty. But he was content with insinuating his sentiments, calling forth a blush and a glance of amazement, to which he responded by heavy witticisms and broad jests. He declared that no one would ever catch him paying court to a subordinate, and he spoke the truth. All his severities were directed toward scruples of conscience. He regarded any such timidity as a personal insult, as he did also the least show of respect for any authority other than the State. The inspector delighted in his functions, which gave him an opportunity for seeing the country, and meeting "representatives of various races, but all equally French at heart." He was most impressive as he uttered this formula. It was these functions which had brought him to Ardésie, in the place, as he explained, of "my dear disabled colleague."

When he had minutely examined the pupils' note-books, he passed judgment on a couple of maxims of civic morality, and declared that, in his opinion, Mlle. Birot was a little too much of an idealist.

"Mademoiselle," he said, "I have just shriven

the directress; it is your turn now. Will you
step outside with me?   We shall be able to talk
more freely in the garden."

"Shall I accompany you, Monsieur?" asked
Mlle. Renée.

"It is needless, Mademoiselle."

The inspector and the assistant proceeded in
silence to the garden, where after casting a glance
at his bicycle to assure himself that no one had
touched it, the functionary seated himself on
the low wall surrounding the vegetable garden,
and made a sign to the assistant to seat herself
on the other side of the gate.   She, however,
remained standing a few paces distant, and although he repeated the gesture she had an air
of not comprehending him.   Thereupon he contracted his brows, looked up to the sky above
Davidée's head, and spoke as if he relished the
words: "I should be sorry to give pain to a
young assistant who needs to have a feeling of
security as to her future.   But I have to warn
you of certain accusations which have been
brought against you."

"By Mademoiselle Renée?"

"I have named no one.   Do not aggravate
your case by dragging in your superiors.   We
have a dozen ways of knowing what takes place
in one of our schools.   I will not enlarge upon
the misplaced familiarities attributed to you."

"Conversations, perhaps; familiarities, no! I
cannot accept such an expression addressed to a
respectable girl!"

"Oh, Mademoiselle, *your* expressions also may

be out of place. I have the right—I ought to have it—to pass judgment on your private conduct."

"Take the right, Monsieur, but do not judge me before you have questioned me."

"Precisely! I have no intention of questioning you on any such subject. But I repeat, I should have a perfect right to do so."

"Do it then."

"How hasty you are! You are very young, to be sure. No, Mademoiselle, I refuse to discuss with each of my instructresses in turn the principles of private morality which they profess and practice. In any case short of scandal I have never intervened in the South; I do not propose to do so in the North."

He ceased to contemplate the white clouds above him, and turned his imperial face, and his eyes, which were of the same bluish black as his beard and hair, upon the young girl, who was expecting that look intended to terrify her, and met it without faltering. One could look deep into the eyes of Davidée Birot as she stood very erect beside the gate, her hands hidden in the pockets of the white apron with red polka-dots which she had thrown on over her dress. A ray of sun just touched her head and turned her hair to chestnut.

"What I have to reproach you with, as a breach of professional duty, is your attitude toward the curé of Ardésie."

"I beg pardon, Monsieur, I do not quite grasp the meaning of your accusation. Since I have been here, I have only once set foot inside a church, and that was on the occasion——"

"I know; you cannot give me any information."

"I was brought up in a family where religious practices scarcely existed. I do not judge my father and mother. If they had brought me up otherwise I would tell you so; I should have no fear of saying it."

A keen smile passed across the severe mask. "Bravo! I admire sincerity. But you see, by your own admission, you do not know whether you have done right or wrong in abstaining from religious practices."

"It is true. I have had no time to concern myself with these subjects."

"I hope you may never have. They are idle questions."

"So I have been taught; superrational."

"Precisely! Ah! you have attended the courses of Mademoiselle Hacquin, one of our great thinkers, although in the primary department. But for the very reason that you have not taken a decided stand, you are being led astray. Innocently, I am willing to believe, but seriously. For there is the example, Mademoiselle! You were in charge of your pupils and filling an official position, when, several weeks ago, you held a long conversation with the curé, at the entrance to the cemetery."

"I was there about one minute. I was thanking him because I loved the child."

"Meanwhile your pupils were wandering unprotected along the road."

"Oh, Monsieur!"

"Yes, unprotected, until the sound of passing
wheels at last roused you from your forgetful-
ness and broke off your parley with the priest.
Moreover—let me finish, I beg—moreover, you
were carrying an ostentatiously large prayer-book
in your hand."

"Oh, Monsieur!"

"Ostentatiously large."

"I should have preferred it smaller, but it is
all I have."

She paused a moment, and the spirit of Père
Birot—who was not an easy man to deal with—
appeared in his daughter's look, in the tone of
her voice, in the movement of her hands as she
clutched her dotted apron. "And so you would
forbid my entering a church if I felt any such
desire!"

A laugh of good-natured scorn accompanied
the answer. "Oh, no, Mademoiselle; liberty, you
know!"

"You would at any rate forbid my carrying
a prayer-book? The only one I own! I should
not have the right granted me to do as every
one else does—to pray for my dead? I must
request you to inform me plainly what you call
my duty, Monsieur, in order that I may perform
it, if possible. I beg you to define it."

It was the inspector's turn to take time for
reflection. He appeared to be absorbed once
more in watching the white clouds which were
rolling up, and now hung above the house-tops
like a gleaming glacier.

"I do not wish to encroach upon any one's liberty, Mademoiselle; that would be to belie my whole public career. What I would order you, or advise you, which amounts to the same thing, is not to walk about carrying a big book which is a manifestation in itself, and to converse as seldom and as briefly as possible with the curé or the vicar, if there is a vicar. You understand, do you not? There are certain fine distinctions I can only hint at. No, I see that you persist in misunderstanding me. You are said to be intelligent—you are so—take care not to pass judgment on too many subjects!" And, so speaking, with a sudden heave of his broad thighs, he sprang down from the wall, and resumed the tone which he regarded as that of a man of the world, as he begged the assistant to relate to him the principal incidents of the strike. The directress, who had been watching for him, came out of the door at once to accompany him as far as the road. He was extremely cordial in his reiterated promises to Mlle. Renée to secure promotion for her. He expressed less clearly his benevolent intentions toward "an assistant whose spirit was somewhat too independent, but who was full of excellent intentions and had a future before her as instructress."

Davidée felt herself condemned on the spot, and at short notice.

"Well, child," said Mlle. Renée, when they were alone, "are you satisfied?"

"Delighted!" replied Davidée.

"I did all that could be done for you. We

have had occasional misunderstandings, but all that shall be forgotten, shall it not?"

"Yes, Mademoiselle."

Davidée, while concluding her afternoon classes, thought over all the words spoken in the morning. She could have no doubts now in regard to the denunciation of which Phrosine had warned her, nor of the dismissal which would be the most certain result of the inspector's vague promises. She had her enemies, she, the young girl who had entered the normal school, not from necessity, in order to support herself, like so many of her companions, but led by a sort of maternal instinct, a gentle taste for training children and an ambition for social service. She said to herself: "I will not be imprisoned or, as Maïeul said, 'caught in a thicket.' I will come out of my difficulties by going to meet them, and not being afraid. And to begin with, I will go this very evening to see this curé, who will perhaps be questioned; who can testify, in any case—if I am reduced to such wretched expedients—as to the words that passed between us. It revolts me to think that any one considers me so base and poor-spirited that I would consent never to meet, on the village street, the curé, or Maïeul, or Phrosine, or any other of those excommunicated ones on the list they choose to make out for me."

Davidée Birot's cheeks were almost as scarlet as her lips when, at six o'clock, having put on the hat like an inverted harebell, she sallied forth to pay a visit to the mother of one of her little girls, who lived opposite the church. With-

out explaining why, she lingered there a while,
which the widow thought very kind on the part
of the young assistant. It was she who sustained
the conversation, explaining the hard conditions
of a washer-woman's trade, which she had
entered upon at fourteen, and over which, at
sixty, she was still labouring, with cracked and
bleeding hands.

"It holds you more than you would think,
this work at the tubs," she said. "If you begin
a washer-woman, you end a washer-woman; and
it's all very well when we are soaking our clothes
by the river—there we can talk to the current as
it rushes by, and say, 'There you go gallop-
ing away, with your edges curling like lace,' and
little things of that kind. But here, where we
have to dip our clothes in holes which the sun
never warms, and where the water doesn't know
how to flow, the business is not so gay. It is
not enough so for the young; but formerly——"

Davidée knew how to answer, because with
her the heart always listened; so by brief words
and nods and little signs of sympathy, she showed
that she understood. But the young girl, pleased
as she was to find her presence so welcome,
was actually waiting for the end of the service
at which the curé of Ardésie officiated, having
rung his own bell at that golden sunset hour
which comes at seven in summer and in winter
as early as five. From the widow's cottage they
could hear the responses of his flock, as they
implored God to protect their slumbers, making
of them a means to fresh labour and to salvation;

and to deliver them from the snares of the
tempter who makes the night his especial domain.
Through the open door there entered not only
the warm air, laden with odours of new mown
hay and of the marshes, as well as of freshly
baked loaves from the baker's close by, but also
a vision of the Virgin and Child painted on
the stained glass window of the church. Davidée looked up at the Child's three fingers lifted
in blessing and, without owning it to herself,
she felt happier at being there, within the immediate influence of that protecting gesture.
She had never before noticed that there was a
stained window in the Ardésie church, where the
Mother was represented triumphant and glori-
ous through her Child.

All at once the colours of the stained glass
faded; the abbé must have extinguished the
candles on the altar. Men and women poured
out of the church, their faces wearing the resolute expression peculiar to believers who live in
the midst of opposition and hostility. The curé
must have lingered to set the chairs in order and
tie up the cord by which he rang his bell. He
came out a moment after the last of his flock,
turned the key in the door and then stopped to
gaze up at the sunset sky, splendid with torn and
flying clouds of purple and crimson; then lowering his eyes, he was amazed to behold Mlle.
Birot standing before him. A few people who
still lingered in the church porch were looking
on. Returning the abbé's bow, the assistant
spoke very distinctly, emphasizing each word,

so that it might carry far: "Monsieur le Curé,
do you remember a conversation I had with you
near the cemetery gate the day of little Anna Le
Floch's burial?"

The curé began to laugh. "I could recite all
your words, Mademoiselle, and the lesson would
not be long, as we exchanged barely three sentences."

"It appears that these sufficed for a teacher
to be denounced as a clerical. But I do not intend to let them do as they please with me. Would
you kindly write down those words, in which I
expressed my affection for my little pupil?"

"Certainly, Mademoiselle."

"That is all I have to ask of you, Monsieur le
Curé; many thanks."

She was moving on when her attention was
arrested by a woman approaching from the village, walking at a rapid pace, weary and travel-
stained, dragging behind her a child who was
constantly falling back and letting her feet trail
in the dust. On the woman's other arm hung
a soup kettle. As they reached the houses whose
dwellers were standing on their door-steps, the
child took heart once more. She pointed to a
dog which was following them, and seemed to be
as worn-out as they. "How dirty he is!" she said.

The mother shook her violently, exclaiming, as
she looked about her:

"Not so dirty as these people here. Come
along, you brute!" she cried with an oath, whereupon the child began to laugh, and this morsel
of a creature echoed the blasphemous words. As

they passed on the curé turned his face toward the church saying in a low voice: "My God, you were a prisoner for the love of such as these, and they know it not!"

Silence followed, and the group of people on the porch gradually dispersed, while only a few neighbours were left standing on their thresholds in the sunset light which streamed across the road.

From the Green Diary; the same day.—"I have not faith, but I will not endure having the contrary spirit forced upon me without the liberty to cast it aside. I am wounded and humiliated for the cause of education, the dignity of which has been attacked in my person far more seriously than it could be by my chance interview with Maïeul Jacquet. The man who objected to a large prayer-book, but was willing to tolerate a small one while despising equally the text of both, could drive me to doing anything except what he demanded. My mind is made up; I have decided to what method of defence I will intrust my cause. If I am not successful I shall renounce my profession. In the meantime this hypocritical violence has influenced me to reopen the forbidden volume. I have just been reading parts of the mass and the service for the dead. It seems to me beautiful that we should be buried to the sound of those words full of compassion, of pardon, and of the eternal dawn. There is a nobility about them to which I am not accustomed. The inspector shall not prevent my returning as often as I please to this source of inspiration.

"I still think of a word, spoken, I believe, by the curé himself, upon the secret of peace and joy in this world: 'The solution of the social problem lies in the development of the supernatural.' That saying is beyond my comprehension; but who knows if it be not true? I am amazed at the fund of love for the people which seems to exist in this priest's heart, although so few care to draw upon it. It seems that the strike is almost over; I do not know how an arrangement was brought about, but as to the mutual hatred, all the causes for it subsist and are still at work; an actual permanent peaceful settlement has not been reached. What a lesson life in the midst of these labouring people is for a girl like me, who troubled herself so little about such questions at first, and who is gradually becoming so deeply interested. I would not exchange my position here amid the stones of these quarries for any school they could offer me in town. Here I see the real life of the people; I am a part of it, there is nothing to distract me from it. And I learn to see the poverty in myself as well as in these labourers' daughters around me, whom it is my business to instruct and make over after my own likeness; but the model realizes sadly what a change is needed in herself.

"Twentieth of June, 1909: A letter from Phrosine! I had given up expecting one. I feared that she was lost to me, that weak and violent being whom nothing has ever elevated, no belief in anything, no friendships with her equals; who has had nothing but her duties to sustain her; and these are not sufficient when one has no belief in another life. What might not kindness or good teaching have done to reform such an attractive nature, so easily tempted and tempting, but so frank and honest. Why was there no one to give some rule of conduct, some ideal, to this seeker after joy, who might have learned at last to love justice too? She writes from Vendôme.

"'MLLE. DAVIDÉE:—It is I who am writing. You separated me from the man I loved, and I bore you a bitter grudge for it. I bear it still. But I must write to you because I am in need of help. At first I lived in Orléans; you understand how I mean; I lodged wherever it happened, in the poorer quarters of the town, but not often on charity. I ate in the taverns where the masons drink, eating only enough to make them thirsty. I asked all of them, every one you understand: "Have you met Le Floch, Henri, a tall, bearded man, with a head like a lion, who is a carpenter, and makes beams for mines, or works in wood in one way or another?" They merely laughed, and answered me you may guess how. But there were some kind ones among these men. For my part, I put on an air like you, only with a flash more of petroleum in the eyes and on the tongue, and said: "I am hunting for the father so as to get the son, who is *my* son. It is not safe to touch a mother when she's defending her child, so answer me!" Then they would answer: "Maybe we have

seen him, but at work we only know the mates
by their arms and legs or their eyes, we don't
always know their names. Le Floch, Henri?
I don't remember, though I remember some
bearded ones as you may believe! How old
would your man be? Forty? well now, in 1904
or 1905 or thereabouts, I worked in a wood-yard
with a bearded fellow of about thirty-five. But
it wasn't in Orléans we were working, it was in
the forest of Vendôme. He was no great talker."

"'"That is so!"

"'"But a deep drinker!"

"'"Then it must have been my man."

"'"And he may have had a bit the look of a
lion, but one that goes on the spree a bit too
often. You might look there for him—" So
from one village to another I finally reached
Vendôme, where I'm writing you. And yesterday, after I'd questioned a lot of men, there
came to the lodging a young fellow from the
Vendôme country. I can't hide from you that
this one gave me a kiss. I am not you, Mademoiselle, and I haven't a sou left, nor a scrap of
courage. After we had talked awhile, he said:
"I have met him." "What! Le Floch?" "Yes,
over three months ago, in the Forest of Vouvant, which is in Vendée, and the finest forest
you ever saw, a forest as handsome in its way
as you are in yours."

"'"Don't talk such stuff! Was it Henri?
Are you sure?"

"'"He had a boy he said, who was fourteen years
old."

"'"With him?"'

"'"No."'

"'"So much the worse!"'

"'"He only said: 'I had a boy, and I took him away from the Charity Board.'"'

"'"That is he! It is he, I tell you!"'

"'"'Wait a moment!' he said: 'I have a boy and I found a place for him.'"'

"'"Did he say where?"'

"'"No, that he didn't say, he only told me that at first the young brat gave him the money he earned, but now he didn't do it any more, and it was disgusting of him."'

"'As for me when I heard that, I left the fellow at once, and now I'm going to the Forest of Vouvant. But they say it's a long way from here, by the sea. I will write you, perhaps, if I find him, or in case I am dying of hunger, for it was you who brought me to this pass. Send me a little money for the journey, won't you? Thank you all the same for coming with me the day I started and helping to carry my basket. If you had half of my heart to carry you would see how much heavier that is. Good-by, try to be happy.

"'PHROSINE.'

"Thirtieth of June: To-day came another letter, not from Phrosine this time, but from an old school-mate at the normal school in La Rochelle. She writes from Rouergue. Why Rouergue? It is true that she might ask: Why Ardésie? And she begins her letter as if she thought I might have forgotten her. 'Perhaps you may re-

member.' Yes, indeed, I recall vividly that weak,
ardent, tender daughter of Rochelais fisherfolk,
whom we called Élise, after a character in 'Es-
ther.' 'Is it thou, dear Élise? Oh day, thrice
blest! etc.,' and because she was a born confidante.
Those who confided their secrets to that little
ivory casket had no reason to regret it. The
words dropped into her soul like rain-drops into
the water; there remained not a trace of what
she had listened to, of what had mingled for the
moment with her thoughts; and we were all
devoted to her though she gave us nothing in
return. We never knew whether she had any
secrets of her own, and probably she had not.
But the years have passed, and to-day it is she
who is seeking a confidante and asking for protection. I suspected in school that she was a
Christian, or at least was longing to be one. She
said to me one evening: 'Do you never pray,
Davidée?' in a tone implying that she knew far
better than I the upward path. Now it appears
that she has found occasion to renew her question, that she has heard—from whom, I wonder?—
of my differences with the inspector or rather
with Mlle. Desforges, and of my other Ardésian
experiences, and she now adopts a more modest
tone and asks: 'Tell me how you have accom-
plished so much. Is it true that you have succeeded in liberating yourself, and securing your
right to your own religious opinions, both for
yourself and in the training of your pupils? I
suffer so much from opposition on both these
points that I feel the need of an ally. And how

many others there are silently pursuing their careers of devotion to duty, awaiting and hoping for a purer atmosphere in which their souls can draw breath! I am rejoiced to learn that you have known how to defend your rights better than I have done, and let me add, my dear Davidée, that I am surprised at this; I did not imagine you to be so near me in spirit, etc.'

"I answered plainly that I was not responsible for the gossip of a village, spread and exaggerated by my colleagues: 'I have had slight difficulties,' I said, 'which are not yet entirely settled, but I hope to come out of them with honour. I have no method in the matter, no advice to give, nor confidences to make. I have not the faith of which you speak.' And now I hope that she will not return to the subject.

"Eleven o'clock at night: My letter is gone, I have seen it put into the green bag which is now on the mail-carrier's back, and he is off on his bicycle. So my answer is well on its way to Rouergue. And now I regret it. The state of secret irritation I am in has made me act cruelly, and cruelty toward souls is the harshest of all. I think of those unhappy souls like hers who has just appealed to me, who feel themselves watched and hunted, and who dare not light their fires at night for fear the mounting flame and smoke should betray them. They are, after all, better than I, but the cause of their suffering and of my anger are not altogether unlike. I want my personal dignity respected, they wish their religious faith to be so; it is the same underhand methods which offend us both. I open my window, I see the curve of low billowy forms in the ashen darkness. Nothing, or next to nothing, can be called by its name; these misty forms before me to the right, are they shrubs or housetops? If I did not know their look by day I could not tell. And the thought comes to me that we, who try to understand ourselves, are like those who gaze out into the darkness; that I have never seen my soul in the full light of day, and that it has hidden emotions and impulses which I do not understand."

CHAPTER XII.

"BLANDES OF THE GREEN SHUTTERS."

"Blandes of the Green Shutters!" When Davidée awoke very late on a July morning, in the chamber never occupied by any one save herself, where the flowers, picked for her, fading for her, and giving out on her arrival their odour of the moors, had wrapped her in memories, she did not feel like ringing her bell at once. At the first tinkle, it would be her mother who would answer the call; her little mother whom Davidée guessed to be already up and partly dressed, her hair in the familiar tight gray knot on the top of her head and held in place by the old-fashioned comb of light shell which she remembered always; her mother who had grown more tiny each year, who was surely on the watch now in the adjoining room amid the familiar morning sounds, for the unusual, the longed-for cry which would bring her running to the bedside: "Mamma! I am awake, mamma!" No, not quite yet. She rose first, noiselessly, slipped on a wrapper, and threw open her window, pushing up the Venetian blinds through which the light cast a score of little bars of shadow to the right and left, which grew distincter each minute. "It must be past eight," she thought, "and at Ardésie we should be in the school-room at this hour." The north window which she had opened looked out upon the flat shores of a bay without cliffs or beach. One had to bend far out for a glimpse of the oozy tide. Before her eyes stretched a marsh melting into meadows, then distant low hills lost in the mists of the horizon. Trees were a scarcely appreciable feature of this flat shore. The marsh-grass was everywhere, tawny yellow as far as the winter tides rolled in, and greener beyond, spreading out like an endless fan. "Open, eyes! and recognize your youth which is there before you, which rises from the reeds and rushes and greets you with the laughter of your early days!" Davidée had promised herself great delight in this home-coming, in this first good-morning to the landscape of her childhood. She had felt it often before, but this morning, in spite of the sunshine which rolled in warm waves over the grasses and the still tender grain, she remained unmoved—and wondered to find it so— and discovered that she had left her heart behind her in unfertile Ardésie, with her school children, her daily cares, and perhaps with the songs of that Maïeul, who had left it for her sake. She had a sense of disappointment as if she had seen a flower fading in her girdle.

"Good-morning, darling! Good-morning, beloved!"

Mamma Birot had come in and was embracing her child, then drawing back to look at her better. All her disappointment had not had time to disappear from the girl's face; it still cast a shadow, though it was vanishing, but her mother had noticed it.

"You are not well."

"Oh, perfectly, and delighted to be in Blandes. Is papa better?"

"You are tired from your night journey, child?"

"No, I have just waked. From two in the morning until eight is a fairly good nap. No, I am not tired at all, mamma."

"Then you have some trouble; some one has been annoying you, or you have had a dispute with the directress. They are not treating you kindly, is not that it? I guessed it. Those Ardésie people are making my child's life hard. They cannot understand what a treasure they have in her. Poor darling! why did you leave me who understand you? Tell me what they have done to you."

The young teacher smiled; she sat facing her mother in the full light of morning; she had taken in hers the poor, thin, knotted hands which trembled at every heart-beat; she hastened to pour forth the genuine tenderness and gratitude that were in her heart. In her own bright, gay fashion she described the distribution of prizes, the departure, the unemotional farewell between herself and Mlle. Desforges, the night journey from Ardésie to Nantes, from Nantes to Blandes. Her mother, without interrupting the flow of her narrative, and merely because she could not postpone her words of love and welcome, kept murmuring: "You are prettier than ever, though your lips are a trifle paler, Davidée; but how clever they look, cleverer even than they used to,

and they look kind besides. Your pupils ought
to be happy! I believe your hair is turning
chestnut, Davidée, and what quantities you have!
More than when you were a child. What braids!
they remind me of one of the statues in the
museum. Oh, my pretty one, whom I brought
into the world!" But when the narrative flagged
a little, she grew anxious, and interrupted it by
asking:

"What ails you, child? Tell me your secret.
You are not quite the same as when you left us
at Easter."

Davidée would have preferred not to relate
at once the story of the inspector's visit and the
incidents which had brought it about. She had
promised herself that she would let a few days
pass in peace, and choose her hour for speaking
to her father. But the ardent tenderness of her
mother would suffer no delay; her imagination,
which magnified everything for lack of subjects
to feed upon, would be ready on the slightest
suspicion, at a shade of difference in her daughter's eyes or smile, to invent a dozen stories, and
her poor little frame would have worn itself out
in tears and anxieties if the child had refused to
tell her all. It was better therefore and safer,
to tell her the truth at once. As soon as Madame
Birot learned the persecution for her opinions
to which her child was being subjected, she said:

"If it were my case I should yield, since it
does not concern your home life; but you are like
your father, and put all your pride into public
affairs. We must warn Birot this morning."

"To-day?"

"Yes."

She had again become the capable housewife, who orders quietly and with a submissive air, everything which goes on under her roof.

"The day, however, is the most ill-chosen one you can imagine," she said; "I was not expecting you to-night. I had put those flowers in your room so that I might say to myself each time I entered: 'She is on the way, she is coming, they will be fresh when she arrives.' But I did not think you could get here so early. Listen! this morning, in a few minutes, the doctor will be here."

"Is my father not so well?"

"No, he is very ill, and has been so a long while; ever since he gave up his business. It is sad for an intelligent man like him to have nothing to do, and he is killing himself by drinking. His hands tremble and refuse to do his bidding; his head shakes; he still tries to attend to business but he takes more time to accomplish much less than formerly. His brains are as good as ever, you know; he is as much feared as in his youth, and more terrible, only his enemies are in greater numbers; he has no longer a chief to fight but an army which is on the watch for him to die or weaken, and he feels it. As I tell you, he is terrible. The house is filled only with my silence and his tempers." Then she added, while her lips, accustomed to self-control, scarcely ventured to form a timid smile:

"And yet with me he is gentler than he used to be."

They chatted a few minutes together until the door-bell announced the doctor's arrival.

"Come, dearest!" said the mother.

In his office, with its pitch-pine wood-work and chairs covered with cretonne of oriental designs, Monsieur Birot was dozing when Davidée entered.

"Oho! the little one!" he cried, while the blood rushed to his face, and two tears rolling down his cheeks betrayed his broken condition. The quarry-master had risen to embrace his child, bending his great head to kiss her first upon the right cheek, then on the left; then he had seized her by the shoulders and was hugging her, bear fashion, as he said:

"You are going to make me well! They never let me know that you had come. Why didn't they tell me?"

At this moment the door opened again, and Madame Birot entered, followed by the doctor.

"Confound it!" cried Birot, "what does this fellow want of me?" And with another sudden rush of blood, swelling and purpling his face, he made signs expressing absolute refusal to see the doctor, casting furious glances of defiance at him meanwhile, and pointing toward the door, though no words came.

Suddenly he burst into a great laugh, and fell back into his cretonne arm-chair; and having gradually recovered control of his lower jaw, which opened and closed mechanically, straining the muscles of his neck:

"Egad! my girl," he cried, "you shall see how little these gentlemen know! You expect to cure me, do you, doctor? You came at Madame Birot's request? Yes, I understand. She has undoubtedly told you all my complaints. I have several, but what she has already told you will serve to shorten your visit. What do you order for me? Let us see!"

The doctor, a red-haired man with a sandy beard as stiff as a sheaf of wheat, patient with the combined patience of his peasant stock and of his profession, answered slowly:

"We must first, Monsieur Birot, feel your pulse and examine your lungs."

"Do it then!"

With a vigorous movement, as if he were breaking stones, the Mayor of Blandes tore off his collar, unbuttoned his vest and opened his shirt.

"Here's the chest!" he said. And looking over the head of the doctor, who was bending forward to sound him, he glanced at Davidée, as if to show her that what he was doing was solely on her account, and out of obedience to her wishes.

"Well," he said, when the examination was ended. "Now what do you advise, doctor? What do you want me to do? I know it all beforehand. My wife has already prompted your prescription: 'Give up drinking.'"

"That is exactly it."

"Give up living then!"

"On the contrary; live much longer."

"Go on living without any resources, any companions, any pleasures! Look here! I have toiled forty years to earn my fortune; I have worked harder than any of my mates; I have been steadier; I have been helped, too, by an economical wife."

This was the first time he had ever openly done justice to his wife, who remained silent in her corner of the room, but gave a little nod of agreement, with a glance at her daughter, who was there to judge between them.

"The men at the stone-works," Birot went on, "my workmen, all drink; why shouldn't I who am rich, drink too? What do you want me to do, then?"

The young doctor who, somewhat intimidated by Davidée's presence, sat rubbing his knees with his hands, made a little grimace at this, which expressed many things.

"There are dozens of things for an intelligent man like you to do, Monsieur Birot."

"Such as what?"

"You can read."

"What shall I read?"

"Whatever you like, novels——"

"They bore me to death, they are all about a world I know nothing of."

"The newspapers."

"They all say the same thing one after another."

"Works of popular science."

"I can't understand them. See here, doctor! you are wasting your time. I was born to work in stone, to give orders to my workmen, and then to rest by getting tipsy with them; but as to reading, no! It's my daughter there who reads for me, and I drink for her; that's the way we conduct our lives."

Here he burst into another laugh, feeling that he had made a telling retort.

"Work in the garden," pursued the doctor; " a garden like yours——"

"After an hour of it I am done up."

"Travel then! spend your money in taking journeys."

"I have tried that already."

"That is true," said Davidée; "we went to Biarritz during the last long vacation."

"Yes, and stayed in grand hotels; but what she doesn't tell you is, that I felt like a fool in them."

"Oh, no, Monsieur!"

"You needn't try to convince *me!* I am just a workman—a stone-cutter—and I have a workman's habits; one can't make oneself over, and change all one's ideas of enjoyment; they are a matter of habit and in the blood. Why don't you advise me to be a doctor?"

"Why not play cards, rather?"

"Because as soon as I lose ten sous at 'Manilla' I feel as badly as if I had lost my house. That's in the blood, too—frugality! I can't go in for high-life, I can't play cards, nor dress, nor talk as those people do, nor take part in their amusements. Leave me alone, will you?"

He rose as he said this, heavy and solid still. His patience and good-humour were exhausted. "Let me alone with all your drugs! I have a mighty thirst on account of the stone. A man dies of his job; I shall die of mine, for stone-cutters always drink too hard. Enough said! It's time to go out and find my mates."

"Wait a moment," said Madame Birot, while Davidée was seeing the resigned doctor out. "I have something to tell you."

"Say it later then."

"It is about our daughter, who has been unjustly treated."

"Oh, that's different! If any one touches our child, that's a thing I can never forgive."

Davidée had just re-entered. "What is it, little one?"

"The primary inspector——"

Birot who was bending his back to sit down again, stopped half-way, and gave her a sidelong glance. "It's some business with a curé, I bet."

"Yes, papa."

"I don't like that sort of thing, but come, all the same."

The girl had seated herself on a chair close beside her father, and patted his hands, feeling that the cause was gained. The longer she talked the stronger grew his admiration for this daughter who was so like himself; who was afraid of no one; who could hold her own and maintain her rights, and who, besides, could talk so well. His eyes grew animated; his lips were compressed, and an occasional brief oath burst forth. Birot expanded body and soul, rejuvenated by his wrath. He was inwardly exercising his argumentative faculties; the words he planned to say threw their reflection across his face. He shrugged his shoulders from time to time, he drew himself up and began tugging at his huge moustache, which would soon rise and bristle

under the torrents of violent words he would be
hurling full-mouthed—at whom? He knew already, he had planned the whole affair, he had
prepared his arguments, as he suddenly exclaimed,
patting Davidée on the cheek:

"I shall certainly not go to the tavern this
morning. Mamma, give us an early breakfast.
I am off to see the prefect."

"What! At La Rochelle?"

"Yes."

"Remember that only yesterday you could not
walk, you had the gout so badly."

"I haven't it any longer."

An unaccustomed sense of enjoyment gave
freedom to Birot's movements, and showed in
the tones of his voice and the flash of his eyes
which had been dulled for weeks. When he left
the house, wearing his broad black felt-hat, and
a suit of heavy tweeds, which was his full dress
attire summer and winter, with the addition of
a red necktie, and carrying a stick in his hand,
his wife said to him:

"Birot, one would swear you were going to a
public meeting."

"Precisely; that is just what it is."

"But you cannot go all the way on foot, you
know! Ask Caderotte to harness his mare and
take you; he cannot refuse, he is under such obligations to you."

"My poor wife! If I did that, he would consider them all cancelled. Let me manage this
business."

He had reckoned on the fact that at the hour

when he would be starting—at about eleven—
there would be every chance of his encountering
on the road some neighbour's gig, or at the worst
a market cart or fish cart which would offer him
a lift. It was in fact the poulterer who came in
sight first and took the big man along as extra
baggage. He had a horse that trotted as fast
as a young colt following its mother, so that at
ten minutes before noon Monsieur Birot entered
the antechamber of the prefecture.

"Shall I announce Monsieur Birot?" said the
usher.

"Leave off the 'Monsieur' and say 'Birot is
here.' When I have no fine speeches to make
I prefer to call myself plain 'Birot.'"

"As you like."

Accordingly the Mayor of Blandes was introduced into the prefect's office, where that official,
who was a young man, though already somewhat
bald, came forward to greet him with extended
hand, but with an air of reserve and without
effusion. He was of a cautious nature and never
showed cordiality except to a parting guest.

"My dear Monsieur Birot, I have only five
minutes to spare."

"That will be sufficient, Monsieur le Préfet."

"Pray be seated. Is it a harvest permit you
have come to ask me for? If so, it is granted."

"No."

"Indemnity for a dead cow then?" and the
great man laughed at his own wit, but Birot did
not smile.

"No, it is a permit allowing a teacher to carry

a good-sized prayer-book when attending the
funeral of one of her scholars."

"You are laughing at me, I infer."

"Not at all. I am making an appeal to you;
the teacher is my daughter."

"Mademoiselle Birot?"

"Yes, Davidée, who is assistant at Ardésie. She
has been denounced, and I do not choose to have
her bothered. You understand. I won't have it!"

"But this is entirely outside my jurisdiction,
Monsieur Birot. I can do nothing for you."

Birot, who had buried himself a little too deeply
in the easy-chair offered him by the prefect, now
sat forward on its very edge, with both hands
supported on his thighs and his fingers extended.
Above the glasses which he had planted on his
nose, he glared for a moment at that functionary
as he was in the habit of glaring at his opponents
before replying to them. He almost invariably
succeeded in cowing them, so much did the fury
in his eyes add force to his words. His hands
were clenched at his sides merely to conceal the
violence with which they shook. The prefect,
on the other hand, was leaning back in his wicker
chair with his lips pursed as if he held a cigarette
between them.

"Monsieur," said Birot in a voice which he
controlled with difficulty, "I am applying to you
because you are our clerk——"

"Your clerk! Upon my word!"

"Perhaps I express myself badly, but I know
perfectly well what I mean. You are a clerk
appointed to get your constituents out of dif-

ficulties whenever they need you, to help along
our side and destroy the others."

"That is a simplified conception of the office,
Monsieur Birot!"

The prefect's laugh as he said this was displeasing to the stone-cutter, who no longer restrained his voice.

"Simplified or not, I don't care a hang! I am
addressing myself to you because I hold you in
my hand, and it is not my place to apply to others.
Outside of the department, what is Père Birot?
Nobody. Whereas, just here, I am a power——"

"A man who has rendered great services, I do
not deny it."

"Services? No I don't call them that. I am
a man who rules other men, who knows them
far better than you ever will, who knows all their
special weaknesses, who sees how they live, and
gets them to vote for him, or to vote as he does.
I serve myself first, and I don't mind serving you
later. But on one condition——"

"I cannot admit threats of this kind."

"That doesn't matter! I can execute them. I
tell you that this inspector who has denounced
my daughter must repair his injustice!"

"I cannot concern myself with your affair."

"Very well then! I will concern myself with
yours. Do you understand?"

Birot had risen to his feet and was shaking his
fist in the face of the important functionary, who
had risen also, stupefied and vaguely alarmed at
seeing these clenched fists and blazing eyes so
near him.

"Monsieur le Maire!"

"I am going to demolish it for you, your commune of Blandes! I will fix your administration for you! I will let them know how you refuse me justice and how you treat the democracy!"

"Monsieur Birot, you are asking an impossible thing."

"So you think me superannuated too! You think I am done for! They have been telling you so? Well, Monsieur le Prefét, this will perhaps be my last campaign, but I swear to you that I will win it. I have the honour of bidding you good day!" He took up his hat, clapped it on his head inadvertently, and stalked toward the door.

The prefect touched him on the arm.

"I am distressed to have to refuse you, but you must be aware that *directly*, I am unable to give you satisfaction."

The Mayor of Blandes made no reply beyond a shrug of his shoulders, as he withdrew. He marched away triumphantly with his adverb. "Didn't he have a bad time of it, getting out his '*directly*'?" growled the good man as he descended the stairs. "Didn't he though! I began to think it would never come."

It was late afternoon, and the exasperating hours, when flies, wasps, and hornets are reaping their invisible harvest in the air, were giving place to the languor of evening before the refreshing breezes rise, as Birot, whom no one had heard enter, approached the arbour where his wife and daughter were sewing in the shade. The

sand crunching under his feet made more noise
than the whole village of Blandes together, so
that the two women raised their heads and stayed
their busy needles. "Well! what news?" asked
Davidée. Madame Birot asked nothing, but it
was to her that the big man made reply, out
of breath and mopping his face, but with eyes
flashing keenly above his handkerchief as he
passed it across his cheeks. "I have no need
of a doctor yet, Mamma Birot. I can still *down*
my prefect like a younger man!" and patting his
daughter's cheek, he added: "I am sure they
will write to you, little one. It won't surprise
me at all if they order you, in future, always
to carry a huge *antiphonaire* when you attend
funerals! I will tell you all about it, but I must
go and take my coat off first."

Davidée thanked him by a deep glance of her
dark eyes, a glance that seemed to say: "Why
are you, who can direct others, so weak where
you are yourself concerned, my poor father;
you, who are on the road to madness?"

The industrious needles began again to fly
along the white seams, and beneath the branches
of the honeysuckle, moist with drippings of
honey and haunted by bees, the talk was resumed between Madame Birot and her daughter
—their first leisurely, confidential talk. "It is
true then, mamma, that you have never felt the
need of religious belief?"

"Your father would never have allowed me
to think differently. He has his political views;
I should only have broken up our household.

Besides, I *am* a believer, such as we all are around here. What do you call believing, child?"

"Accepting God and through Him rising above the life we lead and judging it."

"I leave it to your father to judge, and I also accept the judgment of the neighbours and of my own conscience. Doesn't your conscience suffice for you?"

"No, it is so hard to be sure, without some fixed standard. When you were at a loss, did you not seek counsel?"

"Never."

"You have never known my difficulties, that is evident."

A bee half drunk with honeysuckle wine, and clinging to a dead leaf, fell upon the white cloth, and Davidée brushed him off with her thimble.

"I am trying to train consciences, dear mother, and I feel that they escape me, that they are perishing like new-born babies who have been entrusted to my care, and for whom I have no nourishment. I have nothing but maternal anguish."

"What are you saying? Do you not follow the school programme?"

"Oh, mother! I follow it only too closely! I ignore everything outside it. I am in doubt about all the essentials of life. I have merely intelligence enough to see the great problems, not to solve them. And so I am tempted to believe and to pray."

"You, Davidée?"

"And yet I remain doubtful and troubled,

and that leaves me neither wise enough nor good enough, neither a true guardian, nor a sister, nor a mother, and my brood is immense and cries at my knees, and I ask myself why I was sent to these little ones, destitute as I am."

"If your father heard you, how angry he would be!"

"To such questions, mamma, anger brings no solution. It seems to me that I have been given tiny lighted candles, like those which you used to put round a Savoy cake on my birthday: at nine years old, nine little candles; at ten years, ten little candles, and so on. And I have not blown them out, oh no! but they have all gone out between my fingers, and the odour of their dead flame haunts me."

Madame Birot, who always worked as busily as a spider, never stopping when she had begun to spin her web—white or black—now let her two hands fall idly in her lap.

"Davidée," she said gravely, "you worry and grieve me, because I cannot follow where you are going, I ought not; but I know where you will end!"

"But I do not know, mamma. I am sure only that I no longer have the thoughts of my youth. I can no longer *sleep*, as they sleep here in Blandes."

The mother sighed, as she took up her needle again, and bent over her work with reddened eyelids.

"I would rather not talk of that," she said sadly. "Leave me my sleep, which I call peace!"

"Peace means to me to draw the deep breath

of certainty, so full and pure and calm! I have not attained it."

"Let us talk of other things, Davidée. All this is beyond a poor old mother like me."

They spoke no more. Never had words like these passed between them, under the shade of the vine-clad arbour, never had such words been uttered by them in the white house, and none of the neighbouring houses would have understood their meaning.

From the Green Diary.—"July thirty-first: My father was to tell us at dinner of his conversation with the prefect, but fatigue and, alas, other reasons—of daily occurrence—barely suffered him to utter a few broken phrases and disjointed words which meant nothing. The most painful part of it all was my father's consciousness of his declining faculties, and of the cause, and how irremediable it is. My mother tried to talk with me and fill up these painful gaps in the conversation, but these attempts irritated father, who saw in them merely an interruption and a lack of attention toward himself, appealing to me to sustain him in this view. It grieved me to feel that mother had longed for this evening—my first at home—looking forward to it as the greatest joy of the year, a compensation for many other evenings. At eight o'clock she went up to her room to make sure that my father had gone to bed and had not yielded to the temptation to rejoin at the cross-roads of Blandes those whom he calls his friends. When she left me I went out for a walk; the evening was still warm and bright. In the half-lighted cottages I could see mothers passing back and forth, and catch white gleams from the dishes they were carrying, or the pillows for some little bed. All the youths of the village, and the old men as well, were seated or standing in the door-ways of the freshly painted houses, mostly in dull silence. As I passed they raised their eyes and exchanged a few words between themselves, always the same. I was greeted here and there by a slight nod, but they all made me feel that they no longer regarded me as one of them, no longer as a companion or a friend, and that I had lost my place in the village. It would take long to regain it and it would never be quite the same. I am an outsider now, education and absence have made me an alien here.

"The roads fringed by marsh-grasses, the little paths marking the ancient curves of the shore, gave me a better welcome. I found again their wonted silence, broken only by the creaking of the sand beneath one's tread; and the gleam, like that of the red moon, shed by the setting sun over these open spaces which belong to the sea but once or twice a year, but through the long intervening months are steeped in her brine and sown with her vegetation.

"I saw the sea far off, a sheet of molten silver, not deep enough here to form waves, its endless shallows divided by weirs, like tall black hedges, where shell-fish are bred. The vision of this shore pursued me. In my childhood I had seen only its brightness; to-day I thought: the tides rushed in along these shores once; there were tall ships here, the sound of oars, the track of incoming boats on the water. This was a busy port where men formerly lived lives of adventure and peril. But the shores have risen above the tide, and the bold rovers of the open sea enter here no longer; the water bears only formless craft which crawl along between banks of slime.

"Little by little it came over me that I was destined to the same lot as the landscape; I felt its desolation as a personal grief. No, I will not live here, I will not let the sand invade my open sea! I already belong to the sorrows which I can console and which are life. And the thought stole over me that I might learn to love Maïeul Jacquet. He is without cultivation, but at least his mind is not distorted by the pride of a little learning. He is capable of courage, even of that highest courage which men no longer exert when they believe themselves to be demi-gods. He knows himself to be a man, a poor, weak man; he has listened to a warning voice which was partly mine, but still more that of the dead child, and he has taken our reproofs as showing him his duty, and in order to keep true to his promise, he has gone away. He must be feeling as much a stranger where he has gone as I am here; he must be suffering; perhaps he still thinks of me. If I were sure of him, sure that he would let me guide him, I would seek my path and we would follow it together. He would not hold me back when I strove to be better; he would have con-

fidence in me. I do not know whether I could
rise very high, but he would rise with me.

"August fifth: I have been trying to read
some religious books which I found here at
home. How did they chance to be here on the
shelves of a man like my father, with his strong
anticlerical ideas? Why were they spared from
among the three hundred volumes or so, consigned
to the attic? I did not dare to ask my mother.
But I found two; it is the more modern one by
Gratry that appeals to me most. I find there
a struggling faith, or rather an understanding
of the struggles of seekers after truth, which attracts me. My state is one of trouble, of con-
tradiction, and feebleness of will, the dread of
sinking lower if I do not change, the sick shrink-
ing from effort, and utter solitude of soul. The
contemporary masters of the spiritual life have
known this anguish and it is here that I learn it,
in my father's house.

"August sixth: My mother, who has a gift
for penetrating into the valleys of one's mind,
and who has lost—or never possessed—the taste
for the summits, has been making me describe
to her, in its minutest details, my life as a teacher;
she forgets nothing; she silently classifies names,
dates, and descriptions. This morning, on our
way home from the next village, with a load of
provisions—my arm still aches from the weight
of the eggs, chickens, and vegetables I carried—
we were talking about *me*, that inexhaustible
subject of her thoughts for the last twenty-three
years. She was living over, through the power

of the love within her, nearly all that part of my
life least known to her, such as my years at the
normal school, and especially these last months
in Ardésie. I was watching her look of joy at
being near me; the fulness of contentment expressed in her poor little pale face as she trotted
along in my shadow, drinking in my voice, my
breath, my very soul. It was drizzling, and a
warm marsh mist enveloped us, but she did not
perceive it. She was rejoiced to have her hands
free and to feel that there were two of us, and I
fancied that no thought of the future mingled
with her pathetic happiness. But I was mistaken, she was thinking of my future. She said
to me, just as we reached the Blandes school-
house at the entrance to the village, where she
is used to walking in silence for fear of echoes:
'You must marry, Davidée. Your father has not
long to live, I cannot take care of you. Your
brother hardly belongs to the family, and will
give you more care than help. Only you will
not marry easily.'

"'That is your dream, mamma, far more than
mine.'

"'You could do what I have never been able
to do, and that is: educate your husband.'

"'With what? With my alphabet and my
school-books?'

"'No, you have a power in you for raising others.'

"'That is why I left you both. But when I
was put to the proof I recognized my weakness.'

"I have been deeply moved by her words: 'a
power to raise others.'"

From the Green Diary.—"August fourteenth:
Phrosine is calling for help. She writes to me:
'Mademoiselle I have found Le Floch, he is working in the Forest of Vouvant, which is indeed
a long way from Sologne. He caught sight
of me and was frightened, and has not reappeared at the lodgings where he was in the habit
of coming once a week to change his clothes and
sleep in a bed. I know that he said: "She
wants me to take her back; but if I find her here,
I shall leave the country." He did not have our
boy with him, but I know that he is alive, and
is on a farm, but I cannot find out where. Come
and help me! you would not have a very long
journey to make. They tell me that we are in
the Vendée here. You can talk to Le Floch for
me; he would not listen to me. If you do not
come, my child is lost, my only one. I may as
well tell you also that I have no money left, that
I owe several debts, and that I've come to the
end of my courage.'"

The letter was dated at a little village on
the borders of the great Vendean Forest. Davidée hesitated. What service could she render?
Would they ask anything more of her than the
payment of a baker's bill, or a week's lodging?
And into what company would she be thrown?
Why should she leave Blandes? And as she
still hesitated, she remembered the words spoken
by little Anna! "I give mamma to you." And
so, as soon as the Feast of the Assumption was
over, she set out.

CHAPTER XIII.

THE MEETING.

THE forest began a short distance away, and stretched across the whole horizon. It covered the hills and valleys as far as a distant knoll crowned with lofty old trees, which dominated the scene, and whence poured across the plain the breath of the sea and the sunset light. The sun was descending rapidly below the forest, and the colonnade of massive oak trunks was crimsoned by it. It was a wonderful moment of illumination for the roots and mosses and low bushes springing up in the deeper glades, bringing their share of light to all the recesses buried in shadow. Beyond the forest, on the outskirts of the village, stretched a plain partly clothed with stubble, partly given over to patches of potatoes and strips of maize which had not yet raised their tiny tufts very high; a straight road crossed these cultivated fields. Along this road, all through the winter, carts descended laden with tall tree trunks whose tips trailed behind, tracing scrawls in the dust. Now, in the late summer, the harvest being over, hardly a creature was visible on this long ribbon of road, stretching pale between its violet banks. Two women, however, were seated in the window of a room over the

Café of the Wood-cutters, watching the sinking sun and looking out for the man whom they expected to see approaching.

He had said to the hostess the previous Saturday: "A week hence, mother, have my two shirts ready for me, and a pound of lard." And on the strength of these words, Phrosine and Davidée sat waiting for him, in great trouble of mind. For the last quarter of an hour thay had looked anxiously up the road for the figure of the wood-cutter descending the gentle slope. First he would be a tiny speck on the dusty expanse, gradually drawing nearer, until the wife could recognize the face she had not seen for so many years, and the man would have to tell his secret, upon which her whole future depended. "You must let him sit down to table;" Phrosine said; "when he has ordered a bottle of wine and begun to drink he will not be so rude to the people here as to go away without giving an account of himself. He is a rough man, but more so with me than with others."

"Then shall I show myself?"

"Yes, you can appear before him on the staircase there. When he hears the stairs creak he will think it is I, and will half rise from his seat. Do not be afraid of him if he looks ugly; that will only be for me, not for you. When he catches sight of your white hands he will see that they are no washer-woman's hands, and he will be polite enough; perhaps he will even be afraid of you."

"But when I tell him you are there?"

Phrosine shivered, and without ceasing to gaze up the road said:

"He will fly into a rage, and all will be lost—perhaps forever."

She had bent forward, leaning on the window-bar, while Davidée was standing behind her. The sun was now glowing red between the oaks, and its rays no longer falling on the plain, were mustering an array of clouds above the forest. "That means a hot breeze to-morrow," said Phrosine. "The reapers will have a hard time cutting the last crops." Then she was silent for a while. "What if he doesn't come? My eyes are as tired already as if I had been sewing all day."

"Do not look at that red sky. Stay inside the room, I will warn you when he is coming."

"No, I must see my fate the moment it appears. Don't you see somebody at the edge of the forest there?"

"It is only a bush. The darkness changes everything."

"He is afraid of me! Of me, whom he once courted."

The shadows were now falling and making all things alike. Voices could be heard calling here and there to summon a loiterer home. Smoke was rising from the farm-house chimneys showing that supper was ready. The two women were silent, and now as they looked down, they saw beneath the window on the narrow road bordered by hedge-rows, a young girl appear. Where had she come from? She was waiting, grave and trembling, turn-

ing her head also toward the sinking sun. She was
leaning over a stile and presently on the further
side of the hedge a young man came in sight, tall
and agile, striding over the furrows of the next field,
but with no sign of haste. He was evidently flattered to find the girl waiting for him, and his thin
face, which was already losing its youthful fresh-
ness, beamed with self-satisfaction. The girl, on
seeing him approach, half closed her eyes, as if
for her only, at this evening hour, the sunlight
was too bright to bear. The sweetness of her
dream of love wrapped her about, brought a
smile to her lips, and held her motionless. When
he was quite near, her two virginal hands, those
hands which shared her dream, were stretched
out to him across the hedge, like two lilies opening in the shade. He scarcely noticed the tender gesture, but springing over the gate, caught
the child in a passionate embrace; but the few
ardent words interchanged between the two died
away before reaching as high as the window where
the two women sat watching. Only a murmur
of voices rose on the air, and floated away, as
they disappeared across the lonely trackless
plain. Phrosine followed them with a bitter
glance. "Oh!" she cried, "how happy that
miserable girl is!"

At that moment Davidée caught sight of a
man's form detaching itself from the gloom of
the forest, and beginning to descend the slope.
"Some one is coming along the road," she said.
The other made no answer. "He is walking
rapidly, carrying a small bundle on a stick across

his shoulder. He has just reached the cross which stands in the midst of that field of maize."

"Look what he does! If he bows his head it is not my man."

"He has passed without glancing at it. His head is turned toward the tavern."

"Then it is he!"

Phrosine had already drawn back into the darkest corner of the room and Davidée stood to one side of the window, but both continued to gaze out at the figure approaching in the dying day, and when he was too near to be visible from above, they listened to the sound of his heavy shoes on the threshold, and the creak of the latch under the sudden jerk of his powerful hand.

"Well, mother!" a loud voice called out, "is my linen ready?"

"Certainly, Monsieur Le Floch, we have not forgotten you."

"Serve me a bottle of white wine then, as usual. There is nobody here at least?"

"You are my only customer, you see!"

The women in the room above did not stir, for fear of giving the lie to the landlady's words. They held their breath in order to hear every movement which told them that Le Floch was taking his seat at the table and making himself at home. The landlady uncorked the bottle, and he, having filled a glass, tossed off the contents with a gurgling sound audible all over the silent house. Having set down his glass, Le Floch drew a long breath, and puffed and panted, as if overcome by the fatigue of the day's work

and his long tramp. The woman of the house
excused herself, saying that she must attend to
her work; a door was heard to open and shut
behind her, then the wood-cutters' café seemed
wrapt in sleep for the night. At that moment
Davidée descended the stairs, the boards creaking slightly beneath her tread. From the darkness of the stairway the wood-cutter saw by the
light of the one lamp suspended overhead, first a
skirt trimmed with fine embroidery, then a white
and delicate hand grasping the banister. The girl
paused a moment, with her heart beating rapidly,
then descended the remaining steps and advanced
to meet the man. The surprise was sufficient
to arouse his violent temper, and deepen the
furrows on his thin, sallow face. He no longer
resembled a lion; a narrow, yellow beard fell over
his shabby velveteen waistcoat; his eyes were
blue and hard, and, apparently not in the least
intimidated by this unexpected apparition, seemed
to ask: "Who are you? What do you want with
me? Have I ever done you any harm? What
have you to charge me with, since you are evidently not afraid of me?"

Davidée came straight to the table and said,
as the man raised his hand to his felt-hat:

"Monsieur Le Floch, I am a friend of your
wife's."

Instantly his face assumed a hostile expression. "Is she here then? I suspected as much!"

"She has sent me to speak to you, and you
must listen to me, because she forgives everything,
and what she asks of you is merely justice."

This sudden recall of the wrong he had done, this appeal to justice, and the youth of the speaker, made some impression on the wood-cutter's mind; but a disagreeable smile crossed his thin lips as he said:

"She doesn't want us to come together again, I suppose?"

"No."

"She doesn't want a divorce?"

"No."

"So much the better! That always gives a lot of bother."

"She only wants to know her son."

"Oh, well! that's a different matter. We can talk that over."

"Here she is," replied Davidée, drawing back.

The man's face turned ghastly pale on seeing the woman who had suffered so much at his hands. She was half laughing, awkwardly, and without meaning to do so, but in order that he might not fear her, and that hatred might not have the first word between them.

And, after all, she was a woman, and in spite of everything she remembered that he had once loved her. Upstairs in the dark room she had already smoothed and pushed back from her forehead the hair which brightened her face—still young and bold—whose anxious expression was ready to change at the least sign from the man before her.

Timidly—at least in appearance—she drew up a stool and seated herself between the two rows of café tables. "It is years since we have seen each other," she said.

The wood-cutter shook his head, as if to say that it was no use trying to move him.

"Without doubt; what then?"

"And yet I must explain to you how things are. My little girl is dead——"

"Ah, so much the worse!"

"*Our* little girl, she whom you never knew. She died on the fifth of May."

"Of this year?"

"Yes, just three months ago."

The man appeared to be reflecting, "Where was I at that time?" but he merely said:

"If I had known it, I would have sent a wreath. But when people are separated as we are——"

"Yes, I know."

"Are you still a maid at the school-house? I heard about that through Flahaut, who is from Ardésie, and Père Moine."

"Yes, but that doesn't give me enough to live on."

"I am poor, too; we were both made for poverty it seems."

"Perhaps so. But I cannot be reconciled to the death of my child, unless the other is given back to me. I wasn't always a good wife, but one does as one can, Henri! I am not in the habit of lying, as you know, and I own that there are things you can reproach me with; but I have always been a mother. Say, Le Floch! tell me where my boy is, that I may go and fetch him."

The man, in spite of his boldness, hardly knew how to answer when the past was brought up; there were wrongs to his account too. But when it was a question of this living son who was still dependent on him, and whose whereabouts he alone knew, he was more at his ease.

"I see what you are after, Phrosine. You want to profit by the boy's wages?"

She answered "No," with a shrug of her shoulders.

"He earns a good bit to be sure, but it won't be for you."

"I only want *him*. He can keep his money if he chooses."

"Bah! Nobody can fool me; I had difficulty enough in getting him away from the Charity Board. They didn't want to give him up, just because he had turned out a big, promising lad, and because I had the appearance, it seems, of a man who knows the duty of children toward their parents. It took a lot of visits, and threats too, before they would let him go."

The wood-cutter's impudent laugh resounded through the room.

"For the first year or so the boy was pretty reasonable, and helped his father along. But at present he has changed his mind. He gives nothing for nothing. One would think he was a bastard, the money sticks so to his fingers."

"He is not much like you, certainly."

The man shook his head and his lips curled in a spiteful grimace.

"You want to get the better of me, Phrosine. But you shall not have what I couldn't get. I will not tell you where he is."

"And what if I find him?"

"I will prevent your carrying him off! There

are gendarmes about! It would please you too much to make a fool of me. I say no!"

"I implore you, Le Floch!"

"Not much can be got out of me by prayers, as you know."

She was about to throw herself at his feet when Davidée stepped forward from the shadow of the staircase.

"Say yes, Monsieur Le Floch," she said. "Tell us the name of the farm where the child is, write on a page out of my note-book that Phrosine is his true mother, and in return I will make you a present of this."

And holding out a hundred-franc note, she laid it on the table.

"My soul! but you've got rich friends, Phrosine," said the man. He unfolded the bill, blinking as if the sight of it dazzled his eyes, then said: "Give me a pen. But I warn you that you will get nothing out of him. You are making a bad bargain, you women! He has a will of his own."

Davidée tore a page out of her note-book and gave the man her pencil, while Phrosine looked on in stupefaction, as the heavy hand wrote:

"Maurice, farmer's boy at La Planche, near-by, the woman who will hand you this letter is your mother, Phrosine. She and I didn't agree, but she is your mother. You can obey her if you choose.

"Your father,
"LE FLOCH."

It was Davidée who took the written sheet from him and replaced it in the note-book from which she had torn it. For a moment not a word was uttered in this room where the fate of several beings had just been bought and paid for. The lamp swinging on a chain from the ceiling cast its circle of light upon the group. Le Floch was the first to recover full possession of himself.

"I mustn't linger," he said, turning toward Phrosine, "there is some one who will be jealous!"

A strange gleam of cruelty shot through his hard blue eyes. He felt that he was alienating his son, and was avenging himself.

"She won't have her man passing the night in a tavern. It's queer, Phrosine, she has hair the colour of yours, fox-colour."

She drew herself up. "Wolf-colour, you mean. All the same she may not be as handsome as I, the wench! There is a chance of it!"

She spoke insolently, with her arms akimbo, looking handsome indeed, her somewhat waning beauty rekindled by excitement. The man studied her face, not without complacency; he seemed to be recalling the sweetheart, the bride of old days, when the neighbours called Phrosine "the beautiful she-wolf." Then he rose with a sneering laugh, exclaiming: "At least she is younger!"

And that was the end of all between them. Phrosine recoiled. "You are the same as ever," she murmured, "you have not changed." But she did not say it too loudly, for fear the man should repent having signed the letter. He, meanwhile, was pouring himself a parting glass, which he tossed off at one draught, after saying to Phrosine, as it behooved him to do: "Your health!" Then he called the hostess.

"Give me my washing, mother."

"Here it is."

He untied the bundle on the end of his stick, put in the clean shirts in place of the others, and saluting Davidée with his hand to his forehead, and without a glance at his wife—though he was conscious of her in every drop in his veins—he turned toward the door.

Then pushing it half open, and letting a blast of night wind blow through the room, he said in a hoarse voice which hid some emotion:

"Now I go back to the forest. You won't hear of me again."

And he went his way, the sound of his steps echoing like fingers tapping on the window pane, as they died away in the distance; and the vast night poured over village and fields its silent tide of wind and darkness.

Davidée scarcely slept. She was thinking: "No moral wretchedness has ever moved me like this. This man and woman while young, were drawn to each other by a mere physical attraction; they called this love; and the time while it lasted, marriage. Other temptations came, and they had no souls to resist them. What an ending to that which should have been eternal!"

At daybreak the two women, who had risen while the village was still slumbering, were walking along the road which skirted the forest to the east, making slight détours wherever it encountered too steep a hill, then resuming its direct course like a compass that has been shaken. They were saying to each other: "Which of us shall speak? We are equally unknown to him, you and I. And which would be the better plan, to enquire for him first from the people at the farm, or to take him by surprise at his work?"

"If only his father has not lied to us?" exclaimed Phrosine.

"I do not think so," Davidée answered.

"You do not know all his wickedness, any more than you know mine."

"Why do you speak like that?"

"Oh, my poor girl! There are bad people enough in this world, he and I among them. They called me the 'she-wolf' and they were right."

"The sun is rising," said Davidée, "it is already tingeing the tops of the poplars. The working day is beginning; shall we turn here?"

"Yes; the woman at the inn said: 'When you see great meadows with tall trees on them, leave the high-road and follow a cart track leading up to the pond of La Planche.'"

They followed the road along which the winter's cart-ruts had hardened, and the seed, which had fallen into them, had sprung up here and there in grain of many sorts. The fields had grown barer, dropping on the left-hand into a narrow valley, enclosed between two spurs of the forest. They were mostly stubble fields of wheat or oats, but here and there was one whose crop was not yet garnered, which made a ruddy

spot on the paler slopes. In spite of the early
hour, waves of heat were beginning to quiver
along the valley and the air was filled with an
odour of fresh straw and ripe plums. When
Phrosine and Davidée had followed the cart track
for a hundred yards or so, they discovered that
a causeway, overgrown with bushes, intersected
the road, and that beyond it was a pond fringed
with reeds, and above the pond, at a height
where the winter floods could not reach them,
rose the buildings belonging to a great farm—
dwelling-house, stables, barns, and sheepfolds—
surrounding a hollow square.

"This must be La Planche," said Davidée.

And shading her eyes with her hand, she looked
around for living beings, men or animals, amid
this silent scene. Phrosine, standing mute and
downcast, apparently lost in memories of the
preceding day and of a remoter past, and dread-
ing the thought of how the next few moments
might affect her whole future, left all to her companion.

"I see far-off on the plain," said Davidée, "on
the shady edge of the forest, a flock of sheep with
a shepherd leading them. And across the pond,
half-way up the slope, I can see two reapers.
To which shall we go first?"

"To the nearest," replied Phrosine.

They accordingly drew nearer, crossing the
causeway, and standing motionless beside the
wheat-field where the crop was half cut and
half standing. The reaper who approached them
first, his body swaying with the motion of his

scythe, clad only in a half unbuttoned shirt, and
trousers supported by cords over his shoulders,
was a very young fellow, strong and rough, as
appeared in the vigour of his movements, who
did not relax his activity on catching sight of the
two strangers standing at the edge of the field.
Were they pleasure seekers, or women from the
nearest town, stopping to ask the way to the
fountain or the village, or to enquire at what house
in the neighbourhood they could buy fresh milk?
He had seen many of their kind, here and there,
wherever he chanced to be working. His consciousness of masculine superiority and his natural shyness combined to make him ill at ease
in such encounters. Having seen that these were
women, he immediately pulled his hat down over
his eyes, so that his face was hardly visible.
He drew himself up at the end of the row of
sheaves, seized the handle of his scythe close to
the blade, and with a rapid motion struck it in
the ground, so that the steel rang out as he called
to them:

"What are you staring at me for? I am at
work, is there anything surprising about that?"

"His look is hard and his voice deceitful. He
is like his father! It is Maurice! I am sure of
it," Phrosine said to herself, as she stood directly
facing the reaper. She made no attempt to
attract him, she forgot all the words she had prepared to say when looking forward to this possible encounter, but without a movement, with
no sign of life except her tortured gaze, she studied
every feature in the face of the child, grown to

manhood; the forehead, the restless eyebrows,
the close cropped hair forming a point above the
nose, the lips without a curve, strained tight even
in repose, and those eyes—above all—gleaming
blue beneath the swollen, reddened lids, dissatisfied eyes always seeking to bathe in some fresh
source of light and passion. The young man
now turned toward Davidée, and seeming to find
her appearance pleasing, asked with a shrug:

"How does she know my name?"

"How do I know your name?" cried Phrosine.

"Yes, who told it to you?"

"I gave it to you; I am your mother!"

The reaper merely shrugged his shoulders again,
with a look of disdain for this pair of advent-
uresses, who were making him waste his time.

"I don't know what that is; I never had a
mother."

And he turned away, lowering his scythe and
preparing to get to work again. His companion
was not far off, and they could hear the swish
of the falling ears as he drew near.

"Come, you women, move along! I have no
time to spend listening to you."

But the mother had already stepped in amid
the wheat he was about to reap. Her eyes
were wet with tears, her hands clasped in appeal,
as she approached her child without venturing to
touch him.

"I am your true mother, who has come all the
way from Ardésie to find you! Your father must
have spoken to you of Ardésie, where I live!"

"No."

"Never? Well, it was he, all the same, who told me where you were at work, Maurice. I had a hard enough time finding you. I am all alone now; do not send me away; do not be as hard to me as others have been. I want you to know me at least, and to talk a little with me."

Another voice, that of Davidée, who was standing a little further off, now joined with hers.

"It is quite true, all she is telling you; you may believe her."

But Maurice Le Floch, fearful of ridicule, knowing that he was observed by the farmer's boy, who had looked up from his reaping and could hear all that was said, merely repeated:

"Come! step out of the wheat! If you, too, want me to give you all the money I earn, I warn you that the other didn't succeed."

"I don't want any of your money. I want you to know me; and when we know each other, I want you to come and live with me, if you will. I cannot force you to come, but I want you to love me."

Having said this, she drew back, for he had bent forward, resting his hands on the two handles of his scythe, and was saying:

"Come to La Planche after the nooning. You can talk to Master Ernoux, who is my employer." Then with a half-circular sweep of his blade, he cut down a swath of ripe wheat, and burying himself in the crop, with his head scarcely rising above the sheaves, he vanished more rapidly than he had appeared, leaving the two women to go their way. But he could still hear Phrosine crying, and being young, his heart was somewhat stirred.

"I will go with you as far as Ernoux's farm," said Davidée, who had been trying to comfort Phrosine, "then I must be on my way back to Blandes, or they will be growing anxious about me."

She was happy, but not with that complete happiness which she had hoped for. She would have been glad if Phrosine had said: "I will not leave him. It may be, he, too, will try to escape from me, but I shall win him over, you will see! He does not know what it is to have a mother. Oh, I will never touch his money! I am still young, in spite of what Le Floch said; I can work; I shall bring him back with me." But Phrosine was silent, disappointed at having found the son so like the father; and Davidée wondered within herself as she walked along beside her: "Would she have come if she had known her son?"

The summer breeze blew through the forest, over the harvest-fields, and the pond where the broken stalks of wheat were dipping their heads in the water. It was past two o'clock when the two travellers, after breakfasting in the village, presented themselves at the farm of La Planche. Ernoux, the farmer, who was expecting them, received them civilly, and in order to do them the greater honour, showed them into the best room, where the highly polished wood of three wardrobes, a chest of drawers, and a carved bedstead, gleamed in the midst of a tranquillity which was seldom violated.

He was a short, stout man, whose shaven face resembled that of a pettifogging lawyer. He had just come from the barn, where he had been sleeping with all his family when the watch-dog's bark had roused him; he even had a few blades of straw left sticking in his hair. He listened with a judicial air to Davidée's narrative, appearing to attach especial significance to the paper signed by Le Floch, and never taking his eyes off Phrosine, while her companion was speaking. Then he called Maurice and made him sit down opposite the window, facing the light.

"Maurice," he said, "I believe that she is your real mother."

"That may be."

"She has a paper saying so; and then there is the resemblance between you, which no one can deny, though it would be hard to say where it lies. It's not the eyes, it's not the forehead, it's not the nose."

"I have nothing to say to that!" replied the lad, "but what does she want of me? I am well-off here, but as soon as my father found me I was obliged to give him all my money. Now that my mother has found me, I am resolved to give her nothing. That's what I say, nothing."

"I approve of that, my boy, but all the same if she is your mother, she has the rights of a mother. She can carry you away into her own country."

"Oh! If that is all there is to fear!"

"But later on, when you have finished your time with me, you might go with her! Mean-

while I have hired you, you are satisfied with
me and I with you; there's no reason why you
should leave at present."

"Moreover, how do I know that at her house
I should have my own room?"

Phrosine was not greatly surprised at this bar-
gaining. All her life she had been governed
and oppressed by the selfishness of men. First
of her father, then of her husband, then of her
lovers and even her neighbours, who had made
free use of her hands at the tubs; and yet the
mother had not thought that her first interview
with her new found son would be like this. Certainly she had reckoned that her child would help
her to earn a living, but above all, she had rejoiced through her maternal tenderness, bereft
as she was of her dead child; and for once the
disappointment was too much for this fiery nature, which injustice and suffering revolted, but
could not crush.

Bending toward her son, Phrosine now saw
only him; she had but one thought, and her child
did not understand: "When will he throw himself into my arms, my first-born, for whom I have
suffered? He, the only one left me now; he
whom I have sought for, amid distress which no
one knows; he whose kisses I have missed for a
dozen years? Oh, Maurice! Maurice! To-morrow I will be your servant and will wash your
clothes; to-morrow you may reproach me if the
soup is too thin, or the wind whistles under my
door; to-morrow you may insist on my giving
you all the wages earned by your aging mother to

whom you will give nothing; but to-day only embrace me!" He remained seated stolidly in his chair, with a look of suspicion on his face, his glance constantly seeking Farmer Ernoux, whom he knew to be a shrewd man and hard to deceive. One would have thought that he was discussing the terms of a contract which had been proposed to him, and that there was only one question to examine and decide: "Would the new place be worth the old one?"

It was Davidée who replied to him, as his mother was silent.

"Will there be room also for my bicycle?" he asked.

"The house is large enough," answered Davidée, who was thinking of the house on the Plains. "The bicycle can easily be sheltered there."

"And is the land over that way harder to work in than here? The woman says nothing," and he pointed to his mother. "She cannot guarantee that I shall have well-paid work, at the same price as with Master Ernoux. Does one have Sunday free, at least, on those farms? Do they give meat and wine when the work is hardest?"

"The labourers there look contented," said Davidée; "they do not complain more than elsewhere."

It was the farmer of La Planche who first understood the mother's silence. He was in haste to resume his work, having caught sight, through the window, of a wagon going out empty to the fields beside the pond, where the harvest was not yet gathered.

"Come along," he said. "You shall go when autumn comes. Embrace your mother there! You can see well enough that that's all she's waiting for."

The youth hesitated a little, Phrosine had risen, he rose too. Suddenly he felt himself enveloped in an ardent love such as he ignored as yet; he was pressed to this heart which was beating for him, and words he had never before heard reached the ears of the friendless waif.

"My Maurice! My dear one! Embrace me again! Tell me that you are going to love me!" When he had escaped from the maternal arms, Maurice Le Floch only said: "It changes me to have a mother! I shall get used to it, perhaps, but I shall not give her my money!"

Picking up his straw hat, which he had thrown on the floor, he shook himself like a dog that has been patted, and remarked aside to Farmer Ernoux: "I must know, all the same, whether the pay is good over yonder; without that—" And Phrosine heard him.

Late that same evening, Phrosine and Davidée returned to the village which they had left in the morning. Phrosine was no longer the mother ennobled by the hope of winning back her son. She had judged her child, and found him too much like his father. Her future would never be brightened by him nor her daily task lightened. All that she had expended of fatigue and time, money and ingenuity and baffled hopes, had only served to discover this calculating being, through whom she would have to suffer still more. She would take him away with her! Oh, that was certain, at whatever cost! That was her victory over her husband. But this victory promised her no joy, gave her no strength.

Then, out of her evil past, old sins awakened, and she listened to their voice. Davidée heard her laugh, but did not understand. Phrosine was thinking of festivals and betrayals, and of the snares she would lay, and what she could do to attract Maïeul; her heart was irritated, savage and wild as a wasp on the brim of a wine-vat. As she stalked along, with her bold free stride, chewing a spray of mint which she had gathered beside the road, the penetrating odour floated in the air behind her. The village had come in sight, in midst of the plain, the hour of parting was near and Phrosine decided to speak; she said without looking at Davidée:

"I have made up my mind! I shall settle down near La Planche until November; I do not choose that Maurice should stay with his father. He may help me or he may not; I will not leave him to Le Floch. We shall go away from here together, and afterward—we shall see!"

She was silent a moment. Then suddenly changing her tone, which now became as aggressive as in the worst days of the past:

"Have you any news from the slate-cutter of La Fôret?"

She did not name Maïeul.

"No."

"But I have, though!"

"From himself?" asked Davidée quickly.

"No, but if I had chosen to hear directly from himself I could have done so. It appears that he is successful."

"So much the better!"

"There's a rumour that you are going to marry him." Davidée drew away from the woman walking beside her along the highway.

"Why do you speak to me of him, and spitefully, as you are doing?"

"I told you that I was bad. Look out for me!"

"Phrosine, what I may wish to do some day I do not know, and it concerns no one but myself."

"I beg pardon! It concerns me in the first place, for I have rights over him."

"But he left you!"

"And for whose sake? Do you think such things can be forgiven?"

"For the sake of the child whom you were killing, between you."

Phrosine stopped, and throwing away the spray of mint, she turned upon Davidée:

"I can no longer live! My husband has left me for another, my son will not share his daily bread with me. Did he not say so often enough? Did you not hear him? Now you want to take away my lover!"

"Phrosine!"

"I let him go, but I did not give him up to *you*."

Davidée's voice rising, clear and ardent upon the air, replied: "Well, then. try to take him back now that he loves me!"

Their words seemed to gallop, like a pack of hounds, across the plain. The two women heard them dying away in the distance as they parted.

Phrosine returned to the village, to which the farm of La Planche belonged, and Davidée went on alone to the wood-cutter's inn. She was not greatly troubled, though Phrosine's threat had made her speak at last and utter words she did not know she had even thought.

She had owned her love, and although it was not to Maïeul, she felt herself already a betrothed, who has said, "I love you, I am yours," and who looks with security and wonder at the brightness which that new light casts over a dark and troubled sea. The beam does not destroy the unknown, but shines through it. She had set out on a rapid walk on leaving Phrosine; as she approached the houses she saw, at the end of a street, one lighted window, and instantly the vast night was without ambush and without fears. This was the only sign of life visible; the girl now advanced more slowly; not a sound was floating through the warm air which gently stirred the leaves and shook the last sheaves in the wheat-fields. The light of the stars shed a peaceful gleam over the tiled roofs, while all beneath was in shadow.

"I was obliged to speak! By loving him I defend him against her, against himself. Is not that the ambition I have always had? To raise, to draw souls out of their weight of misery. I shall have won him. I shall ask of him only good-will. What matters it if he is poor and

ignorant? If he obeys noble counsels he is noble.
He has already parted from this woman. To
breathe the same air as his former sin must be a
cause of weakness to him. I have made an
avowal which is startling even to myself, but
what strength will be needed for two! Where
shall I find it? I feel myself so ignorant of all
that which I love best and which attracts me most.
My secret is not yet his. It is only mine, and
that of the enemy to whom I tried to be kind.
I have given a promise, but only to my own heart.
I came to save a woman whom her maternal
instinct led for a moment, but whom it no longer
upholds. She lacks that which I would gladly
have—the knowledge how to sacrifice oneself.
I have gained no influence over her, she hates
me! And yet I regret nothing. May the source
whence my youth drew an impulse of devotion
to others open anew! May I see my road, in
order to lead others! May my love reach out,
first of all, toward truth—even afar off—truth
of which I have caught a ray, like that which my
eyes receive from the stars! May I not fear to
see! May I be a woman, obscure indeed, but
capable of good!" Then she became conscious
that she had prayed. The one little light in the
village had gone out, and she was obliged to
awaken the hostess of the inn.

Early the next morning Davidée turned her
back on the country where the forest of Vouvant lay, already glowing with warmth upon the
hills.

CHAPTER XIV.

THE RETURN TO ARDÉSIE.

OCTOBER, the golden month, was reviving, on the mounds of Ardésie, the sprays of broom which blossom twice a year. The damp mornings, the mild, bright afternoons, the leaves whose mission was no longer to give shade, but which now helped the sun and turned to sunbeams, the fear of coming winter which prowls at night and flies before the day, the desire to see once more the old friendly faces, the custom prevailing in Ardésie of visiting the families of new pupils: all these reasons, together with her mere delight in exercise, moved Davidée to take long walks on her free days, which were Thursdays and Sundays. On her return from the vacation, she had received a letter from the principal inspector. He announced first that he had been promoted to a superior position in the neighbourhood of Paris, a position which was at once a promise and a reward. Then, having spoken of himself, he added: "As for you, Mademoiselle, you have no idea of the vigilant and sympathetic care with which I have defended your cause. You have been, I will not say merely threatened, but actually the object of certain suspicions which I have dispelled. Nothing will

survive, I am persuaded, of these suspicions, which
I successfully opposed, if you will consent to
exercise extreme prudence in the manifestation
of sentiments which are undoubtedly permitted,
but which should not be shown too zealously.
In whatever way I can serve you, believe me,
Mademoiselle——"

The assistant, after reading this letter, had
smiled and exclaimed aloud, amid the flood of
afternoon sunshine pouring into her chamber:
"Thanks, Papa Birot! it was you who gained that
cause!" And the official letter would soon have
been forgotten, if other letters had not come to
recall it to life. These last were not written by
persons of importance, but by young school-
teachers who asked for counsel; some timidly,
some directly, according to the temperament,
the feelings, or the age of the writer. The first
of these letters, which she had received before the
vacation, had almost irritated Davidée, but these
repeated confidences revealed to her a band of
sisters whose existence she had not suspected.
She felt, in consequence, less solitary in spirit,
and a deep sympathy was called forth in her for
these unknown friends, whose faces she would
probably never see. She understood the noble
suffering which a select class of the daughters of
the people in France was sharing with her. How
did these letters chance to be addressed to her,
and why had these strangers taken her into their
confidence? Who had made it known that, among
the blue stones of Ardésie, there dwelt an assistant
teacher who was solicitous for the souls of her

little charges; who had one day dared to carry a prayer-book under her arm, without asking pardon for the offence? Were they enemies who were jealous of her, or secret admirers, or babbling employés? Who could say? Wherever a wire is stretched above the earth, the swallows are sure to light upon it.

These were some of the letters:

"Mademoiselle, I am a young girl of your own age, weak and hesitating by nature. I envy you, for I know that you have had the courage to own yourself a Christian. I have more than once failed to do so, and yet I have greater faith than the people among whom I live. I have been deterred by a timidity which humiliates me. I desire to be more useful, more truly an educator than I am now. I suffer at the thought of giving of myself only that which is least good, least wholesome, least true. Advise me, Mademoiselle; speak to me, point out to me the books which I should read and which would confirm me, not only in my faith—which is imperfect as yet—but in my duty as a teacher, which I would not have out of harmony with my life, as I feel that it has been hitherto. To see all the evil about one without daring to say where good is to be found, or to utter mere formulas of well-doing which touch only the memory—do you know this trouble? I have some friends—only a few— whom I know or guess to be like myself. Will you answer me? I venture to hope so."

*　　　*　　　*　　　*　　　*

"I live very far from you, Mademoiselle; I
know nothing of you, save through one of your
friends, Mlle. S., who was your fellow pupil at
the normal school, but that is enough to inspire
me with confidence in your kindness and dis-
cretion. We have held, during these last days,
many eager discussions in this large city school,
where I am an assistant. I am argumentative by
nature; I maintain my opinions with an ardour
which I try to express courteously, but I often experience, afterward, the need of fortifying myself in
a position which I believe to be just. We were
talking of morality, the directress and I, her husband and the other assistants. I maintained, that
after having by degrees eliminated from education the fundamental dogmas of Christianity, such
as the idea of personal immortality, the idea
of God, and consequently the entire Christian
system of morality, which cannot be separated
from these beliefs, we had sought to create or
disinter other moral systems. Many men of
talent and of passionate ardour have engaged
in this work, and these attempts have been many.
My contradictors recognized that these chance
systems of morality have not held good, but we
were divided on this point: I maintained that
the search had been abandoned; that we had renounced the attempt to found a moral system.
I said that this was a deplorable treason toward
parents and children alike, and that our ambition,
which is to prepare ourselves for life, could no
longer sustain us, as it had once done; that this,
the first spring of action within us, was hopelessly

warped; but to this they would not agree. Tell
me your opinion."

*　　　*　　　*　　　*　　　*

"Mademoiselle, I have been reading some irre-
ligious books which have troubled me greatly;
one especially, well-written, but so cruel and so
hopeless! I laid it aside when I had read it half
through, because I said to myself that I had not
sufficient knowledge to criticise or to confirm
what I was reading; but a certain disquietude
has remained within me. I was attracted for
the moment by the idea of a religion without
dogmas, consisting only in an inner aspiration
of our souls toward God; but on reflection, I realized that this would be mere anarchy: the opposite extreme to the ideals of a religious society
and a common morality, and yet my mind, in its
weakness, returns to this argument which I feel
that I have refuted. Have you experienced this
contention within ourselves, which is so hard and
wearying, especially when we have no one in
whom to confide? Among my companions at
the normal school, there are surely some who are
passing through the same crisis as I, and who no
more dare to avow it than I do. There are others
who have need of affection, to whom I would
gladly hold out my hand, but our days pass by
too rapidly, often full of interest, though many of
these interests are merely outward and superficial;
and it is only on returning to my evening solitude that I feel conscious how little light my soul
has shed on any other soul, and how little it has

received from others. Help me, will you not? The courage of one often avails to sustain many. I come to you seeking the strength to remain myself, and to rise to something better."

*   *   *   *   *

Mlle. Birot also received several visits at this time. On the day before the reopening of school, there had even appeared a young man, an instructor from a neighbouring town.

"Well, my dear!" Mlle. Desforges had exclaimed, "you are indeed becoming celebrated; what with piles of letters and visits every day! I do not envy you, and I doubt very much whether you will find all this profitable for your career. There is a young man in the court-yard asking for you. Do you wish me to send him away?"

"No, I will go down and see him."

"But you have not unpacked your valise yet."

"I will do that when I come back," Davidée replied.

She found her visitor to be a very young man with ruddy cheeks and curling hair, carefully dressed, and of studied speech, who addressed her, at first, merely as a comrade, and as if he had no reason for coming to see her beyond the attraction felt by a youth for a pretty, intelligent girl; but before leaving he held out his hand, and speaking more seriously, said:

"We are not too numerous, those who think as we do; we ought to know each other, and, besides, courage such as yours is always good to see!"

In her diary Davidée wrote: "What is the

matter with them all? What have I done that
is so wonderful? Why do they come to me?
Alas, if they knew the whole truth, they would
see that I am far from being the Christian they
imagine me to be. They force me to interest
myself in these religious problems, they leave me
no peace; they are helping on my spiritual progress far more than I am counselling them. My
dear sisters! you of the tender, troubled souls!
how I wish that I could visit you in your school-
rooms, in your chambers: those plain tidy cells
where you find comfort in the solitude which is
so welcome to us all at first! You weep there
sometimes, I know, for you have to bear ridicule,
insult, and injustice, as well as the silence of companions whom you care for, and the cold aloofness
of the self-satisfied and ignorant. I am only one
of your number, and not the one who has suffered most. I merely look forward and divine, I
struggle and aspire, and accept each day's lesson as it comes. I have been where God is not,
and the vision was a terrible one. You have
been sent to me, so that I might know that beautiful spirit of tenderness which concerns itself for
the future of every stranger child, asking incessantly: 'Shall I have given strength to these
little ones? Will the mothers be true mothers?
The wives, true wives? Can I arm them with
virtue? Is my own sufficient—uncertain and trembling as it is—based only on instinct and good
examples?' I, too, have always before me the
unknown futures which I am preparing; I feel
that for these children, and for myself, I must

develop an inward life through which we all can
live. My sisters! as yet I have only prayed
timidly, and in moments of anxiety and emotion,
to Him who can give or increase this grace. And
you do not know this! How parched and dry
the spiritual world must be, if a drop of water
such as I have to give, preserved I know not
how, can attract these thirsting souls and seem
to them a spring!"

Davidée paid many visits, at this time, to the
parents of her new pupils. All received her
kindly, and she once more repaid the confidence
these mothers reposed in her and the facile tenderness of the children with the same interest
and care she had shown to her last year's scholars.
Several women, whom she had not been to see,
called to her from their door-ways: "Well, Mademoiselle! You are too proud then, to step in?"

She was not proud, poor Davidée! but she was
a little sad in these days, because Maïeul had not
written to her, and had never come back.

She was somewhat surprised, when on a late
October afternoon—it had been rainy all the
day before, and the crows were flying over the
leafless hedges—little Jeannie Fête-Dieu, who was
watching for her outside of one of the neighbour's doors, greeted her with the words: "Grandmamma sends you her love, Mademoiselle. It
seems she has news for you, if you can only find
time to come in and see us."

What news? The answer in her own mind
was immediate. It must be a message from
Maïeul which the old woman had to give her.

Davidée had only to follow the narrow path through the broom, over the mound of La Gravelle, and descend into the hollow where the house and its tiny garden lay hidden.

Lying in her bed, which the sun could only reach for one short half-hour during the day, the invalid held a sprig of box in her hand, with which she was trying to drive away the last flies of the season which were still tormenting her. She had no more power of motion than usual, but she called herself better, and her eyes were alight with a passing youthful gleam.

"Well, here is a term that opens finely!" she exclaimed.

"Why so, Mère Fête-Dieu?"

"Because they are all welcoming you back as if you were the month of May! 'Good-morning Mademoiselle Davidée! Do come in and see us!' is the cry in all the villages."

"How do you know that?"

"Jeannie has ears for me as well as legs, and a heart which remembers every word that is spoken of you. And what would you say, Mademoiselle Davidée, if I told you that there is some one else who is longing to see you?"

The young girl answered sadly: "I should scarcely believe you."

"But if he had sent you a message by me?"

"Give it then, Mère Fête-Dieu."

"Hasn't he written to you himself?"

"No, never since he went away."

"He is afraid to write, because you are so learned."

"Is that the reason why he has never been here since I came back to Ardésie a month ago? La Fôret is not far off, only two hours from here by railway."

The invalid slowly stretched out her hand and touched the girl's bare arm with the sprig of box, like a mother who is playfully correcting her child.

"You have too little faith in life, my dear."

"It is because I know it too well."

"Not all of it! You have seen only its worst side, or nearly so. There is a remedy for *us* and for all who are of good-will. There is succour for us all."

"Where, Mère Fête-Dieu?"

"In Paradise, my dear."

"I do not know the road."

"It is easily found, child. But listen to something else I have to tell you. I have seen Maïeul."

"He has been here then, and has not tried to see me?"

"You were away on your vacation. He talked to me as if he had been my son. Ah! how handsome he looked, with such a resolute look on his face, and dressed like a gentleman."

"And what about the heart, Mère Fête-Dieu? I care little for the coat!"

"Wait till I tell you. Maïeul has worked so well over there that he has been promoted. He has been a foreman for the past week, and they say that he may be paymaster some day. That is a fine place."

"Undoubtedly, but how about the heart? Is that cured of its malady?"

Little Jeannie, at a sign from her grandmother, had left the room, and her shadow could be seen, flitting back and forth across the garden-beds. Joy had vanished from the old face, but not its look of calm, nor that sort of security which belongs to the agéd who have been upright, and have won the victory of the soul.

"You are not greatly to be pitied," she said. "There is only a little weakness left and some fear of himself."

"No, of her!"

"Well, of her, if you will have it so."

Poor Mère Fête-Dieu shook her head on her piled-up pillows, saying to herself: "It is no use trying to hide anything from this young lady from the school."

"I am sure she writes to him."

"Yes, my dear, she does."

"She has been writing to him since August?"

"Yes, and even before that; she has tried her best to win him back, but he does not answer her. He is counting the days now, and if he does not venture to come back, it is out of respect and friendship for you."

"He pretends that it is so."

"You may be sure of it! He left Ardésie because he could not live so near to her who had been the cause of his sin. Here, to my very face, he said: 'I shall not return until the day when I can say: I will live in Ardésie and I will no longer meet my remorse there!'"

"Did he say remorse?"

"Yes, my pretty one, and he is a man who will

not lie. If he comes back, he will not go away any more. You can trust in him."

"As much as one can in a man."

"You may well say: a man. But such a well-meaning one! Only listen again! I said to him, just to see: 'What if Mademoiselle Davidée were to become a good Christian, Maïeul?'"

"It is quite true, Mère Fête-Dieu! It is that way I am tending. What did he answer?"

"He said: 'That doesn't frighten me! If I were married I should be like her.'"

The assistant rose, and caressed the drooping hand, wearily holding the sprig of box, and the serious face, stamped with a look of deep compassion for the sorrows of youth.

"Mère Fête-Dieu," the girl said, "I shall send no answer by you. I shall not write nor let others write for me; I shall simply wait. I cannot promise what my answer will be if he asks me; it may be that I am destined to mount the steep path alone. I will not take a step toward him, I will not seek him if he turns away from me."

At the further end of the garden, Jeannie, who was waiting to see her pass, was amazed that her teacher's eyes were red, since grandmother had been talking to her of Maïeul. She was busily engaged in hammering a nail with the heel of her sabot, by way of proving that she had not been listening. On seeing the assistant, she ceased this demonstration, and put her sabot on again, saying: "Good-night, my poor demoiselle!" In the village the greetings of the housewives met with no response, beyond a wave of the hand. The girl was in haste to go in-doors and weep.

She wept a long while. How helpless she was! To whom should she turn? There were beings then, insensible to every proof of friendship, like this Phrosine and her husband, incapable of loyalty or justice; and other beings so weak that a pure love alone could not save them, that rescued once, they turned back to evil ways. Vain hopes of the summer, useless tenderness, which had thought itself so strong! How hard it was to live amid such hearts, and try to make them live! Had she not tried? But what a mockery! And to-morrow, next year, until the age of retirement came, she must persevere in this superhuman effort, cherish these illusions, continue to offer this hollow show to fathers and mothers who had entrusted their children to her care!

Her two griefs appeared to her as one; to be abandoned and to spend her soul without reward! Not to be happy nor to be able to make others happy! Davidée opened her drawer and reread some of the letters which her unknown sisters had written her; everywhere she read the same words: "You, the Christian!" she recalled Mère Fête-Dieu's saying: "There is help in Paradise!" The road has been pointed out to me, she thought, and opening her prayer-book, she took from it a little picture of the Crucified One and held it in her hand. She sought for a moment the place to lay her lips, there on the wounded heart, then she said: "Help me!"

That same evening, with the chill wind blowing around her, she went out again, and sought through quiet by-paths the house on the Plains. It was deserted; the plum-trees were bare of leaves, but the pyramids of the pear-trees, in the growing darkness, rose here and there like red and golden flames.

CHAPTER XV.

THE PERMISSION.

THE November fogs, chill, heavy, and tenacious, were dragging down to earth the last decaying leaves; for weeks the pear-trees had lost their look of lighted torches, the winds were walled in all day by heavy banks of cloud, and the smoke from the chimneys curled and twisted in spirals beneath them, when one morning, the house on the Plains flung open its window and door, looking out upon the little yard. But no smoke rose from this chimney, and amid the neighbouring cottages this one alone stood silent.

Phrosine was making the rounds of her lower room, where the white mould lay like patches of soapsuds upon the floor. The poor forsaken cat had died, its mummified body lay stretched on the ashes of the hearth, and the stench of death hung about the walls and rafters.

Phrosine did not enter the small inner room, but went out and stood upon the threshold, wrapped in the icy fog, listening. For the last hour or two, Maurice Le Floch had been tramping from one of the neighbouring farms to another, trying to find work for the winter. His sheepskin valise was lying in the middle of

the narrow path, now overgrown with tall grass
never mown. He was likely to return, at any
moment, bringing the wished for news, but Phrosine was expecting another visitor. It was for
this latter that she had dressed herself, and arranged her hair with extra care, before leaving
the little inn on the outskirts of the village where
she had passed the night. He could not long
delay, for had she not written two days before?

"MONSIEUR MAÏEUL JACQUET,
"At the Slate-quarry and Town
of La Fôret, near Combrée.

"I am expecting you, dearest. I shall be at
the gate of our house, waiting for you. I wish
at least to bid you good-by, for you cannot have
forgotten me."

She had no doubts as to the result. She had
reckoned that on leaving the railway train he
would take the tram from La Pyramide, and a
little after mid-day would appear on the road
through the orchards. When he was once more
with her who would know how to hold him, they
could settle down together, either here at Ardésie
or at La Fôret, she did not greatly care.

She was listening intently; it was the noon-
hour, when work stops in all the factories and workshops and on the farms, and she could easily
have caught the sound of a man's step descending
the slopes of Château-rouge, toward the fields of
blue stone, if the wind had not gathered in its
course all the noises of the town, as well as all

the wailing and creaking sounds of branches and gables and of hedge-rows pruned close to the ground, whose twigs were sharpened to tiny whistles. All their life together in that house was in Phrosine's eyes, all the days that she had lived there with Maïeul, except those when a great grief had made her weep, for she did not choose to recall sorrow.

And shortly after noon, a tall and handsome young man turned out of the highway leading to the town, which was invisible from where she stood, into the road which she had been watching so fixedly. She hastened to the edge of the straggling, grass-grown orchard, and leaned her arms upon the gate. The passion within her had made her face fresh and young again; she felt her power, since Maïeul had come back to her, and an alluring smile played round her lips.

Far below in the village, the young assistant was presiding over the children's play-hour, little dreaming that Maïeul was so close to Phrosine.

On catching sight of the woman lying in wait for him, Maïeul turned pale, and slackened his pace. In a moment of combined weakness and over-confidence in himself, he had obeyed Phrosine's summons. At a distance it had not greatly moved him and he had merely said to himself: "Certainly I will go and say good-by to her, I cannot do less."

Poor fool, who fancied that the past is ever dead! Since early morning he had been journeying toward this dangerous moment and this woman; and all the way, his dread of her had been growing. Now that he saw Phrosine before him,

on this very spot, to which he had returned evening after evening for months as a husband to
his wife, he was seized with terror at the sudden
throbbing of his heart. His throat was dry;
Phrosine's smile called him with a terrible unes-
capable spell. She did not speak until he had
approached near enough to read her eyes, grown
wide and bright with an evil charm, then she said:

"I knew you would come to me. Come, my
great one! We were happy once. Come!"

She gazed at him as she spoke, so sweetly, so
sweetly, that he felt his heart reel within his
breast; then she opened the gate slowly, so that
he might see only her eyes, and hear only the
words which should hold him captive. But
when the gate was open and the pathway free,
Maïeul looked on the ground; he saw the tall
grass and the straggling plum-trees beneath
which little Anna had lived her last days; he saw
before him the child whom their sin had driven
from that house and who had died of grief because of it. Then he, who had been so weak and
wellnigh lost, felt himself sustained by a new
strength. Davidée's prayer succoured him, and
little Anna's sacrifice came to his aid. He began
to turn aside from the woman and the house, as
he said:

"I have come to say good-by to you, Phrosine,
for now all that is over."

"Already! We ought not to part so quickly,
you who came from so far and I, too! Come, my
Maïeul!" She hoped that he would look her in
the face once more, but he turned his head quite
away.

"Phrosine," he said, "I must no longer be as I have been."

"Who forbids it?"

"One who has the right."

"Yes, I know her."

"You have known her well, it is your dead child!" He had already drawn back from the hedge, and he now started toward Ardésie. Phrosine ran after him, crying in fury:

"It is not the child, it is that other woman! Ah, the wretch, she has stolen my lover!" But she did not attempt to overtake him; and at that moment a much younger man emerged from the narrow road between the farms, and she cried out to him: "Maurice? Have you found nothing?"

"Nothing!"

"No more have I! Come on! pick up your traps, we will go further afield!"

In the school play-ground, Davidée was still superintending the recess. The children were nearly all assembled, and one of them, approaching her shyly, said: "There is some one at the door, asking for you." She did not know who might be asking for her, poor Davidée Birot! But as there was one memory which never left her, she turned very white on opening the little chestnut-wood door. Maïeul Jacquet stood with uncovered head, partly hidden behind a pillar, clad in his Sunday clothes. He was so deeply moved, he too, that no words came to his lips, and he stood silent as a pilgrim who has reached the city of his dreams. "It is I, Mademoiselle Davidée," he said, at last. This girl had no smile for him, and no tempting glances; she was deadly pale, because her fate was about to be decided, and by herself.

"Oh!" she said, "I had long given up expecting you."

"I could not come back before, but it was for you that I was working."

"I thank you."

"I am a foreman at La Fôret. They will give me work in Ardésie whenever I wish."

He understood at once that she was awaiting something more.

"Mademoiselle," he said, "I can live in Ardésie now."

She made no answer, but a wave of pity for herself swept over her, as over one whose pain has just been lightened.

"Yes," he added, "now I can hire the pavilion of La Gravelle again, only I must have your permission."

Seeing that the girl could not speak, because of the grief over the past which still held her: "It would be more than my happiness if you consent, it would be my salvation." And he added below his breath:

"In this world and the next."

Davidée raised her eyes toward the bank of fog which the sun was at last about to scatter, and answered: "You may hire the pavilion of La Gravelle, Maïeul Jacquet." And at that moment the school-bell rang.